Spotte

Poker Face
House Edge
Double Down
The Squeeze

The Pinch

Spotted Pony Casino Mystery
Book 5

Paty Jager

Windtree Press
Corvallis, OR

Windtree Press
Corvallis, Oregon
http://windtreepress.com

Cover Art by Covers by Karen

PUBLISHING HISTORY
Published in the United States of America
ISBN 978-1-962065-39-9

Special Thanks
To my dear friend Karen McBride who didn't hesitate when I asked if she wanted to help me research "murder and mayhem" at an Oregon Coast casino.

About the Book

This series is usually set in and around a fictional casino on The Confederated Tribes of the Umatilla Reservation in NE Oregon. The reservation is real. I have researched, and while I've made up people and where they live, I will try to stay true to the life people live on the reservation.

This book is set in a fictional casino in Lincoln City, Oregon. While I visited a real casino and did use some of the logistics from the casino for my story, none of the characters are in anyway a representation of the people who work, run, or visit that casino. They are all people my imagination made up. The operations of the casino in my series are all my own common sense, not a complete knowledge of how any casino is run.

Chapter One

Dela Alvaro strode into the Siletz Bay Casino. The sights and sounds felt like home, yet she felt out of place without her uniform. This wasn't her casino, the one where she was head of security. Her friend, and head of security at this casino, Enos Apash, asked her to do a walk-through.

His staff didn't know who she was or why she was here. She'd meet up with him later today and give her findings.

Her ability to see problems and train her employees to also observe and cut off trouble had spread through the other Tribal casino security communities. Dela had never thought her job at the Spotted Pony Casino on the Confederated Tribes of the Umatilla Reservation would get her involved in solving numerous murders on the reservation and getting a name for herself in the casino security circle.

She stood ten feet inside the main entrance of the

casino, scanning the area for security personnel and to get a sense of the security and atmosphere in the establishment. To the left was an area where casino patrons could receive help and turn in their points for gifts. It consisted of a counter with three customer support employees. There were three short lines of casino-goers waiting for help. She noticed an entrance beyond the lines. The door said employees only.

Farther into the casino on the left was the gift shop and beyond that the concert hall. Near the concert hall was a sign that said FOOD. Fifteen feet directly in front of her, the escalator chugged up to the second floor.

A wharf atmosphere surrounded the escalator. Water whooshed like waves up to a sandy shore and retreated revealing sea creatures in tidal pools. A wood pier had a taxidermized seal basking in the sun. Music and the sound of waves battled with the voices and machines.

To her right, slot machines flashed, played music, and cajoled, trying to persuade the people passing by to feed their money in. She moved onto the gaming floor at a leisurely pace taking in where the security members were stationed and keeping an eye on the people playing the slot machines. It was mid-afternoon on a Friday in May. The machines hummed, shouted, and jingled as she wove her way through the people in various stages of anxiousness and party attitudes.

One of the security staff members held his hand to his earbud. His facial expression tensed. She wondered what had happened as one by one all the security personnel moved through the casino, their heads rotating back and forth as they scanned the patrons.

Her phone buzzed. A glance showed the caller.

Enos.

"What's up? Your staff is searching the gaming floor," she answered.

"We have a missing child. I wouldn't be too alarmed but it's the son of someone you don't want to mess with. Can you come to the surveillance office? It wouldn't hurt to have fresh eyes on this." From the man's tone of voice, he was feeling overwhelmed with the task at hand.

"Sure. How do I get there from the gaming floor?" She'd yet to have a guided tour of the establishment.

"I'll have Reuben show you up." The call ended.

Dela stood where she was and a tall, thin man with a thick brown mustache walked up to her. His uniform was dark blue, enhancing his light blue eyes.

"Boss said to bring you up to surveillance." He pivoted and led her through the gaming floor and over to the Winner's Circle. They went around the small lines and through the doorway, making a left and continuing to a staircase.

Dela wished she'd put her shoulder-length brown hair in a ponytail. She'd left it down to look like a customer and not someone official. She'd liked having short hair in the Army but after discovering her father might be Native American and not Hispanic as she'd been told, she'd started growing her hair out. She tucked the swinging, blonde-highlighted strands behind her ear and followed Reuben. With the prosthesis on her right leg, she had to take the stairs slower than the long-legged guard ahead of her. She'd learned about a month after getting out of rehab that she had to place her right foot a certain way to not lose her balance on stairs when she climbed them.

Rueben stood at the top landing, his hand on the doorknob as he watched her ascent. "You scared of heights?" he asked.

She shook her head. "My legs aren't as long as yours." It was rare for her to tell a stranger about her missing lower limb or the fact she'd lost it in Iraq.

He smirked and opened the door when she stood on the landing.

The room looked a lot like the surveillance room at the Spotted Pony. Lots of monitors with people watching what was happening in each one. Scanning the people working in the room, she noticed three-fourths of them weren't Native American. She was happy that at the Spotted Pony nearly three-fourths of the employees were Indigenous.

"The boss is through that door to the right," Reuben said, disappearing back the way they'd come.

Dela headed to the door and was nearly run over by a young woman in a security uniform.

"Sorry!" she said as she hurried through the monitors and toward the exit.

Stepping into the room, Dela immediately knew the parents were there. A blonde woman with her hair piled abstractly on her head, sat with one leg crossed over the other. The large-patterned harem pants hung like curtains from her legs. A short-sleeved shirt tied in a high knot showed off her flat belly. She blew into a tissue and dabbed at the corners of her eyes. The man's dark hair was shiny from the styling product he used. The shiny hair and shiny loafers appeared to hold together the wide shoulders in a hunter-green polo shirt and tight brown slacks that stretched over muscled legs. The man was clean-shaven, though a five o'clock shadow had started to darken his tanned skin. His gaze darted to Dela when she entered the room.

"Dela, please come over," Enos said, motioning for her to join him with the couple.

She'd met Enos Apash at a consortium for tribal casino head of security officers. He'd been fun, telling stories about his family and the people who worked under him.

She walked over and peered into his eyes which were straight across from hers. He was average height with a pot belly and long braids that hung down the front of his business jacket. "What's going on?" she asked before smiling at the couple.

"We have a situation. This is Mr. and Mrs. Benedict. Their son, Asher, is missing. Mrs. Benedict was just telling me how she'd left him playing in the sitting area of their suite while she went to take a shower. When she came out, he wasn't in the suite." Enos waved a hand. "I have surveillance scanning the footage from the time she went into the shower and when she came out to find out when he wandered off and in what direction."

"How old is Asher?" Dela asked.

"He's five," Mrs. Benedict said. "He knows all about strangers and not going anywhere without his father or me when we are at places like this." She blew her nose, wiped, and said, "It doesn't make sense. He was watching his favorite cartoon when I left to take my shower."

Dela shifted her gaze to the father. "And where were you when this happened?"

"Are you accusing me—!"

Dela put her hands up to stop him. "I'm only

11

asking if you were nearby and he possibly heard your voice and tried to find you." The man's outburst made her wonder if he was feeling guilty. She knew all about that, having left her best friend in Pendleton while she went to basketball practice and later learning Robin was found murdered along the freeway.

Shaking off her guilt, Dela waited for the man to cool down and reply.

He drew in a deep breath. "I was here, in the casino visiting with a friend. When I left the suite Felicity and Asher were doing yoga. I'd ordered their lunch be delivered."

Dela peered at the woman. "Did room service come while you were in the shower?"

Felicity stared at her.

"Was there any sign someone had brought food to the room?" Dela added.

"I-a" Felicity stared at her husband. "I don't know. I was only looking for Asher, I didn't notice…" She burst into tears.

Dela centered her attention on the husband. "Mr. Benedict, did you go to your room when your wife called you?"

"How do you know she called me?" he accused.

"Because that would have been the first thing I would have done." She stared into his eyes and thought she saw a flicker of—she didn't know what, but it wasn't remorse. "Did you go to the room?" she asked, again.

"Yes."

"Did you notice if the lunch you'd ordered had been delivered?" Dela was beginning to think the two didn't deserve a child if they couldn't keep any better

12

track of him than they had.

"I—no. I didn't see any food or trays," he finally said.

Dela directed her next words to Enos. "Call room service and see if anyone delivered a meal to the Benedict suite. Do you have everyone checking all the buildings and the beach?"

"Yes, I pulled half of the security off the gaming floor to check everywhere and I called in half a dozen people who had the day off." Sweat dotted Enos's forehead.

"What time did you notice Asher missing?" Dela asked Felicity.

"One. Well, that's when I took my shower."

"That's when you started your shower? What time did you realize Asher was missing?" Dela noticed the woman's cheeks deepen to a red.

"Two or there about."

"You left him alone for an hour?" Dela bit her tongue before she said something that would alienate the couple and have Enos escort her out of the casino for lecturing the casino's clientele. Instead, she glanced at her watch. It was three-thirty. "What did you do for the hour before you came here?"

"I looked all over the suite, then called Hugo. We looked again and asked everyone we found in the building." Felicity peered at her husband through tear-spattered lashes.

"They should have seen something in surveillance," Dela said, excusing herself and motioning for Enos to follow.

Out in the surveillance room, she asked, "Why haven't you asked any questions?"

"You're doing fine," he said.

"But it's not my casino, it's yours. You should be coordinating more searchers. If he got in the water, he could be out to sea by now." She shivered thinking about the little boy walking into the water and being swept away by a wave. He wouldn't have a chance. And while it had been a warm spring, the nights with fog and wind could be cold. The boy could freeze to death if he laid down.

"Let's talk to Oscar. He had eyes on the surveillance cameras in that building." Enos walked over to a long-haired man in his forties. "What did you find on the surveillance tapes?"

The man drew his attention from the eight monitors in front of him. His round face flushed when his gaze landed on Dela. "I didn't find anything. No one went into the room and only a couple of people walked down the hall. Didn't see a kid anywhere."

"That doesn't make any sense. He had to have left that room through the door." Dela studied the man. His gaze didn't meet hers and he flicked a glance at Enos before returning his gaze to the monitors.

The woman next to Oscar said, "I didn't see him go into the play area or the arcade."

"You know the child we're looking for?" Enos asked.

"I saw his mom take him to the play area yesterday. I heard a child was missing. When the mom came walking in here without the boy, I figured it was him." The woman smiled.

"That's good deductive thinking," Dela said, returning the woman's smile. "Where else might a small boy go?"

The woman shrugged. "Watch the water at the entrance. Unless he is fascinated by the slot machine noise and colors."

Dela faced Enos. "One of your guards would have noticed him by now if he was wandering around the entrance or gaming floor."

Her stomach grumbled. Since this wasn't her casino and not her problem, though she knew it would nag at her until the child was found, she said to Enos, "I'm going to get some dinner. If you hear anything new give me a call."

"I thought you'd want to help find the boy?" Enos's tone sounded deflated.

"I'm here to help you with your security, not help you find a lost child. After I eat, I'll do a run through the casino and see how your staff is handling the added emergency of a missing child"

Chapter Two

Dela sat in the Steakhouse and lounge, waiting for her dinner to arrive. Her mind was still trying to figure out how a young child could get out of a room on the third floor without being seen. She sipped a light Oregon beer as she watched the Pacific Ocean shimmer in the setting sun.

"That can't be you. The Dela Alvaro I know is either home on leave or went AWOL."

Dela turned to the familiar voice and peered into the sparkling eyes and mischievous smile of Rowena Maxwell. In place of the inch-long afro her friend had worn in the Army, Rowena's face was framed by long thin braids weighed down by silver beads. As her friend walked toward her, the silver beads bounced and shimmered like stars against her ebony skin.

This was the way Dela had always imagined Rowena. Her friend had a hard time following all the Army's rules. This hairstyle showed the free spirit Dela had known was under the Army uniform.

"Rowena, what are you doing here?" Dela rose and they hugged before her friend dropped into the padded chair next to hers.

She pulled two straps over her head extracting them from her braids, placing an expensive camera and a camera bag on the table beside her. "I'm a freelance photographer. The casino hired me to shoot promotional photos."

A waiter arrived with Dela's order. She hesitated. Should she dig in or wait and see if Rowena would order?

"That looks good. I'll have the same and bring me the house white wine, please." Rowena busied herself with stowing her camera in the bag next to another camera. She straightened as the waiter returned with her wine.

Dela decided to eat her food while it was still hot. In between bites, she asked Rowena where she lived and if she'd married.

"I have an apartment in Portland, but the casino comped me a room here for the weekend so I can get some good photos. You know, different lighting and moods. The sunrise this morning with the fog hanging low was gorgeous. I have some really good images of that." She studied Dela. "Why are you asking all the questions? Did you break out of the Army and need a place to stay?" She sipped her wine when Dela didn't answer. "No, you wouldn't break out, you were going to be a lifer. I bet you're home on leave. Is that it?"

Shaking her head, Dela put her fork down and sipped her beer. She and Rowena had no secrets when they were bunkmates in boot camp. In fact, they'd had a good time trying to figure out the secrets of the other young women in their barracks.

"You look like I asked if your dog died," Rowena said. Bracelets on her arm jingled as she placed a hand on Dela's arm. "What's going on?"

"I received an honorable medical discharge four years ago when an I.E.D. blew up the Humvee I was riding in and took off my right leg." She gulped a swallow of beer and continued. "Life has actually turned out better than I'd thought it would when I was stuck in the hospital and then the rehab facility. I'm the head of security for the Spotted Pony Casino at the Confederated Tribes of the Umatilla."

"Where you grew up," Rowena said and smiled. "I knew you'd go back. You talked about everyone on the reservation with such love and admiration. I figured you'd end up back there." Her gaze dropped to Dela's leg closest to her. "So, you're coping with the loss?" her voice softened as she asked.

Dela smiled. A genuine smile. Leave it to Rowena to ask a personal question with care in her voice. "Yes. It took a while to shake off the shock and the pity party, but I'm doing fine. I also have a hunky Tribal Officer for a roommate and possibly more." She nodded her head as if they were talking about a secret.

Rowena studied her for a moment then squealed and tapped her feet in a happy dance. "It's that boy you were going out with in high school. The one whose heart you broke when you joined the Army."

At that moment the waiter placed Rowena's dinner on the table.

"Yes. Heath returned to Nixyaawii to fill a position on the tribal police. He's now a detective. And if he asks me to marry him, I think the answer might be yes.

But he also knows I'm marriage/commitment-shy, so it could be a while. Which is fine. We're still getting to know each other again." Dela wondered if she should say anything to Rowena about her suspicions about who she thought was her biological father. She decided this wasn't the time or place. One of the other reasons she was on the coast was to see if she could find any records from a jail that had burned down shortly after a mugshot of a man, she believed to be her father, was taken. Heath had discovered which jail the mugshot came from and learned of the fire. He was told all the files had been burned. She wanted to make sure that was true.

"Let's exchange contact information." Rowena dug into her camera bag and pulled out her phone.

Dela recited her phone number. Rowena typed it into her phone and recited hers back to Dela.

"I'm staying in the Otter in room two-eleven," Dela added.

Rowena glanced up from her phone. "You're kidding?"

"No. You?" Dela picked up her beer and sipped.

"Otter. Two-nineteen. What's the possibility that we'd be in the same building, same floor, and have dinner together?" Rowena smiled and squeezed Dela's arm. "I've thought a lot about you since I left the Army. I wondered how you were doing and if you were climbing up the ladder like you planned."

"I've done the same. Wondered what you were doing and how life was treating you. It's good to connect again. Let's not wait another ten years to find each other again." Dela tipped her glass of beer toward Rowena's wine glass when her phone buzzed. It was

Enos. "Damn, I need to take this. I'm here for work."

"You answer your call, and I'll order us dessert."
Rowena raised a fork full of salad toward her mouth.

"Thanks. Be right back." She strode out of the restaurant and onto the sidewalk in front of the building to hear better. "Dela."

"It's Enos. We're starting to think something happened to the boy. I could sure use your help."

"What makes you think something happened to him?" Dela asked. Worry started gnawing at her gut. If they didn't find the boy soon, he was going to be outside in the dark and could very well have something happen to him.

"We found his stuffed dog. His mom said he takes it with him everywhere he goes."

"I'll be there in fifteen minutes." She didn't like the sound of things. If it was an abduction, they needed to know the Benedicts' financial status and look into who would have known the right time to find the boy alone.

She walked as quickly as she could back to Rowena.

"I know that look. Something is wrong." Rowena held a fork, with a bite of cheesecake on it, halfway to her mouth.

Dela sat down and leaned toward her friend. In a quiet voice she said, "A small boy has gone missing and since I'm here checking out this casino's security, they've asked me to help with the search."

Rowena sat back, dropping her fork onto her plate. "I can help."

"You could, but I think the family and the casino would like to keep this to as few people as possible. I have a feeling it was a kidnapping and there will be a ransom note soon. Anyway, I wish I could eat that, it looks delicious." Dela's gaze landed on the huckleberry cheesecake placed in front of the chair where she'd been sitting.

"I'll have it boxed up and take it to my room. When you quit for the night, call me and I'll bring it to your room and we can catch up some more." Rowena picked her fork back up and slid the bite into her mouth.

"Thank you." Dela smiled at her friend and hurried out of the restaurant and back to the surveillance offices.

♠ ♣ ♥ ♦

Stepping into the surveillance room, Dela noticed the quiet. At the Spotted Pony, the workers would visit as they watched the monitors. She crossed to the door where she'd met Enos and the Benedicts earlier.

"They aren't in there. The security office is downstairs," the woman who had added good information earlier, said.

"Oh, this is where I was brought last time, and thought maybe your surveillance and security worked closer together than we do at the Spotted Pony." Dela walked over to the woman. "How do I find the security offices?"

"Go down the stairs and take a left. Follow the hallway to the last door."

"Thanks." Dela left the surveillance room and descended the stairs, cursing the fact she'd had to climb them a second time for no reason. The cardio was good for her after the six-hour drive today, but she could tell her stub was swollen from sitting, and climbing the stairs put more pressure on it.

At the bottom of the staircase, she followed the

hallway and came to a door with the word SECURITY. Opening the door, she found Felicity hugging a small stuffed dog.

Dela walked quickly over to the woman. "Are you the only person who has held that dog?"

Felicity wiped at tears and stared up at her.

She felt for the mother but there was protocol to follow if they were going to find the child. "Felicity, we need to bag the dog for evidence."

"What do you mean?" she asked.

"If your son wandered off by himself, then we should only find evidence of him and you on the toy. But if he was taken—"

Felicity wailed and Mr. Benedict jumped between Dela and his wife. "What do you mean taken? What do you know?"

Enos pushed himself up out of a chair. "There's no need to be alarmed. Dela, would you explain how you came to that conclusion?"

Dela sighed. "A boy as young as Asher would have been found wandering around by now if he was alone. Someone would have contacted the authorities. As long as it's been, I have a feeling that someone took the child." She stared into Mr. Benedict's eyes. "Do you have enemies who might use your son for coercion or money?"

His mouth twisted into a sneer. "No one would dare use my son against me."

Felicity stood up, clutching the dog. "What have you done, Hugo?"

The man spun to face his wife. "Nothing." He turned on Enos. "Who the hell does this woman think she is upsetting my wife more than she is already?"

Enos shrugged. "She's solved several murders as head of security at her casino. I think she knows quite a bit and can help us find your son."

Chapter Three

Dela stared at Mr. Benedict. Three hours arguing with him about calling in the FBI was getting them nowhere. "Don't you want to find your child?" she asked the man as she tried to keep her cool. Why was he being so belligerent about bringing in more help?

"I don't want any law enforcement brought in, other than the casino. I'll not have my family dragged through the news!" he shouted and stormed out of the security office.

Felicity dabbed at her eyes and peered up at Dela. "I don't care what my husband says. I want Asher back. I don't care what the police find out about my husband. I just want my child back."

"The quickest way is to get the FBI involved. I have a friend who works closely with me on reservation incidents. I can get him to see if anyone has threatened your husband lately or would have a grudge against him and want to use your son as leverage."

Felicity sobbed and blew her nose. "If Hugo's

business caused this, he'll never lay eyes on our son again." She stood. "Call your friend. I want my child."

As Felicity walked out of the security office, Dela scrolled through her contacts. She hesitated thinking about the love/hate relationship she had with Special Agent Quinn Pierce.

Sighing, she tapped his number and he responded on the second ring.

"Dela, I heard you were living it up on the coast. To what do I owe this call?" Quinn answered.

There was the arrogant man she hated. The one who overrode her authority in Iraq and took a rapist from her prison and set him free to try to catch a bigger fish. She'd hated him ever since even though she had moments where she still felt drawn to him physically.

"I believe one of the resort clients had their child abducted. We've searched everywhere and all we've found is his stuffed dog near a bush."

"That's not good. A lost child would cling to that." His tone softened with worry.

This was the man she'd lusted over. She shook herself. He wasn't the man for her. Heath was the man who would stick by her for the long haul.

"That's my feelings. And why I finally convinced the mother I should get the FBI involved."

"Where are you and who are the parents?"

She heard him click a pen. All business. That was what made him a good FBI agent. "I'm at Siletz Bay Casino in Lincoln City. The parents are Hugo and Felicity Benedict."

Quinn whistled. "There could be a multitude of reasons that child was taken. Benedict has his hands in lots of illegal dealings and we've been trying to catch him for a few years."

"Does that mean you won't help find his child?" Dela asked, realizing that the child was being used as a pawn against his father and the mother was the one suffering.

"Oh, we'll find the boy. But I hope we can find out something to get that bastard once and for all."

"Great! You are going to use finding the boy as a reason to fulfill your bad guy quota," Dela scoffed, feeling uneasy about calling in the FBI now. "What exactly are Hugo's illegal dealings?"

"I'll send a write-up on him to your phone."

"Thanks. And let me know what the Feds decide to do about this." Dela ended the call and peered around the room. The only person left was Sidney, the security guard on duty in the office who had brushed by her so fast earlier.

"Is the FBI coming to help find the boy?" she asked.

Dela nodded. "But don't let it out. It seems Mr. Benedict isn't a law-abiding citizen."

Sidney nodded. "I know all the guards watch him when he's here. I think he uses the casino as a public place to meet people."

"Really?" Dela wondered if Quinn knew that. "I'm headed back to my room. I'll catch up with Enos tomorrow. Good night."

"Night. And I won't tell anyone you're here to watch us, though I think most of them have a clue since you were drawn into the search for the boy."

Dela had figured as much. Why else would their boss ask her to join in the hunt, and he'd told them she was head of security for another casino.

The Pinch

It was ten-fifteen. She knew Rowena wanted her to call and she wanted to call her old friend, but she wasn't sure the woman would be awake.

Opening her door, she stepped on a piece of paper. Dela picked it up and unfolded what appeared to be a page from a notepad with the casino's logo.

I don't care what time you come in. Call me. R

She smiled and closed the door. Sitting on the bed, she scrolled to find Rowena's number in her phone. She hit dial and the phone rang once.

"Are you done for tonight?" Rowena answered.

"I am. Unless they find the boy." Sadness filled her chest thinking about the child spending a night alone or with someone who was using him as a bargaining chip.

"I'll be right over with your cheesecake." The call ended.

Dela decided she didn't mind Rowena seeing her with one leg and took off her prosthesis. She placed it in the closet as a knock sounded on her door.

"Just a minute!" she called and quickly pulled on a pair of sweatpants and grabbed her crutches. She swung over to the door and opened it.

If Rowena was surprised, she didn't show it. "As promised, your cheesecake." She held out the to-go box with a flourish.

"This will hit the spot after the day I've had. Come in." She held the box and a crutch in one hand as she swung over to the small table with two chairs.

"I also brought hot chocolate." Rowena pulled a carrier with two cups out from behind her back. There was also a spoon.

"I remember calling you a Girl Scout in the Army because you were always prepared." Dela smiled at her

27

friend. She hadn't realized how much she'd missed some of the women and men she'd gone through boot camp with.

Rowena laughed, set the carrier on the table, and took one drink out for herself. She settled on the bed, her back against the headboard. "I had days when I'd wished I'd stayed in and followed you around. But I have more days where I'm happy I left the Army and took up photography."

"You always took the best photos," Dela said between bites. The cheesecake was rich and the huckleberry topping was perfectly sweet and sour.

"It was something I was good at. I definitely wasn't good at being a soldier." She scrunched her nose.

Dela laughed. "No, you weren't."

Rowena laughed and sobered. "Did you learn anything more about the boy?"

Dela shook her head. "I called in an FBI friend to look up information about the parents. I think someone kidnapped the boy."

"For money?" Rowena asked.

"I'm not sure why, but his stuffed animal was found. A lost child wouldn't leave their favorite toy behind. They would take it along for company." That thought had been playing in her head ever since she'd learned about the discovery of the dog.

Rowena nodded. "What was the stuffed toy? An animal?" She leaned forward.

Dela set her spoon down and studied her friend. "Why?"

"When I was taking photos out the window of my room, you know to get some views for the casino, I saw an older man and a small boy walking toward the beach. The boy was carrying a stuffed dog."

Dela pulled the notepad sitting on the table over and grabbed the resort pen next to it. "When was this?"

"Before two? I don't know the exact time. I just know the light wasn't quite right to take the photos. But I kept looking at things through the lens to see what would make a picturesque scene." Rowena shrugged.

"Did you see them again?" Dela asked after writing down *2 p.m.*

"Not the two of them. Just the man. And there was a boat close to shore at that time, but it wasn't there when I took my photos."

Dela believed her friend had seen the kidnapping. "Did you take any photos at two?"

"Yeah, I always snap a few. To see the difference in the lighting and to capture the scenes I want to get in good light." Rowena shrugged.

"I'd like to come to your room tomorrow morning and look at the photos you took." Dela finished off the cheesecake.

"I can go get them now," Rowena offered.

"It's getting late. I can come look at them first thing in the morning and if they have evidence, I can show them to Enos and send them to the FBI agent." Dela sipped her hot chocolate. "Do you have anyone significant in your life?"

They talked for another fifteen minutes about all the near misses Rowena had encountered over the years with men.

When Rowena left, Dela texted Heath about running into her friend and what was going on at the casino. She knew if he was working, she wouldn't hear back from him until morning. He could also already be asleep. She hoped Mugshot and Jethro didn't wake him too early.

♠ ♣ ♥ ♦

In the morning, Dela tried to call Rowena to see if she wanted to meet for breakfast. It rang and went to voicemail. She decided her friend was taking a shower.

Her phone rang. She smiled seeing who the caller was. "Good morning. Did you get my text?"

"I did. This Rowena, isn't she the girl you wrote to me about before you quit sending letters?" There wasn't any accusation in Heath's voice. While back then, as a teenager, he hadn't understood her need to go into the Army and get away from what she thought of as accusing stares, he now, as an adult, understood.

"Yes. It was fun talking to her and catching up. She's a freelance photographer and is here taking publicity photos for the casino."

"Small world. I'm glad you ran into someone you can hang out with." Heath cleared his throat. "What is all of this about a missing boy?"

Dela filled him in on what she knew so far, having called Quinn to look into the parents, and that Rowena may have a photo of the boy with a man.

"That could be the best evidence you could have. Go catch up to her and I'll get started with my day."

Jethro's hee-haw-heee echoed through the phone.

"You must not have fed Mugshot and Jethro," she said, smiling. The dog and donkey were hers and she loved them more than she'd thought she'd ever love an animal. They had saved her life and she would forever be thankful to them.

"I was getting there and thought I'd give you a call before I got busy and forgot."

"Thank you for thinking of me. I'll let you get back to the boys."

"Call me tonight," he said and the phone went quiet.

She pocketed her phone, made sure she had the room keycard, and walked out of her door and down the hall to Rowena's room.

Dela knocked.

There wasn't a sound coming from the room. She leaned her ear to the crack in the door and listened. No shower running, no television, or coffee maker.

She tried the phone again. A song played inside the room.

Chapter Four

Dela called security looking for Enos.

"He won't be in. He's on vacation," the person on staff told her.

Dela couldn't believe the man would go on vacation when the casino had a missing child. And now something could have happened to her friend. She held back her frustration and said, "Then could you send whoever is in charge over to the Otter building, room number two-nineteen, with a master keycard."

"Who are you?" the woman asked.

"Dela Alvaro. I'm here checking up on your security policies. Thank you for asking who I was before sending someone with a master keycard. However, I believe there is someone in need of assistance in room two-nineteen. Please send over the person in charge when Enos is gone with that master keycard." She waited what felt like an hour before the woman sighed and said, "I'll send Trent over." The call ended.

Dela waited ten long minutes as she listened to the song play over and over inside the room when she dialed Rowena's number. Each time she heard the tune, dread circled tighter around her chest, squeezing and making it hard to breathe. She couldn't lose another best friend.

An average-sized man wearing a security uniform strode down the hall toward her. "Why do you want to get into this room?"

"My friend, Rowena Maxwell, is in this room. We visited last night and she told me to come over this morning. Only she's not answering the door or her phone, and I can hear the cell phone inside ringing. After the boy went missing yesterday, I want to make sure she isn't here and left without her phone." Dela stood back and the guard tapped the keycard to the lock box.

The whirring sound of the door unlocking skittered apprehension up her spine.

The guard stepped inside and swore.

Dela slipped around him and stifled a moan. Rowena, wearing the same clothes she'd had on the night before, was face down on the bed, a piece of cotton cord still around her neck. "Call Enos and the local police. I'll stay here and make sure no one enters or touches anything." Dela used as much authority in her voice as she could muster while staring at a friend she'd loved like a sister.

"Why are you giving me orders?" the guard became obstinate.

"Call Enos, tell him what happened, and that Dela Alvaro is waiting for the local police to arrive," she said, with anger dripping from each word. She was more than angry, she was frustrated. If she had come over last night and looked at the photos, Rowena wouldn't have been alone when she'd returned and surprised whoever was looking for the photos. But who knew she'd taken them? She'd only told Dela about possibly having them when the mention of a stuffed animal came up.

Her gaze landed on the smashed camera on the floor. Had anyone heard the sounds of a struggle or the destruction last night? A time of death would be good. If it happened when Rowena returned to the room, Dela would forever feel guilty she hadn't accompanied her friend.

The guard talked on the phone as she did a sweep of the room, looking for anything else that was out of place. Rowena's purse looked untouched as well as her suitcase sitting open on the bed. The camera bag was open and turned upside down on the floor by the smashed camera. She needed to check for the second camera Rowena had yesterday evening when they had dinner.

"Enos said you're a head of security for some casino and have dealt with situations like this before. But I don't think you should be here alone since you were the one who was suspicious and knew the person." The dark-haired guard, with the last name Lawton, crossed his arms. "I told Enos to call the police and I'd wait right here with you."

Dela sized him up and decided he would make a good head of security when Enos retired. She held out her hand. "I'm Dela Alvaro, head of security for the Spotted Pony Casino on the Confederated Tribes of the Umatilla Reservation."

He studied her and grasped her hand. "Trent Lawton."

Her phone buzzed and she glanced at the caller. "I need to take this," she said, walking into the bathroom but staying where she could see both Rowena and the camera bag.

"Things are heating up here," she said by way of answering Quinn's call.

"How so?" he asked.

She told him about trying to contact Rowena and finding her strangled and her camera smashed.

"Dela, why didn't you tell me about her possibly having evidence last night?" Quinn scolded.

"Because we talked about it after I'd talked with you. And since as far as I knew only Rowena and I knew about the possible photos, I didn't think anyone was in danger." She pressed her eyes to hold back the tears stinging them. She wouldn't fall apart. Not in front of Trent or on the phone with Quinn. She'd wait until she could call Heath. He'd know how to console her. Right now, she had to do her job to find out who killed her friend.

"Where were you when you talked about the photos?" Quinn asked. She could tell he was walking as he talked to her.

"We were in my room. Which is about four doors down from hers on the same floor, same building." She chastised herself for not walking back with Rowena. "It appears she was attacked when she returned to her room. She's wearing the clothes she had on last night when we talked. Her bed doesn't look as if she slept in it."

There was a knock on the door and voices. "I have

to go. It sounds like the local police have arrived." Dela hung up and walked out of the bathroom. To her surprise, it was not only the local police but Quinn standing just inside the door.

"What are you doing here?" she asked, using her frustration at him not telling her he was in Lincoln City so he wouldn't know how relieved she was to see a semi-friendly face.

Quinn grinned. "Pleased to see you, too, Dela." He nudged the man in street clothes standing beside him. "I was telling you she's quick."

Dela glared at Quinn and stepped forward with her hand out. "Dela Alvaro. I found the body along with Trent Lawton, security for the casino." She knew how to deal with law enforcement. She'd been an M.P. in the Army and now dealt with the tribal police and the FBI regularly when things happened in and around the casino and reservation.

"I'm Detective Stedman with the Lincoln City Police. We're short-handed today so I'll be taking your statement and Trent's."

"Will forensics be coming in to go through the room?" Dela asked, following the detective to the small table and two chairs, the same as in her room.

"I'm bringing in a team from Portland," Quinn said, standing near Rowena's body. He faced Dela. "You know why."

She nodded but didn't like the insinuation that she might know more about her friend's death than she did.

"Tell me about your relationship with the deceased," Detective Stedman said, hovering his pen over a notebook he'd pulled out of a pocket.

"Rowena and I were bunkmates in boot camp in

the Army. After basic training, we went different ways. Last I heard from her she was going to work with the Peace Corps. Then last night I was sitting at the Steakhouse and someone called my name. I turned and it was Rowena. We had dinner together and then I was called away."

Detective Stedman stopped her. "Why are you here? At the casino?"

"I was hired to check out the security team at the casino. I'm head of security for the Spotted Pony on the Umatilla Reservation in northeast Oregon. There was an incident here yesterday that you may or may not have heard about." She studied the detective to see if had heard about the missing child.

He nodded. "Enos filled us in last night in case someone showed up at the station with the child."

"I was called down to security because they'd found the boy's toy but not the boy. Then Enos and I talked with the parents. The father was adamant that the police not be brought into the investigation." She glanced at Quinn and back to the detective. "When he left, I talked the mother into letting me call the FBI. Special Agent Pierce and I have worked together before and I knew I could trust him."

"That's why I'm here. When she told me who the parents were, I knew this was more than a child wandering off," Quinn said, walking over to the table. He held a steady gaze on her. "Have you had a chance to read what I sent you on the father?"

Dela shook her head. "The only thing I did on my phone this morning was try to call Rowena and call security." She glanced at her friend's body. "Whoever did this will be found."

"Return to telling me about what you and the deceased talked about," Detective Stedman said, drawing her attention away from the bed.

Dela mentally shook herself and told him about her conversation with Rowena when she brought the cheesecake over. "She thought she might have photos of the man and the child she saw. We have no proof it was even the right boy. It could have been any grandfather and grandson on a walk. More than one child has a stuffed dog as their favorite toy." She shrugged. "Rowena offered to bring the photos to me last night, I told her they could wait until morning. We talked some more and then she left around eleven-thirty. I tried calling her this morning to see if she was up. When the call went to voice mail, I figured she was in the shower. So, I finished dressing and walked down the hall."

"What time was this?" Detective Stedman asked.

"About seven-thirty?" She glanced at the clock. It was now 9:30. "I knocked and no one answered. Then I listened at the door to see if I heard the shower running. When I didn't, I tried the phone again and heard the ringtone music. That's when I called security and requested a master keycard be brought up." Dela glanced at the security guard. "That's when Trent arrived and we entered the room."

The detective nodded. "You may go, I'll talk with Trent now."

Dela stood but she didn't leave the room, she drew Quinn over to the door to the hallway. In a whisper, she said, "Whoever did this was looking for those photos and I think they either got them or destroyed them." She pointed to the smashed camera on the floor.

"I'll have forensics go over this room thoroughly and all of the camera equipment." Quinn put a hand on her shoulder. "You know you don't have to be in the middle of this investigation. It's not your job to find the boy or the killer."

She glared at him. "This is personal, not a job. Rowena and I were close and had just reconnected. I won't be going anywhere until the person who killed her is caught." Dela shifted her gaze to the room. "And this is a case of another child gone missing. When someone is murdered or missing, I can't back off. They need to be found and their family needs to know someone cared enough to find the truth."

"We will get to the truth," Quinn said.

Dela swung her gaze back to his face. "Will you? You don't care about my friend's death or the child, you just want to get something on Benedict. I know how you operate."

The muscle in Quinn's left cheek moved back and forth. He hadn't changed from that Ranger in Iraq who'd swooped into her jail and took away a rapist to help aid him in getting the guy he wanted. He didn't care about the young woman the man had violated and how her life was ended by her own hand because her family couldn't tolerate the shame the prisoner had put on their family. And he could care less about Rowena other than using her death to catch someone he'd been after for years.

"I'm here until the boy and Rowena's killer are found." She crossed her arms and waited for Detective Stedman to finish questioning Trent. When they finished, she stepped forward. "I want to help with this investigation."

Stedman looked over her head to Quinn.

"He's not your boss or my boss," Dela said.

Chapter Five

"I've known her a long time and she has an instinct for solving murders," Quinn said, as if Dela hadn't spoken.

"Ms. Alvaro—"

"Dela," she interrupted the detective. "Call me Dela." Since she'd discovered Cisco Alvaro was most likely not her father, she preferred to be called by her first name.

"Dela, this is a local matter. We won't need you to help with the investigation." Detective Stedman moved his gaze from her to Quinn. "But we wouldn't mind help from the FBI."

She had no jurisdiction here, but she'd be damned if she would stay out of the investigation. She pulled out her phone and took photos of the areas that had caught her attention. The overturned camera bag and the smashed camera. A part of her didn't want to tell the two men that Rowena had two cameras but she didn't want to jeopardize the investigation.

"You'll need to find out the make and model of her other camera so you can see if someone pawned it," she said, heading for the door.

"Wait a minute!" Stedman called. "I thought you said you hadn't seen her in years and didn't even know she was a photographer?"

"That's true. But when she sat down to have dinner with me last night, she had two cameras. One on a strap around her neck and one in her camera bag. If there isn't a camera in that overturned bag, then the person who killed her took it." Dela grasped the door latch.

"Wait. It sounds like you could be helpful to this investigation." The detective said begrudgingly.

Dela grinned at the door, then settled her expression into a stern demeanor before she faced the room. "I thought you said I was of no use to this investigation?"

Detective Stedman ran a hand over his face and glanced at Quinn, who sported a grin as if he knew she'd find a way to stay in the middle of everything.

"It appears you know more about the victim and have a strong motivation to dig for the truth, whether we allow you to help or not." Stedman handed her a small notebook. "Walk through the room and write down what you see out of place. Don't touch anything."

Dela nodded and walked over to the detective. She took the notebook from him and walked over to the door, slowly scanning everything as she made her way into the room.

Quinn and Stedman talked to Trent, asking if he'd ever taken statements. It appeared Stedman hadn't been kidding when he said they were low on staff. They asked Trent to go out into the hall and knock on doors asking if anyone heard anything last night after 11:30.

Dela focused on the smashed camera and camera bag. Quinn crouched next to her, holding out a latex glove. She pulled the glove on and turned the camera bag over. The bag was empty other than a long lens, a small rag, and business cards. She documented what she saw and moved toward the bathroom. That's when she saw the toilet seat was up and there were droplets of water on the rim.

"Quinn, Detective Stedman, you might want to come look at this." She faced the toilet and waited for the two to enter the room. "Either your suspect used the facilities, or he flushed the SD cards."

They both swore.

Dela had a feeling they'd never see the photos that caused Rowena's death. But she was going to find out how and who. "Did you ask Trent to call surveillance and see who came into this room while Rowena was in my room? Or at least see who came and went in this hallway all night."

Stedman glanced at Quinn, who grinned, and the detective left the bathroom.

"You better be careful or he'll be offering you a job," Quinn said.

Dela said under her breath, "No one wants a crippled detective." She pushed by him, walking over to the sliding glass door onto the balcony. That could be how the person got into the room. She knew where every surveillance camera was positioned. It had been something she'd asked to see before she came over to assess the security at Siletz Bay Casino. The way the cameras were set up, they would have caught someone climbing over the railing above to drop onto the balcony outside this room.

She studied every inch of the door and the balcony. She didn't see anything out of place. Except… she knelt, studying what looked like sand shoe prints. If the wind picked up these could be whisked away.

"Quinn how soon are your guys getting here?" she called into the room.

He appeared in the doorframe. "Why?"

"I think this sand is in the imprint of a shoe. But it won't last long when it dries and the wind picks up." She pointed to the sand.

He pulled out his phone. "ETA?" he asked into it. His frown told her it would be a while.

Quinn replaced his phone and said, "There's an accident on the freeway and they're stuck in traffic." He spun into the room and talked to Trent. He called on his walkie-talkie for someone to bring them contact paper.

Dela glanced around the room. "Take a photo of the suitcase and bring it out here. We can set it up as a windbreak until the contact paper gets here."

Quinn handed out the emptied suitcase. Dela set it up against the balcony railing to hopefully keep the worst of any wind from shifting the sandy footprint.

When the contact paper arrived, Detective Stedman did the task of placing the paper ever so slowly down on top of the sand. He pressed systematically across the paper, picking up all the grains. When he had them all sticking to the paper, he turned it over and placed another clear piece on top to hold it all together. Then he wrote on the corner where and when he'd made the impression.

"You have a good eye, Dela," the detective said once he had the imprint slid into an evidence bag.

"Thanks. I've looked over every inch of the room. I think I'll take a walk over to the surveillance room and see if they've come up with anything." She used the balcony to pull herself to her feet and didn't miss the puzzlement on the detective's face.

She had only one good leg to push to her feet. By using the railing, it helped her keep her balance. She'd learned early on in rehab to modify things to accommodate the prosthetic leg. She'd let him puzzle or ask Quinn. She didn't want to see the pity in his eyes if she told him.

It was common knowledge at the Spotted Pony that she had lost a leg while in the Army and she didn't let it stop her from doing her job or living a good life. But when she got around people she didn't know, she couldn't help but think they would treat her differently. Hell, Quinn did when he first found out. After showing she could still battle a crazy knife-wielding man, stop murderers, and shoot a man while being without her crutches and prosthesis, he'd gone back to treating her as he had before.

When she left the room, Trent was behind her.

"I'll come too. They might not tell you anything," he said.

"Did you talk to everyone in this hall?" she asked, thinking he hadn't been gone from the room long enough to have taken more than one statement.

"There was only one person still in their room. The FBI agent said he'd have his people question everyone as they came back to their rooms."

She nodded, lost in thought. She'd found important information looking around. Unless forensics found something like a hair, button, or jewelry came loose from the killer when he was strangling… She couldn't continue that thought. It slowed her feet and she almost stumbled.

Trent caught her by the arm. "You okay? She was your friend, you could just go to your room and regroup," he said, stopping her forward movement.

Dela shook her head. "I can't stop and grieve. I need to stay focused on finding her killer. If I don't, it will get filed as unknown. I know how little time a police force this small will put on the investigation."

"You don't trust the police to do their job?" he asked, staring at her.

"Not when it comes to a woman of color. No. I've seen too many women, children, and men who are missing or murdered and no one other than family ever goes looking for them or the killers."

"You must be part of that Indian movement I've heard about." He released her arm and started walking as if he thought the MMIW wasn't worth his time.

"Yes, I believe in the movement. We have finally gotten more law enforcement agencies to take missing and murdered Indigenous people seriously. When we are a small part of the population and yet have the most deaths and violence per capita for our people, there is something wrong."

Trent stopped. "Are those true facts?"

"Look it up if you don't believe me." She stomped past him and out onto the sidewalk alongside the building. She peered over at the casino a good two hundred yards away. Stepping down off the sidewalk onto the asphalt parking lot she headed in a straight line for the building.

"Wait up. We do have a shuttle," Trent said,

jogging up beside her.

"I'd rather walk." She'd yet to get on the beach and if the only sea air she was able to inhale was walking between her room and the casino, then she would get the most of that she could. A thought struck her. She stopped. She hadn't paid attention to the beach area that Rowena could see from her balcony. That might help them find a clue. Like had the dog been found in the vicinity of what Rowena had seen through her camera lens?

Trent realized she'd stopped after he'd taken ten steps. He faced her. "Now what?"

"I need to go back to Rowena's room." She did an about-face and headed back to the building.

"Why?" Trent caught up to her.

"I want to see if the dog was left within sight of Rowena's view from her room." Dela glanced at the guard. "Do you know where the stuffed animal was found?"

"I'll call Sidney. I think she found it." He pulled out his phone as they entered the building and rode the elevator to the second floor.

"What are you doing back here?" Quinn asked as Dela entered the room and walked out onto the balcony.

She breathed in the briny air and stood facing south. She pulled out her phone and started taking a video, moving slowly to the west and up the north beach.

Trent stopped beside her, holding his phone out to her. "This is where Sidney found the toy."

Dela studied the photo and then the area she'd just videoed. "Did anyone search that area?" she asked as her gaze landed on the bush that was in the photo. She pointed. "There." She turned to Quinn. "You need to have a forensic team go over that area. That isn't a place where a grandfather would be playing with his grandson, but it would be a place to hide while waiting for someone."

Quinn took a photo of the area and made a call. "How much longer until you arrive?"

Dela faced Trent. "You go check on the surveillance footage. I'm going to take a walk around down there." She pointed to the area where the dog was found and the beach.

Trent nodded and left.

She caught Quinn by the sleeve of his suit jacket. "Check and see if any unauthorized boats were in this area yesterday. Rowena said she saw a boat close to the shoreline."

"Don't muck up any forensics when you go snooping around," he said in return.

Dela glared, not at him just at his presence, and left the room. This time instead of heading across the parking lot, she walked the path between the buildings down toward the beach. She veered to the south and found the area she was interested in.

There wasn't a path to the area, in fact from ground level it was more of an opening between some bushes. The area wasn't meant for anyone to hang out in. The man who brought Asher here had to have scouted out the area and known it was a good place to hide from people walking the beach and walking to the beach.

To not mess up any footprints or possible evidence, Dela didn't enter the little sanctuary. Instead, she walked around the outside of it and noted impressions in the loose sand leading to the beach that could have been footprints given the distance between them and the placement. Only large indentions. The man must have carried the boy.

She stood, peering out at the ocean. There were half a dozen rocks with waves splashing over and around them. The roar and whoosh of the water as it impacted the rocks made her shiver. How could a man with a child get beyond those rocks, walking into the power of the ocean?

Pulling out her phone, Dela typed *Lincoln City tide chart* in her browser. Yesterday the tide was at its lowest around 2:00 p.m. A glance at her watch showed she had an hour and fifty minutes before it would be low tide today. She'd go grab lunch and come back.

She walked down the beach, piecing together all she knew about the missing boy and the death of her friend. Before she even thought about it, her phone was in her hand and she heard Heath's voice.

"You miss me so much you have to talk to me again," he teased.

She stopped, stared at the ocean rolling in, and swallowed a sob. "She's dead," croaked through her constricted throat.

Chapter Six

"Who's dead?" Heath's calm voice was what Dela needed.

She swallowed the lump, swiped at the tear trickling down her cheek, and filled Heath in on what had happened.

"You think she was killed because she took photos of the abduction?" Heath asked, his tone neutral.

Dela knew it wasn't her fault but all she could think of was nonchalantly leaving Robin in Pendleton and learning the next day of her disappearance and death. Then last night she hadn't gone with Rowena's suggestion they go get the camera and look at the photos she'd taken.

Through the phone, she heard Heath blow out a breath and say softly, "Her death is not your fault. It is the fault of the person who abducted the boy and killed her, not you."

"Rationally, I know that. But Heath, this is the second friend I've lost to violence because I was thinking of myself." She knew it was illogical to think she could never have a close friend for fear they would die, but given that her two best female friends had come to ugly ends…

"You couldn't have made Robin go with you unless you had physically dragged her into the car. And as you said, you thought only you and Rowena knew about the photos. How could either of you have foreseen that someone else knew." He cleared his throat. "Do you want me to take some time off and come to Lincoln City?"

As much as she wanted to say yes, she was not someone who asked for help. "There's no need. I'll pull myself together. I'm helping the local police and Quinn is digging into the father's background. He's been on the FBI's radar for a while." Talking about the incident as an investigation helped to draw her from her grief. "I'll be fine. I just needed someone, you know, who knows my vulnerable side."

Heath chuckled. "Yeah, I know all your sides."

She snorted. "That's not what I meant."

"I know, but it worked. Call any time you need to. If I'm in the middle of something, leave a message about why you called and I'll get back as soon as I can. You know I'll always be here for you."

She smiled. "Yeah, I know. Thank you for being you." She ended the call, squared her shoulders, and headed away from the beach. She'd grab something to eat at the restaurant between the hotel buildings and across from the registration office. She could also inquire if someone took lunch up to the Benedicts' suite yesterday when the boy went missing.

After a quick sandwich and a discussion with the manager, Dela determined that no one at the restaurant received the request for lunch to be delivered to the Benedicts' suite. Which meant Hugo was lying. Why would anyone lie about making a phone call that could be checked up on? She headed to the casino pondering this revelation.

Dela stopped a moment in front of the memorial flag at the entrance and saluted the flag. She'd spent most of her years on this earth defending that flag and was still in awe of it, even though there were many things the government had done over the years that were for a minority of the people and not all the people.

Standing in front of the memorial she thought of Rowena and how she'd been sure Dela was either on leave or AWOL from the Army. She'd never understood Dela's need to belong or feel as if she belonged somewhere. The Army had given her the extended family she'd yearned for.

"I'll get whoever did this to you," she said.

Turning from the memorial, she watched a limousine pull away from the casino entrance. As it passed, she tried to see into it, but the windows were tinted. Who would come to a Tribal casino on the Oregon Coast in a limo?

She hurried up to the valet standing at the podium to the left of the door. "Hi, who just drove away in that limo?"

The long-haired man who appeared to be in his forties, shrugged.

"You didn't see who got into that car?" she asked, studying the man. His eyes were glazed and he reeked of marijuana. "Do you even work here?"

He just stared at her.

Dela dialed the security office.

"Siletz Bay Security, how may I help you?" answered the same woman she'd talked with earlier that day when looking for Enos.

"This is Dela. Are you aware the man standing at the valet podium in front of the casino is high?"

There was a long silence. "Hello? Are you still there?" Dela asked.

Trent's voice grew louder before his voice came through the phone. "Dela, there isn't a valet out there today. He must be a vagrant."

"Can you ask your staff if they saw who pulled away from here in a limo ten minutes ago?" Dela was curious if it was Mr. Benedict. He would be the only one arrogant enough to travel everywhere, even the Oregon Coast, in a limousine.

"Paul said it was Mrs. Benedict and a man he's seen watching her."

"Pull up the video and get the license number. He could be working with whoever kidnapped the boy. I'm headed to surveillance."

She walked into the casino and went left, through the lines and into the back. She took the stairs faster alone, not worrying if she missed a step with no one to see. At the top, she took a couple of deep breaths to slow her breathing and opened the door.

Trent was already standing in the middle of the room. "Over here." He motioned to a bank of monitors above an older man with a gray beard. "Ray, run the video at the front entrance from twenty minutes ago."

Dela stopped beside Trent and faced the monitors. The entrance appeared on the one directly in front of the older man.

A couple walked out. A man walked up to the doors and stood back. The man she'd thought was a valet, walked over to the podium and stood holding it as if he would fall if he let go.

"That's the guy I thought was the valet," she said.

"He's harmless," Ray said. "I've seen him here every day for about a week."

Dela studied the man clinging to the valet podium. While his body appeared weak and wobbly, his head was steady and his gaze fixed.

Mrs. Benedict walked up the sidewalk toward the casino. The limo appeared, stopping beside her. She glanced around and slid in when the door opened. The car pulled away.

"She knew whoever was in there. Was it her husband?" Dela asked.

"No. Their limo is silver," Ray said.

Trent held out a piece of paper. "Here's the plate."

"Thanks. I'll give it to Stedman and the FBI. Maybe they can find out who it is."

Trent's phone rang. "Trent." He listened. "Okay, I'll send her over." He faced Dela. "Registration said someone came down last night and left something for you with them." He studied her.

"Did they say who?"

He glanced around and tipped his head toward the door.

Dela followed him out to the top of the stairs.

"It was your friend," he said.

Dela stared at him for a moment. "Did they say when?"

"I didn't ask. Figured you'd want to question

them."

"Thanks, I do."

Trent led the way down the stairs. When she started to go right, he touched her arm. "We have a side-by-side you can use to get there. Follow me." They went into the security office, he grabbed a key, and they exited a door that led out the west side of the building. Sitting under a small lean-to were two ATVs. He handed her the key. "Unless you want me to go with you?"

He had been more than helpful all morning. "I'd prefer if you drive. I'm not very good with these things." She was proficient at driving many types of vehicles, but she had to experiment with pedal-driven vehicles like this. It required the right amount of pressure with her prosthetic foot.

She slid into the passenger side and Trent slid in behind the steering wheel. They took off, driving on a narrow asphalt path to the front of the building. The man who'd been using the podium to hold himself up was gone.

Trent used the road to drive over to the registration office. He parked at the side and they entered. One woman immediately waved them over.

"When I heard what happened in room two-nineteen I figured security should know about this." She held up an envelope the size someone would send a greeting card in. Dela saw her name and room number written on the front side.

"Thank you. I'm Dela Alvaro." She reached out and the woman handed the letter to Trent, who in turn handed it to Dela. "What time did this get left here?" Dela asked.

"The time written in the top left corner says twelve-fifteen." The woman pointed to the corner of the envelope.

"Is the person who she gave this to, still here?" Dela asked.

"Heavens no. She went home when her shift ended. She'll be back tonight if you want to talk to her."

"Thank you. What's her name?" Dela asked.

"Kristy Dodd."

"Thank you." Dela exited the building with Trent right behind her.

"What now?" he asked.

Dela walked over to the ATV and sat. She opened the sealed envelope and found a note on the same casino stationery Rowena had slipped under her door.

In large looping print it said: *Dela, I know you said we'd look at this in the morning. But I received a call to do a sunrise shot on Mt. Hood. I thought you might need this before I'd get back. See you in a couple of days. R.*

Dela read the note twice before running a finger over the SD card in the V of the note. Rowena hadn't been killed when she returned to her room from visiting with her. She'd been killed while packing to leave.

"Let's go to security and see what's on this SD card," she said.

Trent nodded and slid in behind the steering wheel.

While she was happy to learn that she couldn't have prevented her friend's death, it still hurt knowing her friend's life had ended so soon. And she vowed to find the person responsible.

Chapter Seven

As Trent drove them back to the casino, Dela called Detective Stedman and Quinn giving them the limo license plate number and letting them know she had the SD card. She told Quinn, "Trent and I are headed to the security office to view the photos."

"I'll be there in fifteen," he responded.

Dela ended the call as Trent parked the ATV. She didn't want Quinn telling her to wait for him because she wasn't about to. For all she knew he'd come in and confiscate the card before they had a chance to look at anything.

She shoved her phone in a pocket. "Where would be the best place to take a look at this card?"

Trent paused before they entered the building. "I would say the room behind the main surveillance room. I'll call Sidney up to help us. She worked surveillance before she applied for security."

Dela walked through the door Trent unlocked.

"That's a good idea. Because if there isn't any video of someone entering Rowena's room, that means someone in surveillance helped the murderer."

Trent stopped and stared at her. "Really?"

"Who else would have been able to either scrape the video or turn it off during the time the killer walked down the hall, entered, then returned to the hall and walked away?" She clenched the envelope in her hand. She'd discovered there were surveillance members who would take money to hide crimes. It had happened at the Spotted Pony shortly after she'd started working there. She'd exposed the cover-up and became the head of security.

"Makes sense. I just don't like to think someone who has been working for the casino would do something like that." Trent led her through the security office. "Sidney, call in someone to take over for you. We need your help up in the back surveillance room."

She nodded and spoke on the radio. "I need someone to cover for me, Trent's orders. Jack, how about you come sit for a while."

"Copy," said a garbled male voice.

"As soon as he gets in here, I'll head up," Sidney said.

Trent nodded and Dela followed him out of the security offices and over to the stairs leading up to the surveillance room. She was glad the Spotted Pony had both security and surveillance on the main floor of the casino. Her stub would always be angry and throbbing by the end of a shift if she had to climb stairs multiple times.

At the top, Trent looked back. "You sure you're okay? It had to of been a shock finding your friend."

Dela ignored him and they entered the surveillance room.

"What do you need now?" Oscar asked.

"Sidney will be coming up here to help us," Trent said, continuing to the back room.

Dela noted the other surveillance members kept their gaze on their monitors while Oscar's followed their movements.

When they were in the back room waiting for Sidney, Dela asked, "What do you know about Oscar?"

Trent stopped putting three chairs in front of a large monitor in the room. He studied her. "Why?"

"He's been jumpy ever since we asked him about the surveillance of the hallway to the Benedicts' suite and just now, he was the only one who was interested in what we're doing."

"You think he had something to do with the missing boy?" Trent sat down and motioned for her to sit as well.

"He does seem overly interested." Dela settled onto the chair as the door opened.

"Sorry. It took Jack a bit to relieve me. He was stopped by a guest and felt he should answer the questions."

Dela smiled at the young woman. She liked Sidney's commitment to her job. "That's okay, we had things to discuss." Dela held out the SD card. "We'd like to see what is on this, please."

Sidney started up the computer in front of the chair she sat in and the monitor came to life. "Does this have something to do with the missing boy?"

"There is a possibility." Dela glanced at Trent, wondering why he wasn't taking the lead on this.

"I feel for poor Mrs. Benedict. She loves Asher. She just doesn't know how to be a mother." Sidney clicked on a folder that appeared on the monitor.

Small photos of fog, waves, rocks, and the darkness of the land on the north side of the beach shrouded in the fog. Rowena was able to capture the mood of the foggy morning. Seeing her friend's talent squeezed Dela's heart. Why did those with so much talent to give the world die so young?

Trent put his arm out, pointing to a photo. "That one is from her balcony."

"Yes. Make that larger and don't change the photo until we've searched it thoroughly," Dela said, compartmenting her sorrow and getting back to the reason they studied these photos.

She searched the full photo before seeing the small spot out on the horizon. "Okay, move on but keep an eye on that spot there." She pointed to what could be a boat.

Sidney moved to the next photo. Same scene but the dot on the horizon had been brought up close by a zoom lens. It was a boat. A power boat with some writing on the side.

Her phone buzzed. Dela glanced at the caller. She sighed and read the message.

Where are you?

In the back room of surveillance.

"Be prepared, Special Agent Quinn is on his way up. He'll probably want this card." She had to admit that his tech people could probably blow the photo up with enough clarity to read the name on the boat. "Next photo."

Now the photos were of the beach. In the left lower

corner, she spotted a head. Hard to say if when the photo was enlarged the image would be discernable. "Sidney, can you blow that lower corner up?"

The security guard isolated the section Dela pointed to and enlarged it on the screen. The photo was grainy.

"Does that look like anyone you've seen?" Dela asked.

"It's hard to say. If I could see the body, it might help jog my mind," Trent said.

"Yeah, there aren't any features—"

The door opened abruptly. Quinn stepped in and shut the door with a thud. "What are you doing viewing evidence in a federal case?"

Dela spun around and frowned at Quinn. In a fierce quiet voice, she asked, "What's up with you coming in here and letting everyone in the casino know we have this card?"

He didn't even quell from her reprimand. Quinn stalked up to the back of Sidney and said, "Give me that card." He held his badge out in front of her face.

Sidney glanced at Trent, who shrugged, then at Dela.

She shook her head as Sidney mouthed "*Stall him*."

"I don't know why we can't see what's on the disk, it pertains to a crime committed at the casino," Dela said, standing and moving to make Quinn turn his back to whatever Sidney was doing.

"You know that kidnapping on Indian land is under FBI jurisdiction," Quinn said, crossing his arms.

"You Feds could care less about what happens to anyone on Native American land. You wouldn't be here if the father wasn't someone you've been after for years." Dela had enough anger against this man, and many others who wore his badge, that she could keep this going for as long as Sidney needed to accomplish whatever she had planned.

"You know good and well that we step up and help out when needed on the reservations," Quinn said, a smattering of hurt in his tone.

"Only because there are now laws that require you to." Dela uncrossed her arms and pointed at him. "I want copies of all the photos on that disk."

Quinn shrugged. "You can ask but that doesn't mean you'll get them."

Sidney held the SD card up over her head. "Stop bothering Dela and take your card."

Quinn snatched the card from Sidney and said, "At least someone around here understands authority."

"Don't let the door hit you on the way out," Dela said, dropping into the chair feeling as if she just lost a battle that should have been a victory.

The door closed and Sidney turned the monitor back on. The photo they'd been looking at popped up.

Dela sat up straight. "How did you do that?"

"I started copying the card onto the hard drive when you said he was coming up to get it. It hadn't finished when he arrived, that's why I told you to stall him."

Dela hugged her. "Quick thinking."

Trent cleared his throat. "You think it's wise to go against the FBI?"

Dela waved a hand and told Sidney to go to the next photo before replying to Trent. "He's used to me going behind his back. He'd lose respect for me if I hadn't tried to see the photos or, thanks to Sidney's quick thinking, hadn't kept a copy."

"Is there any way we can figure out who that boat belongs to?" she said out loud.

"My brother is with the Coast Guard harbor patrol. I can see if they saw anyone with this type of boat yesterday." Trent took a photo of the boat on the monitor and sat back typing on his phone.

"Next photo, please," Dela said.

The next photo was of the boy and an older man in the bushes where Dela was sure the man was waiting for whoever was picking up the child. Asher played with his stuffed dog while the man looked out to sea. "That boat had to be there to pick up the boy. But how did they accomplish it?"

Sidney moved to the next photo when the door opened. Dela stood, blocking whoever opened the door from seeing the monitor.

It was Oscar. "Trent, there's something you need to see," he said, his voice wavering and his head tilting as if trying to see around Dela.

"Talk to you later," Trent said and ended his phone call. "What's going on?" He motioned for Oscar to turn around and then stared at Dela as if to say, you might be right.

Dela waited until the door closed before she sat back down. "What do you know about Oscar?" Dela asked.

"He shouldn't work in a casino. He has a gambling problem. When he isn't working, he spends half of his off hours gambling." Sidney clicked to another photo. She pointed, "What's that?"

Dela followed the tip of Sidney's finger and noticed something out in the water. "Do seals come in that close to the beach and rocks?" Dela asked.

"They can, but they are usually out at the spit, not here by the casino," Sidney enlarged the seal. "I don't think seals wear goggles."

Dela studied the enlargement. It was a man in a wet suit. "But how did he get that poor little boy out to the boat without anyone seeing him? He surely wouldn't just haul him through the water sputtering and taking on salt water." Dela had another thought. "Keep looking through those and print out the ones that show us the man in the wetsuit and the best photo of the older man and the boat. I'm going to read through the information that Quinn sent me on Mr. Benedict."

She leaned back in her chair and opened her phone to her emails. She scrolled to the one from Quinn and started reading. It appeared that Hugo Benedict had his fingers in every operation there was in Oregon, Washington, and California that had to do with money laundering and corporate fraud. The reports named people she'd heard linked to the same types of crimes. Everyone had gone to court and won their freedom with money and good lawyers.

"From what I'm reading, he could have pissed off any number of people who would want to get back at him." Dela stopped reading as her phone rang. Detective Stedman.

"Hello Detective," she answered.

"Dela, I have a name on that limo license you gave me. It's Jude West."

She ran the name over in her mind. He hadn't been named in the report Quinn sent her about Benedict. "Do you know anything about him?"

"I figured you'd ask. He's as rich as the Benedicts,

single, and has been seen with Mrs. Benedict multiple times."

"As in lovers?" Dela asked.

"That's the rumor."

She thought about this. Had Felicity called her lover for support when her husband was being an ass? That made sense. "Where can I find Mr. West?"

"He has residences in Portland, Seattle, and Oakland. And rumor has it he owns one of the beach resorts on the Oregon Coast but no one has been able to substantiate it."

"Any chance you could have the state police be on the lookout for his limo? That way I can have a talk with him. I'm sure he wouldn't take Mrs. Benedict very far from here considering she would want to be notified if we hear anything." Dela wanted to see if perhaps the lover got the boy out of the way so he and Felicity could be together without having to deal with Hugo.

"I'll see what I can do. How are you coming along with that card?" Stedman asked.

"We're printing off photos that give us an idea of what happened but I'm not sure how easy it will be to find the two men and the boat." She went on to tell him about the scenario they'd pieced together from seeing the photos. "I want to make sure when these guys are caught that Rowena gets full credit for taking these and realizing they were of importance to the kidnapping."

"I'll make sure of that," Detective Stedman said before he ended the call.

Dela pointed to a photo. "Who is that in the background?" The photo was one taken not of the beach in front of the balcony but toward the north. At the corner of the next building stood a man who looked familiar.

Chapter Eight

Sidney enlarged the photo and Dela could make out the man's build, slouch, and beard. *The vagrant at the valet podium.* What was he doing watching the beach at the same time there was a kidnapping happening? Now she wanted to find him and have a little chat.

Dela pulled out her phone. "What's Trent's number?"

Sidney rattled it off and Dela added him to her contacts before putting the call through.

"Lawton," he answered.

"It's Dela. Can you tell the security personnel who are at the front of the casino to call me when they see that vagrant who was hanging around at the podium earlier today?"

"Yeah. Why? Did you see something?" He didn't add 'in a photo' which made her wonder if he was still with Oscar.

"Yeah. I'll tell you more later." She ended the call

and gathered up the photos Sidney had printed out. "Make copies on two cards and then delete everything from the computer. Give one copy to me and hide the other one. Then give Trent a blank card and tell him I asked that he put it in a safe place."

Sidney studied her. "You don't trust Trent?"

Dela shook her head. "I want whoever is after these photos to think the blank card is the real thing. If Trent knows it isn't, he won't be careful with it."

The young woman smiled and nodded. "Yeah, he's good at giving orders but you can read his face like a kid's book."

Her respect for the young woman was continuing to grow. "Do not tell anyone what we have or did in here today. Make something up, like I thought you should be able to see if videos had been tampered with and wanted you to go over the ones from the hallway outside of the victim's room."

Sidney nodded. "That makes sense. It will also make Oscar or whoever might have helped nervous."

"That's what I'm hoping. Maybe I can catch the person and get some answers out of them or at least who they're working for." Dela grasped the disk Sidney handed to her.

"That's the second copy. I already hid the other one." She smiled.

"Where no one will find it?" Dela asked skeptically since the woman hadn't moved from the chair.

"Positive."

"Delete away. I'm going to see if I can find the vagrant and catch up to Kristy Dodd who works nights at the registration desk." Dela knew she shouldn't be paranoid, but this had her thinking there could be more than Oscar who helped the kidnapper and killed Rowena. She spun on her chair so her back was to Sidney and raised her right pant leg. She slipped the card under the sock on her stub and put her pant leg down. The only way someone would find the card on her was if she were dead.

Dela didn't see Trent when she walked out of the back room, but Oscar watched her. Had the reason Oscar opened the door to the back room been legitimate? She headed out of the room and down the stairs with the decision to wait by the Starfish building for Felicity to return. That would give her a chance to possibly talk with Jude West. And if she was lucky, it would be in a spot where she could keep an eye out for the vagrant as well.

She pushed through the door into the casino area and walked around the people lined up for help. Stepping into the entry of the casino, she scanned the area for the closest security personnel. When she didn't see one, Dela walked into the crowded gaming floor. It appeared the casino had a full house on Saturday afternoons. She wondered what it would look like come evening when the comedy club opened.

She finally found a security guard standing with his hands on his duty belt, feet spread apart, watching the people milling about. Dela strode toward him. She'd yet to meet this person and he studied her as she approached.

"Can I help you?" the tall, broad-shoulder man with a shiny mahogany head asked.

"Where can I find Trent?" she countered.

"Why would you need to speak to the acting head

of security?"

She read his name tag. "Mr. Trainor. I am here at the request of Enos Apash and have been working with Trent Lawton all morning. I wanted to let him know where I would be if he needed anything."

Trainor squinted his eyes and studied her. "What's your name?"

"Dela Alvaro."

He jerked back as if someone had hit him. "The person here to evaluate us?"

She smiled. "Right now, I just want to talk to Trent."

"Last I saw him was early this morning. He hasn't been back out here for some time. You'd learn his whereabouts quicker if you asked surveillance where they last saw him."

"Thank you. You wouldn't happen to know if the vagrant that likes to hang out in the front of the casino has been around lately, would you?" She didn't think from his position so far into the casino he would have noticed the man.

"He usually stands out front from ten to two. You missed him for today."

"Thanks." Dela headed to the entrance. She didn't really need to tell Trent anything but did want to find out what Oscar had said to him. Stepping out into the brisk wind, she ducked her head and followed the sidewalk toward the hotel buildings. She'd gone thirty yards when she heard the rolling of tires on asphalt come up slowly behind her.

Dela turned and found Trent in the ATV.

"Need a lift?"

"Sure." She sat in the passenger side and twisted to

study him as she asked, "What did Oscar want?"

Trent frowned. "It was a lame-ass excuse to get into the room. I'm beginning to think you're right about him being part of the kidnapping if not also the murder."

"He's just being paid to hide the person who is doing it. Can you get someone you trust to go through surveillance footage and see who has approached Oscar when he's off-duty playing the slots?"

Trent's gaze snapped around to her. "How do you know he's been playing the slots off duty?"

"There are a lot of observant security personnel here." She wasn't going to get Sidney in trouble for telling her the truth about an employee. An observation anyone in surveillance or security would know. "Will Enos be coming in to work tonight?" She was beginning to wonder about the head of security not coming in when there was a kidnapped boy and a murder at his casino.

"He's gone on a family thing," Trent said.

It was Dela's turn to jerk her attention from the parking lot to the man sitting beside her. "How long had this been planned?" she asked, wondering why he hadn't told her he'd be gone when she'd settled on this weekend to come do a security check.

Trent shrugged. "It's been on the calendar for six months. Some big party for his father, I think."

"Why didn't he tell me he'd be away? I could have come another weekend." Dela found it odd that the weekend he'd planned to be away, he'd brought her in and two crimes were committed.

"Stop here." She twisted in the seat to look back toward the casino entrance. She wouldn't be able to tell who was going in and out of the building, it was too far away. But then the vagrant had been down here, at the corner of the Starfish building yesterday in the afternoon. She glanced at her watch. It was nearing evening now.

"Have you seen Mrs. Benedict return?" she asked.

"No, but her husband was in an argument with someone in the High Stakes room. That's what Oscar wanted me to break up."

Dela held up a hand. "Was Oscar watching a different set of monitors today?" Yesterday he'd been watching the outside monitors on the building where Asher had been kidnapped. Today he was watching the gaming floor. At Spotted Pony, the surveillance members usually watched the same set of cameras every day. That way they could pick up on irregularities easier than someone unfamiliar with that area.

Trent put his foot down on the pedal and the vehicle lurched forward. "He should have been on the same ones as yesterday. I need to have a chat with him and who he changed with."

When the vehicle started moving, Dela put a hand on the steering wheel. "Stop! Let me out. You can tackle that while I continue looking into the Benedicts." She slid out of the ATV and stood on the sidewalk in front of the registration office as Trent whirred away toward the casino.

Her stomach started growling when a whiff of fish and something smokey reached her nose. She glanced over at the Seafood Grill. It looked like a good place to get a late lunch or early dinner.

Before she walked across to the grill, she stepped into the registration area. Several couples were waiting in line to be helped. Dela didn't see anyone that was in the office that morning. It was after three, and a new shift was on duty.

"What time will Kristy be in?" Dela asked the closest woman.

"Not until ten-thirty," the woman answered and smiled at the couple across the counter from her.

Dela took that as a good reason to get something to eat.

When she wandered into the restaurant, she noticed she could see the fronts of the hotel buildings to the south. She asked to be seated where she could watch the buildings and the ocean. Her back was to the entrance and the people who were coming and going.

Just as her meal arrived, a voice behind her made her skin tingle and her gut clench.

"I'll just sit with her," Quinn's arrogant voice grew closer.

She willed him to head to a different table, but no, he pulled out a chair and sat down, smiling. He held up his hand, fending off the menu the hostess tried to hand him.

"I'll have what she's having, except for the beer. Bring me a dry red wine."

The hostess walked away, and Quinn pulled the cloth napkin from around the utensils and spread it across his lap.

Leaning toward her he said in a low voice, "I must say, you are either not putting your all into this advising other casinos or your friend's death has knocked off your edge."

Dela pointed the serrated knife she'd been about to use to cut into her steak at Quinn. "Says a man who chases criminals for years without finding enough to arrest them," she hissed.

"Whoa," he held up his hands. "Let's call a truce until the meal is over. I don't want indigestion."

"Fine. But if you didn't want indigestion, you should have picked a different table." She stabbed her fork into the bite she'd cut and shoved it in her mouth. Chewing would keep her from saying anything she didn't want him to know.

"True. I was hoping we could civilly talk about this kidnapping."

The hostess returned with his wine and gasped.

"What are you talking about? Who's been kidnapped?"

Quinn put his hand on the woman's arm. "Shh. Nothing to be alarmed about. I'm with the FBI and we have everything under control. It's being kept quiet so we can catch the person."

The woman leaned toward Quinn as if he were her protector. Dela refrained from snorting at the woman's obvious ruse to get close to Quinn. He was handsome. And there was a time when she would have given anything to have Quinn hold her and— Dela shook her head. He'd ruined anything between them with his arrogance.

"You should take care of those people waiting for a table," Dela said, before washing the steak down with her beer.

The woman glared at her but headed to the hostess podium.

"Thanks. There was a time when I'd been all over that, but not anymore." He smiled and sipped his wine.

Dela wondered what he meant by that, but let it go.

"Have you learned anything new?" She had several things to tell him if he didn't try to withhold information from her.

"I have someone watching Benedict. He's going about business as if his son isn't missing. As far as I know, there hasn't been a ransom note, which is odd."

Dela nodded. She'd been surprised nothing had arrived for the Benedicts. "What about the wife? Do you have someone watching her?" Dela asked, wondering where she and her lover could be.

"Yeah. She's with Jude West. They're staying down the coast at a place he has." Quinn sipped his wine and stared out at the water.

Dela studied him as she chewed on another bite, then swallowed. "You know about West and Felicity?"

"Yeah. She doesn't know anything about what her husband does, but she is willing to help us to get away from him. Only this little kidnapping put a kink in the plan."

Dela picked up her glass of beer. "Is she blaming you for not keeping her child safe?" She sipped.

"Something like that. She thinks since we know so much about her husband, we should know who he had take her son."

Dela placed the glass down harder than she'd planned, making it slosh over onto her hand. Wiping the beer off her skin she asked, "She knows her husband had the child taken?"

"Not really. She just thinks because he didn't want to call in the police or FBI, he took the child. I tried to tell her that he doesn't want us getting involved in his business." Quinn leaned back as a waiter delivered his dinner.

"Just when did you have this long conversation with her?" Dela asked, wondering how he'd become chummy with the woman.

"About an hour ago at West's place." Quinn forked the piece of steak he'd sawed off the sirloin.

"West's? How do you know him and that he couldn't be the one who took the child?" Dela picked her drink back up and sipped, watching Quinn. He was methodically cutting his steak as he chewed the bite in his mouth. She figured it was a stall tactic as he tried to figure out just what to tell her about West.

Quinn set down his utensils and picked up his wine glass. He studied her for several seconds before he set the glass back down and leaned forward. "No one, not even Mrs. Benedict knows this so don't tell anyone." He continued to hold her gaze.

Dela kept her face void of emotion but inside she was smiling. He was going to tell her something only FBI agents knew.

"West is an informant." Quinn picked his utensils back up and started shoveling grilled vegetables into his mouth.

Dropping against the back of the chair, Dela stared at him. "You have an informant in love with your target's wife?"

"It's not one-sided. She's in love with him and will tell him anything." Quinn grinned while chewing a bit.

Dela didn't think she could have heard anything lower about the FBI than the history of turning their backs on missing and murdered Indigenous people on reservations. But this! "I suppose you told him by helping you get the goods on her husband he could move in on Felicity?" She had a hard time keeping her voice down. "How could he, you, the damn FBI do such a thing?"

Quinn's chiseled features darkened and his gun-metal blue eyes narrowed. "We do what needs to be done to keep the rest of you safe from parasites like Benedict."

"That's where I'm different. I don't use innocent people to try and catch the bad guys." She tossed her napkin on her plate and shoved them away from her. "I'm not hungry anymore." She stood. "And for the record. We copied that disk before Sidney handed it over to you. We'll get to the bottom of Rowena's death since you only care about getting one person."

Quinn grabbed her wrist as she spun away from the table. He held tight when she tried to pull it away. "I figured as much because you turned me away from the monitor. I'm not stupid, Dela. Remember that."

He released her arm and she teetered on her prosthetic foot for several seconds before gaining her balance and walking away.

Dela wasn't sure where she wanted to go. Once again, Quinn was showing her why she was better off for not having fallen in love with him seven years ago in Iraq. It was as if every time she started thinking of him romantically something came along that showed her why he wasn't right for her. Especially now that she believed she was Umatilla and not Hispanic. She and Heath made a much better union.

Stepping out into the cold foggy evening, she shuddered and hoped the boy had been kidnapped. That would be a safer, warmer place for him to be than wandering around alone along the coast.

Chapter Nine

Dela hurried to her building, cursing herself that she hadn't learned where West was staying. Quinn knew, but she didn't feel like texting and asking him after their argument in the restaurant. It still set her blood boiling thinking of how the FBI had been using Felicity.

Pulling on her jacket, her phone buzzed.

Trent's name popped up.

She answered, heading out of her room and down the hall to the elevator. "Hey, I have some questions for you."

"I have some information for you. Want to meet me at the coffee shop in twenty?" Trent asked.

"I can do that. But can you give me Felicity Benedict's phone or room number, please? And did you give the information to everyone about if they see the vagrant?"

He rattled off the building and room number for Felicity. "Why do you need to talk to the vagrant?"

"I'll tell you when I see you. Thanks." A glance at the time on her phone said she still had almost three hours until Kristy Dodd came to work.

Not feeling like walking across the parking lot, and knowing she had twenty minutes to get to the casino, Dela headed to the beach. She did her best thinking when she was jogging. Not that she could jog very well in the sand, but the briny sea air would be good for her brain.

Taking her time going down the large rock steps, she peered at the rocks out in the ocean where the person in the wet suit had most likely waited until the "grandfatherly" man had handed the child over. But how did they get the boy from there to the boat? She planned to ask Felicity if the child knew how to swim. But why would he go with a stranger? This had been puzzling her all day. Why would a five-year-old first let a man take him from his room and then go into the ocean with another person without making a fuss? When she reached the bottom of the tiered rocks, the sound of quick heavy steps had her moving to her left as quickly as she could with her feet sinking into the dry sand.

Four teenage boys bounded off the last rock and over the sand toward the sea shimmering in the last rays of sunlight.

With the sun going down and no lights on the beach, Dela made her way down to the wet packed sand and strode along toward the steps up to the ocean side of the casino. She'd planned on a relaxing stroll but after realizing being alone on the beach as the sun set wasn't a good idea, she'd headed straight for the casino.

Knowing the door she and Trent had used earlier

would be locked, she headed around the end of the building. That's when she spotted the vagrant standing in the shadow of a corner of the building behind the memorial wall. The lights over two employee doorways didn't reach the corner. A garbage can and a bench along the wall made her think it was a place for employees to smoke.

She took a step forward to have a word with the man when she heard a voice.

"We have to catch him in the act," a deep drawling voice said.

"I've been keeping an eye on him. So far, he's not shown his cards," said the vagrant.

Dela narrowed her eyes. The man wasn't a homeless person, he was either with law enforcement or a private investigator. But if he was working with law enforcement and saw the kidnapping, as she presumed from seeing him watching in the photos, then why hadn't he come forward?

"He got the ransom note at noon. Did he do anything after that?" the man she couldn't see asked.

"Nothing, other than getting in an argument with the manager of the casino but that's all. He hasn't made any attempt to go to a bank," the vagrant said.

That must have been the argument that Oscar had used to summon Trent from the back room. Had it been staged for Oscar to get into the back room and see what they were up to? They had to be talking about Hugo Benedict. Was he trying to get money for the ransom from the casino manager? But that didn't make sense. Why go there and not to a bank?

Dela eased her way over to the sidewalk in front of the memorial. As she walked past the two men, she glanced at the back of the man talking to the vagrant. She gazed long enough to get a good feel for his size and build. She couldn't barge in on their conversation without them getting suspicious. Neither would know who she was and she didn't have a badge or the status to pull them in for questioning.

She walked over to the entrance of the casino and sat on the bench closest to the memorial. A man dressed in t-shirt and sweatpants scooted over and offered her a cigarette. She shook her head and he lit up. She'd never cared for second-hand smoke but in this instance, she needed a ruse to keep an eye on the two men.

Three minutes later the tall man walked out of the dark corner but went the opposite direction, giving her a glimpse of a tailor-made suit jacket and dark short hair. A quick glance at the shadow and the vagrant was gone. Most likely he'd ducked around to the backside of the casino.

Pushing to her feet, she moved away from the smoker and over to the doors. Tonight, there was a middle-aged man in a jacket with the casino logo standing at the valet podium. She nodded to him and wandered in for her meeting with Trent.

She hoped the information he had for her was better than what she could tell him.

Trent sat at a table with a basket of fries in the middle and a burger in his hands. Dela noted there was a paper cup with a straw lying beside it on the opposite side of the table from him.

She sunk onto the hard chair and waited until he chewed and wiped his mouth.

"Wasn't sure what you liked. That's iced tea in case

you weren't a soda person. But if you want soda, I haven't touched mine." He motioned to the larger cup in front of him.

"Tea is good," she said, taking the paper off the straw and swirling the conversation she'd heard moments ago around in her head.

Trent continued to eat, pushing the basket of fries toward her. In between bites, he said, "I can't eat them all."

She shook her head. "I had dinner earlier." She wasn't going to say with whom.

He nodded, finished the burger, and slurped his drink before releasing a large sigh and smiling. "That's better. First food I've had all day. Can't remember when I've had a busier day here."

Dela didn't return the smile. The reason he'd had a busy day was because her friend had been killed. "Have you learned anything more about Oscar or the kidnapping?" she started.

"I wanted to run this by you. Should I ask Oscar to take some time off so we can continue without him always popping in on what we're doing?" Trent picked his cup back up and started slurping.

"No. We need him here. If for no other reason than to keep an eye on what he does and who he talks to. Did you get anything on who he might have been talking to before the kidnapping?" She sipped her tea and put the cup down. It tasted like instant tea. She wasn't a fan.

Trent pulled out a small notebook. "From what Sidney could find, he just talked to some casino patrons and a couple of the security guards. Except for a week ago. She caught him talking to the vagrant you were interested in, twice."

Dela studied him. "The vagrant." Her mind spun. She'd just heard him talking to someone who had said a ransom note had been sent. It made sense. "Get photos from the video of Oscar talking to the vagrant. And make sure you have a guard bring the vagrant into security tomorrow when they see him. Then we'll parade the two past one another and start asking Oscar questions. You might want to tell whoever is in charge of surveillance to have someone on standby who can fill in for Oscar when we bring him down to question."

Trent wrote everything she said down in his notebook. "Good. Good."

Then she said, "Did Benedict say anything about getting a ransom note?"

Trent's head jerked up and he studied her. "He got a ransom note?"

"I'm not sure. I heard it from someone else."

"Who?"

She shook her head. "I don't know. I only heard a bit of a conversation but 'ransom note' was brought up and it sounded like it had been delivered to Benedict."

"Where did you hear the conversation?" Trent leaned both forearms on the table as if he could pull the information out of her head with his desire to know.

"Outside in the shadow of the casino when I was coming to meet you. I doubt there is a clear view from any of the cameras." She'd already checked the angles of the cameras when she was sitting on the bench and didn't have any hopes they would catch either man on them.

"What did you have to tell me?" Trent asked, "Besides what you heard on the way over."

Dela chewed on the inside of her lower lip. How

much should she tell him? To change the subject while she pondered what to say, she asked, "Did Sidney give you the card?" she'd lowered her voice in hopes he would do the same.

He did. "Yes, and I have it put in a safe place." He nodded and winked.

This was perfect if someone was watching them and believed they had Rowena's photos. The ones that had gotten her killed. Her chest squeezed. "Have you heard anything from Detective Stedman or the forensic team?" Remembering Quinn had called in FBI forensics. Damn! She'd have to talk to him to find out anything. She wasn't looking forward to that encounter.

Chapter Ten

"Stedman said he didn't have anything conclusive yet. Which means the FBI hasn't told him anything," Trent said.

Dela nodded. She had to agree. From what she'd found out from Quinn tonight it appeared the Feds knew more about the kidnapping than he'd let on. Which snapped an idea in her head. Could the Feds have instigated the kidnapping to get Benedict to use unlaundered money? That only infuriated her more. Using a child to get what they wanted.

"Hey, you look like you could kill someone," Trent said, easing back in his chair.

"Sorry. I just had a bad thought about the FBI. One that I wouldn't put past them."

"Oh yeah? What's that?" Trent picked up his cup and slurped loudly.

"Nothing that I'm going to tell anyone until I know the truth." She picked up the tea, took a sip, and put it back down. "Can I use Sidney tomorrow to help me dig around on the internet?"

Trent shrugged. "You'll have to ask her. It's her day off."

"Do you mind if we use the computer in the security office?" Dela asked.

"As long as we don't need it for anything."

"What's Sidney's phone number?" Dela typed the number in her phone while Trent read it off his cell.

"Did your brother come up with anything on the boat?" Dela asked, remembering he'd called his brother in the Coast Guard.

"They noticed about four boats close to the coastline on Friday. But they didn't make a sweep along the Lincoln City beach until later in the day. They'd been called out to rescue some fishermen." Trent shook the ice in his cup and then set it down.

Dela added, see if Jude West owned a boat, to her list of things she and Sidney would be looking into the next day. "Did you have anything else you wanted to tell me?"

He leaned forward. "Do you want me to tell you where I hid the card?"

She shook her head. "No. The fewer people who know the better. Just leave it there until we need to look at it again."

He nodded. "Then I'm headed home."

She stared at him. It was a busy Saturday night and he was in charge of security. "You can just leave like that?"

"I've been here since seven this morning and should have gone home at three. I think I've put in enough hours. I'll be back at three tomorrow." He stood.

Dela asked, "Who is in charge when you're gone?"

"Sherman. He's qualified. Good night."

When Trent left, she wandered out onto the packed casino floor. Walking through the smoky room she coughed a few times which got her glares from the people smoking. After finding all of the guards on duty, she took the escalator to the second floor where there were more slot machines, the two large restaurants, and the conference area. She found the security staff on the second floor. None of them were Sherman.

She started for the escalator and spotted Felicity coming out of the steakhouse with her husband. So much for the worried parents, Dela thought sarcastically before noticing the tight grip Benedict had on his wife.

Dela walked over. "Mr. and Mrs. Benedict, could I have a word with you?" She shot her gaze to the man's grip on his wife.

Benedict released the arm and Felicity rubbed it. Tears glittered in her eyes.

"What could you want to talk to us about?" Benedict snarled.

Opening her eyes wide, Dela said, "The absence of your son."

Felicity pressed a handkerchief to the corner of her eyes. "I tried to tell him this was a bad idea. I just wanted to sit in the room and see if someone contacts us."

Dela looped an arm around Felicity's and led her down the hall toward the quiet conference area. As she'd hoped, Benedict followed.

"What are you doing?" he asked, with barely concealed rage.

"I wanted to talk to you where no one else could

87

hear," Dela said and faced Felicity. "I believe there was a ransom note sent to your husband. Did he mention that?"

The woman's eyes widened and she stared at her husband. "Did you receive one? What did they want?"

The man took two menacing steps toward them. Dela pushed Felicity behind her and glared at the man. "Did you receive a ransom note, Mr. Benedict?"

"Yes!" he snapped. "But it's no business of yours."

Felicity pushed around Dela. "But it is my business. He's my son too! You arrogant bastard! You think you can make everyone do what you want. Well, you can't and this is one time when I want you to do exactly what they ask. I want my boy back unharmed." The woman had one hand on her hip and the other pointing a finger in her husband's face.

He grabbed her finger and she cried out in pain.

"Let go of her or I'll have you arrested for assault," Dela said, pulling her phone out of her pocket.

He released Felicity's finger and backed away. "I'll not give in to the kidnappers. They aren't going to kill Asher, he's too useful to them. They'll just up the ransom until I have no choice." He glared at his wife. "You have no idea what would happen to you if I gave in."

Benedict spun around and strode off into the crowd of people.

Dela studied Felicity. She looked as if he'd punched her in the gut. "Do you know what he meant?" Dela asked.

"I'm sure it has something to do with his illegal operations. Oh God! If one of his enemies has Asher…" She started bawling.

Dela put an arm around her. "We'll find him. That's what I wanted to ask you. Who are your husband's enemies and what can you tell me about Jude West?"

Felicity stopped crying and studied Dela. "His enemies are a long list. But Jude? Why do you want to know about him?"

"I understand you and he have been seeing a lot of each other lately."

"Yes, he's a good friend. He's easy to talk to and easy on the eyes." She smiled.

"Are you more than friends?" Dela asked, wondering how much bull Quinn had fed her.

She blushed. "We are very close, but Jude doesn't want us to get caught in bed and have that to be the cause of my getting a lousy divorce settlement if Hugo can prove I was sleeping with him."

Dela held in what she knew. "Have you told Hugo you're divorcing him?" That would give the husband a reason to want to keep his child all to himself. Had he kidnapped his son and that was why he wasn't worried about paying ransom? But then why would the other people involved talk about giving him a note, unless it was posturing on his part?

"I haven't told Hugo, but I've had a private investigator watching him so I could get something other than his illegal dealings. He doesn't keep any of that at home and has refused from day one to tell me anything. I know some of the people he meets but I have no idea why."

"Then you are hoping the P.I. will catch him with a woman?" Dela asked.

"Yeah. If I can prove his infidelity, then I'll get a

larger settlement and full custody of Asher. I don't want him around his father's dirty dealings. I don't want him growing up and becoming his father." Felicity shuddered.

"Who is the P.I.? Dela asked.

"Peter Ferris. He works out of Portland. Why?" Felicity studied her.

"I want to look him up so I know who he is when I run into him. I don't want to ruin things for you."

"That's a good idea. I don't want Hugo to know about him." Felicity nodded.

"I'm going to be working on the kidnapping with someone tomorrow. I hope to have news for you by the evening." Dela led Felicity back to the gaming area and down the escalator. "Want me to walk you back to your room?"

Felicity's gaze moved over the slot machines. "No, I'm going to play some roulette before I go to the room. If I can win using Asher's birthdate and age, I know he'll come back to me." The woman headed along the edge of the machines toward the gaming tables.

Dela strode to the door that led into the hall to the security office. In the office, she found Sherman talking on a cell phone. He ended the call when she walked in.

"I heard you've been all over the casino tonight. Is everything running as it should?" he asked.

"Yes. You have quite a crowd tonight. Do you run things every Saturday night?" She pulled a chair over and sat down facing him.

"About once a month I get to be head of security on a Saturday night. I knew this was coming up when Enos took the weekend off." He smiled.

"What can you tell me about Trent Lawton?" she

asked.

Sherman's eyes widened in his large round face. "What do you want to know about Trent for?"

"Just curious. I'll ask him about you tomorrow." She smiled to take the sting out of what she said.

He studied her a moment, then grinned. "You'd like to know how we got the jobs we did?"

"No, I want to know what you do when you aren't at work." She settled back in the chair, waiting.

"For real?" He stared at her before clearing his throat. "Trent has a wife but they don't get along too well. No kids. But they have two cats and a dog. I'm pretty sure when they split up, Trent will take the dog and leave the cats with his wife."

Dela nodded. "Do you know why he took a job here?"

"No. Why does that matter?"

"Just curious. Does his wife work?"

"Yeah, she's a secretary with the biggest law office in town."

"Do they live over their means?" Dela didn't think Trent had anything to do with the kidnapping or the murder, but it was always good to know as much as she could about the people she worked with.

"Naw. They are both pretty thrifty. They own a small, but nice, house." Sherman studied her. "You going to ask all these same questions about me tomorrow? I can save you time and answer them now."

Dela smiled. "Go ahead, tell me about you."

Sherman told her about his wife and two kids. How they were Siletz Tribe and proud of their heritage. He was glad when he was moved to fill in for Enos because it was a raise in pay. His wife was a stay-at-home mom until the kids were in school. Then she'd take part-time work.

"I'd like to meet your wife sometime. She sounds like a person I'd enjoy," Dela said.

Sherman's face beamed as he smiled. "She is a keeper."

"What can you tell me about Oscar in surveillance?"

Sherman rubbed a hand over his face. "That's one guy I know little about, other than he keeps to himself and eats his lunch outside no matter what the weather is like."

"Thank you for all the answers. I hope you have a quiet night." Dela stood.

"I was sorry to hear about your friend," he said softly.

"Yeah, me too. But I'll find out who killed her and put them in jail." She glanced around the office and realized she'd forgotten about the old man manning the office phone and security radio. He smiled and waved as she walked out into the hallway. Going over what she'd asked Sherman and said to him she didn't see where it could be anything dangerous to Trent or Sherman if the older security officer reported it to anyone.

Chapter Eleven

Dela pulled up the collar of her jacket and shrugged her shoulders to keep the cold wind out of her ears as she walked across the parking lot toward the registration building. It was now close to eleven and she wanted to talk to the registration clerk and take a hot shower.

Several people walked out to a car, laughing and joking. She thought about the last time she'd gone out with friends. She and Heath both worked long hours and preferred to stay home when they weren't working. But after losing Rowena, she had a desire to make time for her friends.

At the registration building, Dela walked in and found three women of various ages dressed in the casino uniform visiting behind the desk.

"Hi, I'm looking for Kristy Dodd," Dela said.

"That's me," a woman with dark hair and the darkest brown eyes Dela had ever seen.

"Hi, Kristy. I'm Dela from room two-hundred-eleven."

The woman inhaled and said, "You're the person room two-nineteen left the message for. I was sorry to hear what happened to her. She was so excited about an assignment she'd received. That's why she said she was checking out." The woman appeared genuinely upset about Rowena's death.

It was hard for Dela to concentrate on what she needed to ask knowing she'd finally run into someone who seemed to feel as devastated as she did. "Yes, can you tell me if she said anything about feeling like she was being watched?"

The woman's head snapped up from where it had been bowed. "You think whoever did it was following her?"

"I don't know. That's what I'm trying to figure out. Did she seem upset or nervous?"

Kristy shook her head. "No. She was just super excited about her new job."

"But you said she checked out. I thought she was here for several more days." Dela pulled the note out of her pocket that Rowena had left for her.

I thought you might need this before I'd get back. See you in a couple of days. R.

"In her note, she said she'd be back." Dela looked up from the note. "Did she ask to reserve a room in a couple of days?"

"No. She just checked out. The bill was being picked up by the casino. All she had to do was sign she was leaving and that was it."

"Would the casino have had a room for her when she returned?" Dela asked, wondering if that was why Rowena hadn't reserved a new room for when she came back.

"We keep a few rooms empty all the time for important people who show up. There would have been a room to put her in when she returned." Kristy leaned forward. "She was a really nice woman. I checked her in when she arrived. It's so hard to think—" She stopped and whisked a tear from her golden-brown cheek. "I've always felt safe here knowing there are all the cameras and security. Not anymore."

Dela understood her fear. A good woman, whom Kristy had barely met, was now gone due to violence. Here in the States, Dela should have felt safer than as an M.P. in Iraq. She didn't. Not since someone broke into her house and tried to kill her. When violence is so close, you start studying everyone differently.

"If you think of anything else give me a call." Dela picked up one of the resort's business cards and wrote her name and number on the back.

Kristy took the card from her. "I will."

"Thanks." Dela left the registration office and headed to her building. She was exhausted yet her mind wouldn't stop flipping through all that had happened today.

Her phone buzzed as she stepped into the elevator. It was Heath. She quickly texted. *Call you in 5*.

Once she was in the room and had her prosthesis off, she reached for her phone and hit call by Heath's name.

"How are you holding up?" he asked.

"Okay and not so okay," she said, dropping back onto the bed and staring at the ceiling. She went on to tell him all that she'd discovered since Rowena's murder, including believing the FBI may have taken the child to get the goods on Benedict.

"Whoa! I hope you haven't said this to anyone else. I don't want you to go missing." Heath's tone told her he was worried.

"I haven't said a word to anyone but you. I don't want it to get back to Quinn that I suspect the FBI. Especially if they did take the boy." Dela wasn't a hundred percent sure but there were too many things that made it feel like they had.

"What about the two you heard talking about a ransom note?" Heath asked.

"Yeah, that's what has me wondering if it's not the Feds. I hope to get some footage of the face of the well-dressed guy tomorrow. And I'm going to look up the P.I. Felicity has following her husband."

"I have a couple of days off. I could be there by morning if you want me to come help," Heath said.

She thought about how much easier it would be to have someone she could work with and not worry she was giving the wrong person information. Also, to be able to split up and do more. "Are you sure you can drive this far without falling asleep? You worked a long shift today."

"I can be there tomorrow with a full night's sleep. Don Turner with the Pendleton Police is flying over to see his folks tomorrow. I'll catch a ride with him. Pick me up at the Eugene Airport."

"That's great but how will you get home?" Dela was happy to hear she would have Heath to help her investigate Rowena's death but worried he would get in trouble with the Tribal Police.

"I told the Chief that if you wanted me to come, I was taking this coming week off."

"And he agreed to that?" Dela asked.

"Begrudgingly, but he also knows how much vacation time I have accumulated. See you at the airport at nine tomorrow morning."

"I'll be there. Thank you for coming, Heath. You know I hate to admit needing anyone, but I really need your support on this one." She blinked at the tears trickling from the corner of her eyes.

"Get a good night's sleep and I'll be there tomorrow. You are my *timnáki*." Heath ended the call before Dela could sputter a reply.

He'd called her his heart. She knew he loved her. He was always ready to jump in and help and had believed her innocent when others had thought she'd killed a neighbor. And if she were honest with herself, she loved him. Not with a hot smoldering passion but with a steady beat like the ceremonial drums.

He would always be there for her and she for him. They'd made the pact as teenage sweethearts and even though she'd shoved him away after Robin's death and joined the Army, upon her return after rehab, he'd also returned to Nixyáawii and things clicked back in place. His embrace was warm and welcome. His kisses tender and sweet. One of these days she needed to tell him she loved him. But not yet. She still didn't know who she was.

While he was here, they could go check out the information they had on the burned jail and records. She had to find out the truth about her biological father without asking her mom. She had just married for the first time at the age of 66 and Dela didn't want to upset her happiness.

Using her crutches, she swung into the bathroom

and brushed her teeth. Back in the room, she checked her phone to see how long it would take to get to Eugene and set her alarm accordingly.

Ten minutes after nine Sunday morning, Heath crossed the tarmac toward Dela. She'd found a place to park near the small aircraft hangars. She'd left Lincoln City at six to give her plenty of time and she'd taken the most direct route over to Salem and down I-5.

Heath walked up to her, dropped his duffel bag on the ground, and wrapped his arms around her, kissing her neck. "I've wanted to do that since you told me about your friend."

His soft voice, warm against her neck, made her feel whole again. She wrapped her arms around him, clinging to his warmth and feeling the beat of his heart. "I'm glad you came. I've needed a friend and someone to bounce thoughts off of."

He tipped her face up, he was a few inches taller than her 5' 7", and peered into her eyes. "You know I am always here for you no matter what you need."

"And I'm very grateful." She raised onto her tiptoes, which wasn't easy to do with a prosthesis, and kissed him.

Her heart swelled when his eyes opened in surprise. It was rare she made the first move, always trying to be strong and not need anyone.

He kissed her back before opening the driver's side door. "Who's driving?"

"I'll let you if you'll listen to directions," she said, teasing and meaning it.

Heath laughed and tossed his duffel bag in the back seat before sliding in behind the wheel. "Straight back to Lincoln City?"

"No, we're going to cut across country roads and then up the coast. I want to have a visit with Jude West. I discovered he has a house at Salishan about seven miles before we get back to Lincoln City. And going this way you won't have to focus so much on the traffic and we can talk through what I know and what I think." Dela motioned the direction Heath needed to turn. "How about some breakfast?"

"I can always eat." Heath smiled at her. "But it looks like we're outside of town."

"Junction City is sixteen miles up the road." Dela wanted to get to Jude West's and back to the casino to see what Sidney had found. This morning on her way to pick up Heath, she'd called Sidney and asked her to look up people and things. That's how she knew where West was staying right now. Only seven miles from Felicity.

Dela finished telling Heath what she knew about Rowena's murder as he pulled into a fast-food restaurant.

"Looks like this is all I see here," he said.

"That's fine. It won't take as long to get food. We can sit inside and eat." Dela opened the car door and stepped out.

Heath grabbed the establishment's door and held it for her. This was the type of thing he did without thinking. She liked that about him and didn't feel affronted as she would if any other man had held the door for her. She wasn't a feminist. Just stubborn and thought she could take care of herself. Heath knew better. He knew her doubts, fears, and insecurities and made her a better person by the way he dealt with her.

Inside they ordered and waited a few minutes.

"Heath!" the server behind the counter called.

Dela remained at the table as he retrieved their breakfast.

While they ate, she asked him who was taking care of Mugshot and Jethro while they were both gone.

"I asked Travis to house-sit. I figured you wouldn't mind him in your house." Heath took a bite of his breakfast sandwich.

"That's perfect. Both animals know and like him and he knows all about my disability since he remodeled the house." She studied him. "You told him to stay in your room, didn't you?"

"Yes. I knew you wouldn't want him in yours." He grasped her hand that was lying on the table. "And I haven't been sleeping in my room much anymore anyway." He smiled and her body warmed.

That was true. The last month, before she'd headed to Lincoln City, they'd spent every night in her bedroom. She was finally feeling comfortable enough with her disfigured body to allow him to see her in all her vulnerability. It was a huge step for her. And one, he had let her figure out on her own, not pushing to become more of a couple than her allowing him to sleep in her bed once in a while with him leaving the room before she got up.

They finished the food and returned to the car. As they continued over to Highway 101, Dela told Heath about her thoughts on Quinn, West, and the FBI.

"From what you say, it does sound like the Feds may have something to do with the kidnapping, but if they did do it, they could face serious charges and I can't see Quinn putting his career at risk to do something like that." Heath glanced over.

Dela had been watching him as she spoke. He'd taken it in and replied with his thoughts, but he didn't know Quinn as well as she did. "He will do whatever it takes to bring someone in. I know. I've seen him take criminals and let them loose so he can get a bigger criminal. He will go against the rules if it will get him the result he wants."

Heath didn't say anything for a few minutes, then asked, "What about this P.I. the mother hired?"

"Sidney, the security guard who is helping me, sent a photo of him. I looked at it while I was waiting for you and he resembles the vagrant I saw hanging around the casino and I believe watched the kidnapping." Dela had let out several curses when she'd seen the photo of Peter Ferris.

"Who is he working for? The wife or the father?" Heath asked.

"Or the FBI?" Dela came back with.

Heath blew out a low whistle. "You have walked into a mess over here."

"That's why I'm glad to have you here to help. I want to find the missing boy and I want to find Rowena's killer." Dela told him to turn right as they came to the Highway 101 junction.

"I have a feeling when we find one, we'll find the other," Heath said.

Chapter Twelve

Dela used the GPS on her phone to find Jude West's vacation home on the Oregon Coast. Heath drove through large wrought iron gates and up a long, paved driveway that circled a small fountain. He parked and Dela sat in the car staring at the three-story house that looked like an old mansion that was being remodeled on a television show she liked to watch when her mind was numb.

"How are you going to approach him?" Heath asked, as the door opened and a man stood staring at them.

"The truth is always good." Dela stepped out of the car and walked up to the door with Heath beside her.

"I'm sorry, we don't allow solicitors," the man said. He wasn't Jude West. She knew that because Sidney had sent her a photo of him.

"We're not solicitors. We're here on behalf of Mrs. Felicity Benedict," Dela said not flat-out lying.

The woman had asked her to find her son. And this was the next person she wanted to question to do that.

The man studied them both. "Your names."

"Dela Alvaro. Heath Seaver," they both said.

"I'll see if Mr. West will see you." The door closed.

"Good thing it's not raining today," Heath joked.

Dela snickered and within minutes the door opened.

"Mr. West will see you." The man ushered them into a large, beautiful entryway. "Follow me."

They walked down the hall and out the back to a small patio in front of a large swimming pool. Dela was impressed. This was a man who had money. Or the FBI was footing this so he could woo Felicity. Either way, he had the use of the house and pool. She'd love to have a pool to exercise, but it wouldn't be in her budget for a long time. Buying and remodeling her house had depleted her savings.

West sat in a lounge chair looking at a laptop. He closed the computer, placed it on the table next to him, and stood. "What do you have to tell me about Felicity?" he asked, indicating a patio table and chairs.

Dela, followed by Heath, walked over to the table and sat. West took a chair facing the house and studied them.

"I'm helping Felicity find her son," Dela said.

"Why did you come here? I don't have him," West countered.

"I've learned you and Felicity are good friends. I was wondering if she might have mentioned to you someone she believed might have kidnapped her son."

Dela settled back in the chair as West snapped his fingers and the man who'd let them in appeared.

"Bring us something to drink."

The man nodded and did a military turn before disappearing into the house.

Dela knew West was stalling. "Has she mentioned anyone in business with her husband that might have done this?"

He stared at her. "She would have told you, if she has you looking for her son."

"Not necessarily. She's distraught and might not think of someone that she might have mentioned before the kidnapping." Dela continued to hold West's stare.

He broke it off and glanced at Heath. "Who are you?"

"Dela's friend," Heath said, also relaxed back into his chair as if he planned to spend the whole day there.

West's gaze moved back and forth between them until the butler, she guessed he'd be called, brought out a tray with a pitcher of iced tea, three glasses, and a sugar bowl. The man poured the beverage into three glasses and handed the sugar bowl to West. He scooped two scoops and stirred with a long-handled spoon. The butler offered Dela and Heath the sugar but they both declined.

When the butler disappeared, Dela said, "You are avoiding my question. Is it because you have something to do with the kidnapping? Or do you think Benedict had his son taken?"

West's eyes widened. "I'm glad I'm not the only one who thinks that. When I mentioned to Felicity that her husband could have taken Asher, she objected, but I could tell she had the same thought."

"Do you think it's because Felicity plans to divorce him and take Asher away?" Dela asked, knowing that playing the man's ally would get her more information than accusing him of anything.

"I don't know if she let it slip or he found out from someone else, but he does know she is planning a divorce. And I wouldn't put it past him to take the boy and keep him from Felicity to keep her from moving on." West's amber eyes narrowed. "He is a man who doesn't give a shit about the law and will do what he damn well pleases."

"I haven't had the chance to ask Felicity and since you have a swimming pool here, does Asher know how to swim?" Dela had decided the child must know to have not been fearful of the ocean as he was being packed out to the man in scuba gear.

"Felicity put him in lessons when he was young. That kid can swim like a fish. He loves this pool." West twisted his head and stared at the calm water.

"Then you've had him here a few times? He and Felicity?" Dela asked.

West nodded. "Felicity is welcome here whenever she needs to get away from Hugo. He is a domineering man with a temper."

"Has Hugo ever beaten Felicity?" Dela asked, thinking about the grip he'd had on his wife's arm last night.

"Not enough to put her in a hospital but enough to make her scared of him and want to get away with her son." West lowered his eyelids to hide whatever emotion he was feeling.

Dela had an idea it was rage or hatred for Hugo

Benedict. "Would Asher have been afraid if someone took him into the ocean and a scuba diver showed up?"

West's eyelids jerked up and he stared at her. "Why do you say that?"

She'd hit on something. "Just a theory I have. But I needed to find out if Asher is scared of water. It sounds like he isn't."

"What's the theory?" West asked, picking up his glass of tea.

"I'm going to run it by Special Agent Pierce before I tell anyone." She finished off her tea and stood.

"Where are you going?" West asked when Heath also stood.

"Back to Siletz Bay Casino. I have a kidnapping and murder to solve." Dela walked toward the door and stopped. "You didn't happen to know Rowena Maxwell, did you?"

The man studied her for a moment and said, "I think she's a photographer. If it's the same person. She took photos of my place in Portland for a magazine. Why?"

"She was murdered two nights ago at the casino." Dela watched him blink rapidly before walking toward them.

"What do you mean murdered? Do you think it has anything to do with Asher?" He seemed genuinely surprised but she didn't know him well enough to know for sure.

"I believe it had everything to do with Asher's kidnapping." Dela stepped through the door and Heath followed.

Once they were in the car and headed up the highway, Heath said, "You just gave away two of your aces. If he is working for the Feds, he'll go tell them you are getting close."

"If Quinn tells me to back off, we'll know for certain they are in this up to their short haircuts."

♠ ♣ ♥ ♦

Heath parked the car and they took his duffel bag up to her room. Dela opened the door and cursed. Her room had been ransacked. She knew the reason. It was tucked in her stub sock.

"I've known you to be messy but this is a vacation side I've not seen," Heath said, stepping into the room behind her.

Dela laughed at the ridiculousness of the scene and Heath's lighthearted comment. When she caught her breath, she said, "Call the Lincoln City Police. I'll call casino security."

While Heath was on the phone with the city police, Dela called Trent.

"I won't be in until three. Call the office. Sherman will take down the information."

Seething, and changing her mind on him making a good next in line to be head of security, she called the casino security office and asked to talk to Sherman.

"Hey, Dela, I expected to see you when Sidney showed up to go through footage for you."

"I went to Eugene to pick up a friend and while I was gone someone trashed my room."

"You're kidding, right?"

"No. I'm calling Sidney next to check footage of this hallway while I was gone, but I need you or someone from security over here to take photos and my statement." She wondered if Enos would have been so nonchalant about a break-in.

"I'll get over there right away."

She ended the call and dialed Sidney. "Someone broke into my room while I was gone. Can you pull up footage of the hallway and see who entered, please."

"That's horrible. Do you think it had to do with what we did yesterday?"

Dela could hear the keyboard clicking in the background. "Most likely."

"Did they get it?" Sidney asked in a distracted voice.

"No. Do you have anything?"

"It looks like a maid went in to clean at nine. The door is open and the cart is sitting in front of the doorway for fifteen minutes. She moves on to the next room." Sidney's voice fades then blares, "Booyah! She doesn't put the cart right in front of the door like she did at your room."

"Find out who the maid is and have her brought up to the security office. I want a talk with her." Dela felt better having someone who was after the card to question.

Sherman arrived at the door where Heath had been standing after calling the police.

"Sir, you'll have to step out of the room," Sherman said.

"Sherman, this is my friend. The one I picked up at the airport. Heath Seaver, this is Sherman... I never caught your last name," Dela said.

"Tulee, Sherman Tulee." He shook hands with Heath.

"Heath is a tribal detective on the Umatilla Reservation," Dela said, by way of letting Sherman know he could be trusted.

The security guard's face darkened. "Then both of you know more about handling this than I do."

Heath shot a glance at Dela. She nodded. "Sherman is third down the line from the head of security. Enos is at a family event this weekend and the second in command doesn't seem to take that position very responsibly. He thought Sherman could handle things when there has been a kidnapping and murder here in two days." She couldn't hide the disgust she felt that no one here seemed to take either of the incidents seriously.

Just then Detective Stedman arrived. Dela made introductions and Sherman said there were too many people, and he'd leave it to the experts.

Dela sighed and motioned for Stedman to enter the room.

"What were they after?" the detective asked.

"I'm guessing the card Rowena left for me at the registration desk." Dela pulled out her phone and started taking photos. It looked like it was up to her to make the report for the casino.

"Did you have it in here?" Stedman asked.

"No. We gave it to Special Agent Pierce." She wasn't lying. They did give the original to Quinn. But she didn't have to tell him they had copies spread around.

"Then why would they search your room?" Stedman asked, studying her.

She shrugged. "I don't know but I hope you can pull up some fingerprints. I'm beginning to think this casino isn't safe."

"Now don't go spreading that around. This casino has been good for business around the whole town." Detective Stedman stopped taking photos and faced her. "There is a reason I come to all the calls from here. The city wants to make sure people know that we do care what happens here and want them to feel safe."

"You coming yesterday for Rowena's murder was to keep up pretenses and not to catch a murderer?"

"That's not what I meant," Detective Stedman said, glaring at her.

"That's what it sounded like to me," Dela turned to Heath. "Is that what you heard?"

Heath walked into the room and put an arm around her shoulders. "Dela, let the man do his job. Have you taken all the photos you need? We'll go see · that person in security you called and come back and right things later."

Dela let Heath move her out of the room and over to the elevator. Once they were inside, she said, "He's only putting on a show. This is why I need you here. The FBI could be the abductors and the local police don't give a piss about Rowena." It always ate at her when law enforcement didn't seem to care about a missing or murdered person. This time it happened to be a friend, which infuriated her even more.

Heath ran his hands up and down her arms. "But we do. Don't lash out at everyone who is either not qualified to know how to work a murder or is overworked."

The elevator did a little bounce before stopping and he released her.

Dela stepped out as soon as the doors opened. She hated it when Heath was right, but that was why she wanted him here. To help her keep a clear head and find Rowena's killer.

Chapter Thirteen

Dela led Heath into the security office. A young man who didn't look old enough to be a security guard glanced up from a book. "Can I help you?"

"I'm Dela Alvaro, here to review your security team. A maid was supposed to be brought in here for me to question. Do you know anything?" she asked.

The man shook his head. "Sherman hasn't been back after getting a phone call from you. Sidney was here all morning on the computer. I'm not sure where she went about ten minutes ago."

Dela pulled out her phone and called Sidney.

"Hi. I wasn't able to take care of that matter. I'm helping the FBI with surveillance. Gotta go." The call ended.

"Crap!" She faced Heath. "Quinn is upstairs bothering Sidney. It's her day off."

Heath stared at her. "And you have her working for you on her day off. That's why he's bothering her."

Dela shrugged. "Do we go up and see what we

can find out or find a way to get him to leave…" She pulled out her phone and scrolled through her contacts. Touching Quinn's name, she waited for him to answer.

"What's up, Dela?" he asked.

"Hey, someone ransacked my room while I was picking Heath up from the airport. Any chance you can spare a forensic person to check for fingerprints?" She waited, while he spoke to someone else.

"I'll bring someone over right away." The call ended.

She smiled. "Let's go watch for them to leave and we'll go see Sidney."

Dela and Heath stood in a shadowed corner not far from the stairs leading up to surveillance. They stood there five minutes before Quinn and another Fed jogged down the stairs. Once they cleared the "Employee Only" entry, Dela led Heath up the stairs, through the surveillance room, and into the back room.

Sidney swung around in her chair. "Wow, if I had known telling him about your room being tossed would have gotten rid of him, I would have said something."

Dela smiled. "Who is the maid? We'll go looking for her."

"Tamara Dorsey. I can call housekeeping and have them send her over now that I'm not answering the FBI's questions." Sidney reached for the phone on the desk.

"Yes call, but ask them to have her come to housekeeping, that won't be as suspicious as having her go to security. And it will keep us away from Quinn a little longer."

"Housekeeping is in the building by the

registration building," Sidney said, before announcing who she was and that someone wanted to speak with Tamara Dorsey. "No, just ask her to come to housekeeping, please. Thank you." Sidney hung up the phone. "They'll contact her and request she come to the housekeeping building. I suggested they not say who was coming to talk to her."

"Good. If she ransacked my room, she's going to be suspicious." Dela turned to the door and then back. "Did you find out if someone diverted the video during the kidnapping and the murder?"

"I'm still going over it, but I do think the cameras were overrode. The FBI wanted to take all the footage but I stalled them by saying I couldn't do it without Enos's okay." She shrugged. "I think Agent Pierce is going to go to the casino board."

"We'll worry about that later. Just keep digging until you need or want to leave. I'm sorry for taking up your day off." Dela did feel bad. Just because she worked 24/7 didn't mean everyone else had to.

"I can hang around a couple more hours, then I'm going to my folks'."

"Thank you," Dela said and opened the door.

"Where are we headed?" Heath asked when they reached the bottom of the stairs.

"By now Quinn will know I wasn't in my room when I called him. Let's go out and walk the beach to the rooms and then walk between the buildings. We'll have to make sure we don't see Quinn when we cross to the registration building. I don't want him butting into the conversation." Dela entered the security office. She asked the young security officer, "Let us out this back door, please."

The young man put down his book and punched in a code to let them out. "Do you want to come back in this way?" he asked.

"Is there a way I can?" Dela thought it might be a good thing to know in the case of an emergency.

The security guard walked over to a desk and pulled out a keycard. "This will get you into any place that is locked on the resort."

She stared at him. "You just hand this out to anyone?"

He shook his head. "No. Enos said if you needed access to the building this week to give you a master keycard."

Dela glanced at Heath and back to the guard. "When did he tell you this?"

"Before he went on his vacation."

She nudged Heath and they stepped out the door behind the casino that faced the ocean. She breathed in the salty damp air and shook. "Enos knew something was going to happen this weekend. Why else would he leave and tell that young man to give me a master keycard this week? I was supposed to go home today."

Heath nodded as they used the steps down to the beach. He directed her out to the hard-packed sand where walking was easier. "It does seem as though he had prior knowledge of the kidnapping. I'm sure he didn't know there would be a murder."

"But the kidnapping. Why would he turn the other cheek and let a child be taken from his parents?" She knew exactly why. The FBI.

"Don't jump to conclusions. Have you checked up on Enos's background? He could have debts that someone like Benedict would pay off if he was gone on a particular weekend."

She had to concede she'd not looked up anything about the man. She'd liked him and believed him to be law-abiding. "I know nothing. Looks like I need to dig into that as well."

She pointed to the steps leading up to the hotel buildings. "Remember, don't just walk out from between the buildings. We need to make sure Quinn isn't going to see us."

They climbed the stairs, with Heath ahead of her. He had offered to hold onto her hand, but her stubbornness refused his help. He waited at the top for her, and they walked between the buildings and cautiously peered both ways.

"There, that looks like a Fed vehicle driving toward the casino. It figures they wouldn't walk over here." She waited until the driver wouldn't see them in the rearview mirror and crossed to the registration building. When she didn't see the laundry, she walked inside.

"Where is housekeeping?" she asked.

"It's that building where the pool is. On the far end," a male registration clerk said.

"Thank you."

Dela led Heath over to the building in the middle of the parking area. Bypassing the pool entrance, she used the keycard to enter the end of the building which appeared to be where the laundry was done.

"What are you doing in here?" a small Hispanic woman asked.

"I asked security to have Tamara Dorsey meet us here," Dela said.

The woman still had her hands on her hips but she nodded. "I took the call. Tamara is in that room." Her head tipped to the right.

Dela walked to the room. The door was open. Two women sat at a table drinking sodas and talking.

"Tamara Dorsey?" Dela asked, walking in and taking a seat. Heath pulled out the chair next to her and sat.

"Are you the person who had me called in here?" a slender brunette asked.

"Yes. I'd like to know why you trashed my room, number two-eleven, this morning?"

Tamara's eyes widened and she set her can of soda down with a clunk.

The other woman leaned away from her. "What have you done?" It was at that moment that Dela realized the two must be related. They had the same shaped face and eyes. The second woman appeared older. Mother and daughter?

"I didn't take anything. I was asked to make it look like someone was looking for something." Tamara faced the other woman. "Mom, I couldn't pass up two hundred dollars just to mess up a room."

"Is that illegal?" her mom asked. "Will she go to jail?"

Dela shrugged. "I'm the one who has to press charges. If she can tell me who asked her to mess up my room, I won't say a thing." She studied Tamara. "Who paid you to do it?"

Tamara glanced at her mom, then at the open door. She shrugged. "It was Mr. Benedict. He said it was a joke he was playing on someone."

Dela leaned back. "Mr. Benedict told you to toss

room two-eleven?"

"Yes."

"How did he know that you cleaned my room?" Dela decided she needed to dig deeper into the man whose son was missing.

Tamara shrugged. "I don't know. He came up to me this morning when I rolled the cart out of the elevator. He asked me if I was cleaning room two-eleven. I said, if the guest wasn't in, yes. He laughed and said, here's two hundred to play a joke on my friend. And told me to make a mess of things like I was looking for something. And not to tell anyone." She peered at Dela from under her fake lashes. "Will you tell him I told you?"

There wasn't a trace of fear. The man must not have threatened her if she told someone, just not to say anything.

"I won't tell him but don't do that again. Or if someone approaches you with a tale like that, go to security and they can determine if the person in the room is really a friend of the joker."

Tamara nodded. "Do I have to give the money back?"

"No. He shouldn't have put you in this position." Dela stood. "Thank you for talking with me."

Heath stopped when they stood outside the building. "What was he trying to do having that girl mess up your room?"

"I think he is trying to scare or intimidate me." She went on to tell him how she separated him from his wife the night before when he had a hurtful grip on her arm.

"He also didn't like me mentioning the ransom

note to Felicity last night. He's a bully and I won't let him get to me." Dela said, noting the security ATV coming their direction.

Sherman stopped the vehicle beside them. "Hop on. Special Agent Pierce sent me to retrieve you."

"Oh joy," Dela said sarcastically and waited for Heath to climb into the back seat before she sat beside Sherman.

"He was upset you weren't at your room when he got there and no one seemed to know where you were." Sherman studied her as he drove through the parking lot.

"That's because I didn't want him to know where I was. How did you know where to find me?"

"Oscar said he saw you enter the laundry building." Sherman glanced at her again. "What were you doing there?"

"Talking to someone." Dela met Heath's gaze over her shoulder. She didn't know who to trust, now believing that the head of security knew what was happening this weekend and the second in command's disinterest in finding a kidnapper and a killer.

"Is it someone we need to be aware of?" Sherman asked.

"No. It was a dead end."

Sherman parked the ATV behind the building at the door where she and Heath had exited. Preferring not to let anyone, other than the young man who gave her the keycard, know she had it, she waited for Sherman to unlock the door.

He motioned for her and Heath to go first. Quinn and another agent stood in the room facing the door.

"Why weren't you at your room when I arrived?" Quinn asked.

"Because I was chasing down leads with Heath." She crossed her arms and planted her feet.

"He has no jurisdiction here." Quinn turned his attention to Heath. "Why are you here?"

"To give Dela support. She just lost a good friend," Heath said in his soft, unassuming voice.

"I'm aware there has been a murder and kidnapping here. Which is why I think you should hand over the copy of the card you made, unless the person who ransacked your room has it." Now Quinn crossed his arms and glared at her.

"The copy wasn't in my room." She noted his eyebrows rose as if he didn't believe her.

"Where is the copy?" He held his hand toward her, palm up.

"I don't know. We gave it to Trent to hide in case we wanted to look at it some more and today is his day off." She shrugged.

Quinn stared at her and one side of his mouth went up. "Like hell you did. Did the person who trashed your room get the copy?"

"No. We discovered the whole event was a ruse paid for by Hugo Benedict. He told the person who did it that it was a joke he wanted to play on a friend. But I see it as a threat. He wanted to show me he had power."

"And why would he be threatened by you?" Quinn asked.

Dela walked over to a chair and sat. How much did she tell a man she believed might have helped or organized the kidnapping?

Chapter Fourteen

Dela waited for Heath to take a seat beside her before she told Quinn about breaking up what looked like the husband bullying the wife the night before. Then she said, "Did you know that Asher Benedict knows how to swim and isn't afraid of the water?"

Quinn shook his head as if clearing away cobwebs and said, "What?"

"Asher knows how to swim. Which means, he wouldn't be afraid if someone took him into the ocean and say handed him off to someone else." She watched Quinn, almost seeing the gears in his head switching to the topic she'd tossed out.

"You think someone carried that boy out to another person waiting in the ocean?" Quinn laughed along with the agent beside him. "Don't you think someone would have seen that?"

Quietly she said, "Someone did and she's dead."

Heath grasped her hand, squeezing it. She took that as an okay to continue where she was going.

"You and I both know what we saw on that disk that you probably destroyed after I gave it to you."

Quinn's brow wrinkled and he narrowed his eyes. "What are you accusing me of?"

"You know." She glared back at him.

"I nor anyone else in the FBI killed your friend," Quinn said, his hands fisted at his sides.

"Ahhh, but you aren't denying kidnapping a person of interest's son which resulted in my friend's death." Dela wasn't going to let this drop until he confessed or told her what he knew. Because it was the kidnapping of Asher Benedict that got Rowena killed.

Quinn grabbed a chair and placed it three feet in front of Dela. He motioned for the other agent to take the young security guard and Sherman out of the room.

"Hey, we need to be in here to do our job," Sherman protested.

"This won't take long," Quinn said and jerked his head toward the door.

The other agent ushered the two security guards out. When the door closed behind them, Quinn sat down in the chair. "This is for your ears only." He waited for Dela and Heath to nod.

"We didn't kidnap the boy, but we may have planted the idea in Felicity's head through West." Quinn let out a sigh. "However, West denies that they set up the kidnapping and Benedict has refused to pay the ransom, which makes me think he got the jump on Felicity knowing he was being followed and she wanted a divorce."

Dela shook her head. "It was West who met with Felicity's P.I. last night. They were talking about the ransom note being delivered. How would they

121

know?"

Quinn leaned back and studied her. "Where did you hear this?"

"Last night outside the casino. I walked up the beach to the casino, came up the steps, and heard voices. I skulked in the shadows and saw the P.I. Ferris and a man talking. After we visited with West today, I realized the other man was him."

Heath said, "You didn't say anything."

She glanced at him. "I just realized it was him. The voice and body shape are the same." She returned her gaze to Quinn. "You might want to look into West. I think he's playing both sides." She stood. "We're going for a drive. Call me if you learn anything new."

Heath stood and they left the security office.

"You can go in now," she told Sherman. "Call me if you learn anything of interest."

"Will do. Where are you going?"

"For a drive to clear my head." Dela followed Heath out to the casino entrance. They stepped out into the air laced with cigarette smoke. "When will they make people who smoke go farther away from entrances," she said, feeling snarly.

"They can put the ash cans far away from the doors but they can't make the people walk that far if they don't want to." Heath led the way along the sidewalk to the parking lot. "Where are we going?"

"First to the restaurant for a late lunch, then we're going to check out the county jail that burned down. I can't believe there aren't records in the courthouse." Dela stopped outside the restaurant across from the registration office. "The food in here is good and service is fast. We can get to Benton County and see where the jail was and decide where we need to go to get information."

They returned to Siletz Bay Casino after dark with a plan. Heath would go talk to someone at the county courthouse and see if he could find out anything about the records that might have burned and then he would go to the local newspaper and see if he could find any mention of the man Theodore (Dory) Thunder while Dela continued to dig for answers to the kidnapping and Rowena's murder.

Before retiring to her room, they entered the casino to head to the security office. Trent strode toward them as soon as they came through the door.

"I thought today was your day off?" Dela said with a bit of sarcasm.

"Day but not the night. Have you learned anything new?" he asked.

"Didn't Sherman fill you in?" she asked, wondering why he hadn't said anything.

"I couldn't find him when I arrived. No one knows where he went or when he left." Trent shrugged.

Dela shot the man a glare. "Has he ever done something like this before?"

"Not that I know of."

She squeezed her fist to her side to keep from punching the man. "There has been a kidnapping, a murder, and now a person who doesn't normally sneak away from work is missing. How dense are you?"

"Dela." Heath cautioned.

She shook her head. "I want you to get on that microphone and ask every security person here if they saw Sherman when they came to work. I'm headed up to surveillance to see if we can find him on video." She stormed toward the employee entrance past the help counter, not even saying excuse me to the patrons she pushed by. Heath's polite voice behind her saying, "Excuse us," would have to suffice. Right now her main concern was losing a kind man with a family because she'd drawn him into her speculation of what happened to the child.

In the surveillance room, she was happy to not see Oscar and that she did see the observant woman who had mentioned where the child wasn't the day he'd gone missing. She walked over to the woman and read her name tag.

"Dede, I'm going to need your help in just a minute." She turned to face the room of surveillance people. "I know you all came on shift at the time Sherman was going home but did any of you see him in your monitors when you came on duty?"

A short, skinny man raised his hand. "I saw him talking to the vagrant in front of the casino."

Dela's chest squeezed. "Did they separate or walk off together?"

"They walked out of my cameras together."

"Which way did they go?" She hoped they found Sherman alive and that he didn't give away they were interested in the P.I.

"North."

"Where there are fewer cameras." Dela glanced at Heath. He nodded.

She put her hand on the woman's shoulder. "I want you to find all the video of Sherman from noon to when he was last seen with the P-vagrant." It was better that few people knew what she did. It appeared that

Sherman may have become a victim because she had told him the vagrant wasn't what he seemed.

"Let's go," she said to Heath. They left the surveillance room, descended the stairs, and entered the security room. Dela walked over to where the keys for the ATVs hung. "We're using one of these," she told the man sitting at the desk by the radio.

"I need to tell Trent so he doesn't think someone stole one."

"That's fine." She handed the keys to Heath and they exited the door on the backside of the casino.

"Where to?" Heath asked, turning the key.

"Head to the north end of the casino. We'll check all the places where a body could be hidden. And while you drive, I'll try Sherman's phone."

She found the number he'd called her from in her contacts and pressed the dial icon. The phone rang three times and a woman's voice answered.

"Hello?"

"Hi, I'm Dela Alvaro with casino security. Is Sherman there?"

"He's in the shower. Do you need him back at work? He was late coming home and tripped over my son's bike. He's bruised and really shouldn't come back to work tonight."

Dela bit her lip and said, "Do you mind if I come to see him?"

"Why?" The woman's voice rang with suspicion.

"I have some questions to ask him about today."

Heath had turned the vehicle around and parked back where they'd found it.

"I'd rather you—"

Sherman's voice in the background asked, "Who are you talking to?"

"Some lady named Dela. Who is she?"

"Dela? Why are you calling?" His voice was hesitant.

"I need to come visit with you tonight. Is that okay?"

"I'd rather not."

"Because the vagrant beat you up?" she asked.

He inhaled and whispered, "How did you know?"

"I need to come see you and visit. What's the address?"

He told her and sighed, "I guess I should have gone back into the casino."

"Yes. I thought you were dead. I'll be there in twenty minutes." She ended the call, her hands shaking.

Heath took her hands in his and rubbed them. "He's alive. He can give us some answers, hopefully."

"But what if Ferris finds out he talked to us?" She peered at his face in the shadow of the roof of the ATV.

"You can't keep everyone safe. You can't control them like puppets. He did what he did to discover the truth. Just as you put yourself in harm's way every time there is an injustice at the casino or on the reservation. That's why you are good at your job." He tugged her out of the ATV. "You told him we'd be there in twenty minutes. Where are we going."

Dela scanned the trees and undergrowth. "I'll tell you when we're in the car." She didn't want anyone to get Sherman's address. She knew Heath would make sure no one followed them.

Chapter Fifteen

On the way to Sherman's house she called Trent and told him she'd found Sherman and to tell everyone he was fine.

Mrs. Tulee answered the door with a glare. Sherman ushered them in and did the introductions. "The kids are in bed so keep your voices low, please." He kissed his wife on the head. "Nina, you can go to bed. I'll be there as soon as I talk to Dela and her friend."

Nina glared at Dela as she left the room.

He shrugged. "She didn't really believe my story of tripping over Danny's bike. Then you called and she became even more suspicious. She likes the money I make at the casino but has been worried I would get caught up in violence."

Dela took in the cut lip, red eye with black and blue bruising, and his defeated demeanor. "I'm so sorry you were caught up in this. Was it the vagrant who did this to you?"

"Yeah, after you said to have anyone who saw him bring him in, I saw him when I was headed to the office to clock out. I stepped out the door and asked him to come in. He said he didn't feel like it. I said it didn't matter and grabbed him by the arm. He pulled out his P.I. license and said he'd talk to me in private outside. That he didn't want the person he was tailing to see him talking to security. Like a dumbass, I followed him to the end of the casino with the fewest cameras." He sighed.

"We all get caught up in situations that we know are wrong but it's hard to stop the momentum," Dela said.

He nodded. "When he lured me into some trees, I thought, well he doesn't want to be seen. But he clocked me and grabbed my gun. I have never been so scared. I've never drawn my gun on anyone and I've never been held at gunpoint." He swallowed.

"What did he want to know?" Dela asked.

"Who told me to bring him into the casino? I told him the head of security and he laughed. Said that he knew the head of security wasn't even in town." Sherman studied her. "How would he know that?"

"He is a P.I. His name is Peter Ferris. He would have looked into all of that while watching the place." But Dela also wondered how he knew that.

"I didn't want to put him onto you or Trent so I said the FBI. Since he'd been watching the casino, he'd know they had been in and out."

"That was good thinking." She smiled at the man.

"That got him upset. He hit me in the eye and

said why would they want him. I told him it had something to do with the missing boy. That made him walk back and forth a couple of times. Then he pointed my gun at me and said, if I told anyone about talking to him, he'd hurt my family." Sherman shook his head. "I'm glad I have the next two days off. I can get healed up before I go back, and hopefully, if he sees I'm not coming to work, he'll think I didn't say anything."

Dela peered into his eyes. "Would you have called and told me if I hadn't come to you?"

He dropped his gaze. "I was going to sleep on it and decide in the morning."

"I don't blame you for wanting to protect your family," Heath said. "You had a scare unlike any you'd had before. I'm sure by morning you would have seen that Dela needed to know this. She can tell everyone not to approach the guy now and they won't get harmed."

Sherman sent him a grateful gaze.

Dela knew she should have said that but Heath was much more diplomatic than she was. That's why they made a good team. She stood, put a hand on Sherman's shoulder, and said, "I'm sorry you had to go through that tonight. Get a good night's sleep and tomorrow I'd like you to write down all of what you told me so we have it documented." She pulled out her phone. "Do you mind if I get a photo? It will go with your statement."

He nodded and she took a photo straight on and from each side.

"I am truly sorry. I never thought he would be so violent." Dela gave him a weak smile and followed Heath to the door. She faced Sherman. "To be on the safe side, keep an eye on your family. I think it was just a threat and he won't act on it when it could jeopardize what he is really doing."

Sherman nodded, and she followed Heath to the car.

Once inside, a tear trickled down her cheek. She swiped at it with her hand. She wasn't an emotional person but losing Rowena and then having this teddy bear of a man get hurt because of an order she'd given. She was raw with emotion. Her throat burned from the sobs she swallowed.

Heath backed the car out of the driveway and pulled onto the street. He put a hand on her leg. "It's not your fault. No matter who had confronted him, Ferris. would have acted the same. It could have been you."

"I would have been prepared for an attack. Sherman is a sweet guy who hasn't been trained to do anything other than eject a drunk or separate a fight."

"Maybe you need to suggest all the guards be trained once a month in a situation where they are facing down a person with a gun."

Dela stared at Heath. "That's a good idea. Thank you for coming to help." She leaned her head on his shoulder. "We have to find Ferris tomorrow and talk some more with Felicity. I'm not buying Quinn's tale of West talking Felicity into kidnapping her boy and that Hugo got the jump on her and did it himself."

Heath pulled into the parking lot in front of their building.

Dela's phone buzzed. It was a number she didn't know. "Hello?"

"This is Tamara Dorsey, from housekeeping." The woman's voice was barely a whisper.

"Yes, I remember. What's wrong?" Dela's senses went on alert. Why would someone Benedict had used to harass her before call now, after Felicity's P.I. had assaulted a security guard?

"The person I told you that paid me the other day?" she stammered.

"Yes."

"He gave me more money tonight, along with a listening device to put in your room tomorrow when I clean it. I tried to tell him no, but he said if I didn't do it, he'd make sure something happened to my mom." She sniffed.

"Thank you for calling. Go ahead and put it in the room. No sense in you worrying about your mom. Since I know about it, I can make sure nothing is said that he would want to hear." Dela ended the call and peered across the car at Heath. "Hugo Benedict must be scared we know something. He threatened the poor housekeeper into putting a listening device in my room tomorrow morning."

"He thinks you know something. But about what? The kidnapping or his business?"

"I'm wondering the same thing and why would he think that I know anything unless Ferris is working for him? He could have called or talked to Hugo right after beating up Sherman and they decided I'm the person who knows what they've been up to." Dela didn't like her opponents thinking she knew more than she did. But she'd rather have them after her than innocent people.

Chapter Sixteen

Monday morning, Dela and Heath had breakfast at the grill and he headed to Benton County to dig up any information he could find about the jail and Dory Thunder. Dela wandered over to the casino, expecting to find Trent on the day shift. Instead, Reuben sat in the office sipping coffee and reading a piece of paper.

"Is Trent coming in today?" Dela asked, noting the security officer at the radio desk was the older gentleman she'd seen before.

"He called in sick and it's Sherman's day off. That leaves me in charge. Just how long are you sticking around here watching us?" Reuben's body language, from his glowering face to his ridged spine, said he wanted her gone.

"I'll have my evaluation done today," she said.

He sneered.

"But I'm not leaving here until I learn who killed my friend." She did an about-face and walked out of the office and up the stairs to surveillance. She leaned over Dede's shoulder and whispered, "Keep an eye on the front of the casino and discretely tell me when that vagrant starts hanging out in front of the building."

Dede nodded and pulled up the building entrance on the monitor in front of her.

Oscar sat on the opposite side of where the woman was watching one of his cameras. Dela hoped if he got up, he didn't see they were keeping tabs on his job.

"No one's in there," Oscar said when Dela walked to the door of the back room.

She smiled at him. "Good, I need some privacy to write down my evaluation."

He stared at her as she opened the door and walked in. The room was dark. She flicked the light switch beside the door and studied the room. She could use the computer to the side to do some digging around on the internet. Where would Sidney have put all the information she'd asked her to copy?

Dela walked over and turned the computer on, scanning the desk where it sat. She didn't see a folder or envelope tucked anywhere. Pulling out her phone, she called Sidney.

"Yeah?" she answered in a sleepy voice.

"Sorry if I woke you," Dela said.

"Not half as sorry as I am. I was having a good dream." There was a hint of a smile in her voice.

"Then I'm really sorry. I'm in the back surveillance room and can't find the items I asked you to copy."

Sidney yawned. "Sorry, I stayed up too late watching a movie, which I always do when I don't have to go to work the next day."

"Yes, I understand you worked one of your days off helping me find a kidnapper and a killer. Where did you put the information?"

"It's taped to the back of the top right monitor. Didn't want Oscar snooping and finding it."

"Smart! Go back to your dream," Dela said, happy to have found someone competent to work with at this casino.

"I'm awake now. Want me to come over and help?"

Sherman's bruised face flashed in her mind. "No, it's best if you stay out of it from now on."

"What happened?" Sidney's lazy attitude became sharp and inquisitive.

"Sherman was beat up last night and his family was threatened because he did something I asked him to do. I'll not have anyone else put in the same situation." She hadn't come here to upend people's lives and put them in danger. She came to do an easy job for a friend. *Some friend.* He'd gone on vacation while a kidnapping had occurred under his nose.

"Does it have something to do with the kidnapping or the murder?" Sidney asked.

"Both. I believe they're connected. Maybe you should come in. But don't let Reuben or Oscar see you come to the back room. I told Oscar I was writing up my evaluation where it was quiet."

"Good move. He takes lunch at eleven. I'll slip up there then."

"And avoid the vagrant if you see him. I think he's in on it. He beat up Sherman. When Sherman gets his statement to me, I'm taking it to Detective

Stedman." Dela knew she should have had Sherman call the police last night but she could tell by how frightened he was for his family he would have refused. She had to make Stedman see that this was bigger than they had originally thought. Something was going on and she wasn't sure who was pulling all the strings.

"If you see people in the front who shouldn't see you, call me and I'll let you in the security back door." Dela felt keeping those helping her safe was her main priority. And she believed Rowena would feel the same. Find her killer, but keep everyone else safe.

"Will do. You'll either see or hear from me at eleven ten." The call ended.

Dela inhaled deeply and walked over to the monitor on the far right. The door opened and she spun, facing Reuben.

"What are you doing in here?" His eyes scanned the room, landing on the blinking computer.

"I am getting ready to write my evaluation. The reason I came up here was to not be disturbed. She walked over to the blinking computer and opened up a blank document.

"Why were you walking around if you were writing?"

She glanced over at the man. He'd crossed his arms and stared at her.

"I think best when I'm walking. I was trying to decide what to start with, the good or the things that need work." She returned her attention to the computer screen and started typing. She began with the day she arrived and what she'd found.

Reuben huffed and left the room, closing the door loudly behind him.

Dela rose, walked to the door, and clicked the lock. She was tired of people popping in unannounced. Once she knew the room was secured, she walked over and ripped the papers from the back of the monitor.

She spread it out on the table where the printer sat and put them in order of what she wanted to look at first. Wishing she had a magnifying glass, she rummaged through the drawers and came up empty. She held the photos under the strongest light in the room and studied the boat, trying to make out the name on the side, the level of the water on the rocks, and the enlarged head of the older man. None of the photos were of a good enough quality to make out a thing.

She began reading the information Sidney had dug up on Ferris, Hugo, and Felicity. The P.I. was kicked off the Portland Police for illegal procedures. That didn't surprise her given how he'd treated Sherman last night. He'd been linked to several drug dealers. Could he and Hugo be laundering money for those people? The records Sidney printed out on Hugo were the court cases he'd been involved in and the results. His marriage certificate and pre-nuptial agreement.

Dela tapped her finger on the paper. This was why Felicity was trying to get the goods on Hugo. But she was using a P.I. who most likely told Hugo everything she did and asked him to do. That didn't make sense. Why would she use her husband's P.I.?

The more she learned the more confused Dela became.

She picked up the paper on Felicity as tapping sounded on the door. Dela shoved the papers under a stack of blank paper and crossed to the door.

"It's me," Sidney's voice whispered.

Dela let her in and peeked at who was in the monitor room. None of them looked in their direction. She closed the door and clicked the lock.

"I was tired of people popping in," she said, walking back to the pile of papers.

"I understand. I made sure Oscar was sitting in his usual place eating, didn't see Reuben, and hurried up the stairs. I don't think anyone out there will say anything. They all value their jobs and know you are here to say who goes and who stays." Sidney set a pizza box on the table. "I brought lunch." She pulled two bottles of water out of her purse.

Dela smiled. Her preparedness reminded her of Rowena. "Thanks. I hadn't even thought about lunch."

She picked the printout on Felicity up and began reading. The woman had come from a wealthy family. She was an honor student, cheerleading captain, and went to college for art. She married Hugo six months after meeting him at an art gallery. He used her money to start up a business, that grew rapidly, not from legal means.

Dela tapped the paper. "I don't get it. She signed a pre-nup agreement for Hugo, yet, he used her money to start his illegal activities. I would think she could just walk away, the money is hers."

"I wondered about that, too. But if you look at his pre-nup, if she walks away, she can't divulge anything she knows about his business and forfeits any ongoing profits."

"Then she knew he was going to use her money for illegal profits. Otherwise, she wouldn't have signed. She is greedy and that's why she is pretending to be dumb about his business. She could be hauled in as an accomplice. And that's why the Feds have an informant who is schmoozing and grooming her to give up her husband. They know the best way to get her cooperation is to say she isn't an accomplice." Dela slapped the paper down on the table and walked back and forth. "The FBI may not have put the cord around Rowena's neck but they started the ball rolling on the kidnapping and what my friend saw."

The plastic bottle in Sidney's hands crackled as she twisted the cap. "You think the FBI had something to do with the kidnapping?"

"Special Agent Pierce told me their informant put the idea into Felicity's head. That's enough for me to blame them." Dela sat in front of the computer. "I want to know more about Hugo Benedict's business dealings and more about Jude West. Felicity wants away from Hugo and she has feelings for West. But according to Pierce, the informant is helping them to get Felicity."

Sidney cursed. "That is pretty low."

"Yeah, that's what I told Pierce. He just grinned." Dela opened the computer to the browser. "I'm going to dig deeper into my suspects. Can you check outdoor cameras at the Starfish building the day of the kidnapping and the Otter the night when Rowena was murdered? Even if all you can do is figure out if the cameras were turned off or messed with."

"On it." Sidney sat at the computer in front of the monitors and started clicking away at the keyboard.

Dela typed, scrolled, and printed off information until her stomach started growling. She stopped, stretched, and opened the pizza box. A combination pizza with olives made her smile. "Good choice," she said, plucking a piece from the twelve-inch pie.

Sidney stretched and reached for a slice. "It's my favorite place that makes it and my favorite combination."

Dela's phone buzzed. It was Heath. She finished chewing the bite in her mouth and answered. "Hey, how's it going?"

"Kind of what we'd expected. Everyone I've talked to says the records were all burned in the fire. When I asked how a mugshot from before the fire made it out without a scorch, they just shrugged. I'm grabbing some lunch and heading over to the county library. The newspapers from that time are on microfiche there." It sounded like he took a drink and asked, "How are things there?"

She relayed how Reuben was in charge and had barged in to see what she was doing. She now had the door locked and Sidney was helping.

"Glad you're not alone. It seems like your friend has made some poor choices in his assistants."

"Yeah, I've been wondering about that, too." Dela had lain awake the night before trying to figure out why Enos had brought her here and then took off.

"I have something!" Sidney said excitedly.

"I have to go. Good luck this afternoon." Dela ended the call and walked over to stand behind Sidney. "What did you find?"

"I can say that at the time of the kidnapping, the monitor in the hallway outside of the suite was turned off. There is a discrepancy in the time stamp on the footage. It jumps from twelve-fifty-five to one-fifty-five. Which means that is the time frame when Asher was taken."

Dela smiled. "And that's the time frame in which Oscar turned the camera off. He was the one watching the outside hallway that day. Which means I can have Stedman bring him in for questioning." Dela raised her hand still holding her phone.

"I also looked at the footage for the elevator and the entrance to the building in that time frame."

"Let me guess, it was all cut at the same time?" Dela said, knowing they weren't going to pick anything up from the cameras.

"Yes, which makes it suspicious. One camera going down, that could be a maintenance thing but on different floors and the entrance… That's definitely foul play." Sidney clicked the keys on the keyboard.

"I had an idea that would be the case. We can use this to get Oscar to talk." Dela was feeling better about the outcome.

"Let me go through the footage of the night your friend was killed. Let's see if we can connect him to that as well." Sidney's gaze held hers.

It made sense to pull him in for both if he'd been an accomplice in both. It would also put more against him and make it more important for him to help them. "Keep looking."

Dela continued her digging into Ferris as she ate her pizza. Her phone buzzed. Quinn.
She fluctuated between answering and not answering. She was pissed at him for allowing the FBI to use Felicity but at the same time, she wanted him to know about Ferris beating up Sherman. Reluctantly she swiped the screen and answered.

"How do you plan to ruin my day?" she asked.

Quinn chuckled. "I was hoping to make it better. We've established that the P.I. Felicity hired is working for Hugo."

Dela snorted. "Tell me something I don't know."

"When did you figure it out?" Quinn asked his tone all business.

"Last night when Ferris beat up the security officer helping me and threatened his family."

"I suppose the officer won't come forward?" Quinn asked.

"He's hesitant but is writing up an account of what happened. I plan to give that to Stedman and let him pull in Ferris. It's clear to me that the security officers at this casino haven't been trained as well as they should be." Dela planned to add that to the report she had started this morning.

"From our observations of the casino, I agree with you."

"How long have you been observing this casino?" she asked, wondering if it had been under surveillance before the kidnapping.

"Myself, not until you called me about the kidnapping. But there have been agents here to monitor Benedict's activities."

Against her better judgment, she decided to tell Quinn about the compromised cameras. "We've determined that the cameras in the hall outside the Benedicts' suite and the elevator and entrance to the Starfish lobby were turned off during the kidnapping."

"We'd assumed as much when surveillance couldn't find any decent footage at that time."

She caught the hint of smugness in his tone. "You

assumed or you knew because you asked someone to turn them off?" Anger boiled in her chest and burned up her throat.

"We knew that one of the surveillance personnel had been approached by one of Benedict's people and believed when the kidnapping was reported there would be no footage for us to use to find the kidnapper."

"And I know who you are talking about. Thank you for filling in the hazy parts. I have a phone call to make." She ended the call and immediately dialed Detective Stedman.

Chapter Seventeen

"You're sure the FBI are in on this?" Stedman asked Dela when she told him she wanted P.I. Peter Ferris and surveillance personnel Oscar Xaviar brought into the Lincoln City Police Station for questioning. And she would like to be present when it happened because she knew all the things to say to get at least Oscar talking.

"Special Agent Pierce all but told me they knew Oscar had turned off the cameras during the kidnapping and that his contact who told him to do it was Peter Ferris. He is the vagrant that has been hanging around the entrance of the casino for several weeks." Dela had a feeling once Oscar and Ferris started talking, she and Heath would be going home.

"I'll send two patrolmen over to pick up Xaviar and see if we can find this Ferris. But what if the FBI gets wind of this?" Stedman asked.

"Tell them you had it on good authority that these men were part of the Benedict kidnapping and you are trying to get the boy back unharmed." She smiled at Sidney who chewed on pizza and watched her during the conversation.

"Ok. But if the Chief gets wind that I'm ruffling FBI feathers he's not going to like my doing this without asking."

"If you find the child and a murderer, isn't that what matters the most?" Dela persisted.

"He *would* like to have both of these matters cleared up as quickly as possible," Stedman agreed.

"There you go. Let me know when you have both men in custody. I'll come right down."

"I'll keep you posted."

The call ended and Dela shoved her phone in her pocket. "Let's hope they can get both men today. I'm sure we can get the truth out of Oscar fairly easily, but Ferris will be harder and he's dangerous."

Sidney stood. "Do you want me to keep an eye on Oscar?"

"No. It'll be easy for the police to walk in here and escort him to the police station for questioning. It's Ferris I'm more worried about them finding. He seems to be able to change his appearance and blend in. And he's dangerous. I don't want him to get wind of this and go after Sherman's family."

Dela studied Sidney. "That's who you should keep an eye on. You know who all I suspect. If you see one of them going near Sherman's house or a family member, call me and the police."

Sidney stood, grabbed her purse, and headed for the door. "I'll let you know what I see when I get there."

"I'm glad I can count on a few people who work at

this casino," Dela said as Sidney unlocked the door and disappeared.

Dela sank onto the chair in front of the computer and picked up the paper with the times, dates, and cameras that were shut down during the kidnapping. They'd need this when they talked to Oscar. She folded it and put it in her pants pocket.

They would need Sherman's statement about getting beat up by Ferris when the police brought him in. Did she ask Sidney to get it? Dela doubted Sherman would hand it to anyone but her. She didn't have a car to drive there and didn't want to compromise Sidney.

She'd wait until they had Ferris in custody and then ask Sherman to bring the statement to the police station.

Gathering up all the printed-out information, Dela folded it in half and stuffed it into her shoulder bag. When she stepped out of the back room, two uniformed police officers were talking to Oscar.

His gaze landed on her.

Dela kept a neutral expression and waited to see what happened. The man was arguing he couldn't leave his station.

Ray, the older man on the monitors next to Oscar's, said, "Don't worry, we'll split up your cameras until they get someone in to take over."

Walking over to Ray, Dela asked, "Who's in charge of scheduling the surveillance personnel?"

"Enos has been in charge of both the security and surveillance personnel," Ray said.

No wonder Enos had wanted her to come clean out his team. He was too spread out to make heads or tails of what was going on. "Okay, and I know Trent, who is sick, and Sherman, who has the day off are under him.

145

Is Reuben the next person in line with the highest authority?" She didn't like the idea of that man having that much control of the casino security.

Ray shook his head. "Sidney, having worked both positions would be the next person."

Dela did a mental slap and pulled out her phone. "Reuben was only in charge because it was Sidney's day off?" She asked, scrolling and touching Sidney's name in her contacts.

"Yeah. As soon as Reuben saw that no one was in charge, he took over."

"I'm almost to Sherman's, what's up?" Sidney answered.

"You need to come back to the casino. I just found out you are the person who should be here running security and surveillance, even if it is your day off." Dela kept her tone light. Why hadn't the woman mentioned it earlier?"

A whoosh of air rushed through the speaker of her phone.

"I forgot. It is a newly appointed position. But it's my day off, like Sherman," she reasoned. "If anyone should be called in, it's Trent. He sure became sick all of a sudden after Sherman was beat up."

A light went off in Dela's brain. "You're right, it is suspicious that Trent called in sick today. Go home, put on your uniform, and get back here. You need to take care of things. The police took Oscar away and they are one person down on the surveillance team. You need to call someone in and get the security staff realigned." She added, "When you get here, I'd like to borrow your car to check on Trent."

"Okay. Luckily my place is between where I'm at

and the casino. I'll be there in twenty."

The call ended and Dela glanced around at all the people watching her.

"Sidney will be here in thirty minutes to bring in a replacement for Oscar. Do any of you have any questions for me?"

One woman raised a hand.

Dela nodded at her.

"Have they found the boy yet?"

Her heart sank as she admitted that they hadn't been able to find out anything about the child. "We're hoping that Oscar can help. He turned off the cameras that allowed the kidnapper to get into and out of the building without being seen."

Ray nodded. "I had a feeling he'd done something. He's been jumpy ever since the kidnapping happened."

Dela shifted her attention to the older man. "Do you happen to know who was supposed to be watching the cameras outside of the Otter building the night my friend died?"

"Not Oscar. He always watches the hallways and entrances. But I think he was watching them that night." Ray swiveled in his chair and made eye contact with everyone in the room. "Did one of you trade with Oscar?" They all shook their heads.

"You're the mid-day shift. It would have been the night shift." Again, Dela stopped as a thought came to her. "Is this normally Oscar's shift?"

"Yeah, but he takes over the night shift if someone can't make it in. He lives with his mom and hates going home." Ray shrugged.

She made a note to find out which person didn't come to work the night Oscar took their shift and allowed someone into Rowena's room to kill her.

♠ ♣ ♥ ♦

Heath arrived five minutes before Sidney walked into the security office with her uniform on. Dela had just been getting ready to tell Reuben to go back to his regular position when Sidney swooped in.

"What is she doing here?" Reuben asked with disdain.

"I understand she is the next person in line to be in charge with Enos, Trent, and Sherman gone." Dela glared at him. "Not you. She should have been called in as soon as Trent called in sick."

"I suggested it," the security officer at the radio desk said.

Reuben shot him a piercing glare.

"Joe, call in Shirley Moat to take over the rest of Oscar's shift. I believe she is on the night shift so she can come in early," Sidney said. Then she stopped in front of Reuben. "I believe your shift ended about three hours ago. Go home so you can rest up for tomorrow."

Reuben glared at her, pivoted, and walked through the door leading to the employee's lunch room.

"I'd be careful talking to him like that. He has the look of someone wound up too tight," Heath said.

"He doesn't like women being in authority positions," Sidney said. "He was the first to start bad-mouthing Dela before she even showed up. Just because he didn't think a woman was qualified to make judgments on how our staff performed."

"I'm putting in my notes that he should be one of the first to be let go. Other than the ones that are caught up in the kidnapping and murder," Dela added.

She studied Sidney. "Go do what you need to do,

then find us in the coffee shop and I'll catch you up to date with what I've learned since you left."

Dela led Heath out of the security office and back out to the casino. They headed to the coffee shop and once they were seated with ice teas, she leaned toward him. "What did you find out?"

"The jail and all the records did burn down. However, Theodore Thunder had been transferred to a different jail right before the fire and his records went with him." Heath leaned back, picked up his tea, and drank half the glass.

Dela studied him. "Where was he moved to?"

"There had been so much anger over the reason he was in jail that they had moved him because someone had threatened to burn down the jail if he wasn't executed." Heath reached across the table and took her hand.

Dela felt all the air squeeze out of her lungs hearing that there was that much hatred for her father. When she could breathe, she asked, "When and where was he executed?"

Heath shook his head. "He wasn't. He was sentenced to twenty-five years."

"Then he's been out of jail and hasn't been seen?" She couldn't wrap her head around why he hadn't come back to Nixyáawii and why his family wouldn't talk about him.

Heath shook his head. "He escaped during a transfer to prison. They never caught him, though there were sightings of him across the West and Midwest at colleges. They believe he was a serial rapist." He squeezed her hand.

She shook her head. "No, I don't believe that of

him. Wouldn't I have more desire in that way, if…" She couldn't wrap her head around being the child of a rape victim. Her mom had never treated her as if she were dirty or caused her pain.

"He was identified by several of the women. I have copies of the trial manuscript in the car. They would only let me copy a limited amount of it. I tried to get what I thought would give you the most information." He moved to sit in the seat next to her and put an arm around her shoulders. "Your mom was one of the women who testified against him."

Dela swallowed, unsure if the bile burning her throat would stay down. She couldn't talk, couldn't think, for the images crashing around in her mind.

Sidney strode over to their table. Her smile wavered and concern wrinkled her brow as she sat across from them. "What's wrong?"

"Personal stuff," Heath said.

Dela thanked him by squeezing the top of his thigh where her hand rested. She took several minutes to compartmentalize what she'd just learned and get back to the kidnapping and murder. "Is everything under control now?" she asked.

"As good as it can be with the real boss gone," Sidney said.

"True." Dela nodded. "Heath and I are going to check on Trent. The City Police picked up Oscar, but I haven't heard anything from Stedman about them catching Ferris. Once we check on Trent, we'll go see Sherman and pick up his statement about last night. Then I'd like to go to Jude West's place and see if we can learn any more from him."

Heath nodded.

Sidney asked, "What do you want me to do?"

"Keep things running here and if you see Ferris, send two officers out to detain him for the City Police." Dela rose. "Do not go after him yourself. Sherman is a big guy and Ferris got the better of him."

Sidney's eyes widened as she nodded. "You two be careful, too. We don't need any more kidnappings or murders."

Chapter Eighteen

On their way to check on Trent, Dela called Enos. She didn't think it was a coincidence he'd brought her here this past weekend.

"You have reached Enos Apash, leave a message."

When the phone beeped, Dela said, "I don't appreciate you disappearing on a weekend you knew there would be a kidnapping and leaving me in the dark. It has also escalated into a murder. Would be nice to have you back here helping me discover which of your employees are on the take. I'm beginning to think it starts at the top with you." She ended the call and stared out the window.

"That was a bit harsh, don't you think?" Heath said.

"No. I don't appreciate being used. And that's what he did. He knew the kidnapping was happening and brought me here to clean up his mess." She twisted in the seat to study Heath. "There is no other explanation for what happened and why he has disappeared. And as far as I can tell, Trent is either in on it, or he doesn't have balls enough to be second to the head of security. I think Sherman would if he'd had training. I know Sidney is."

"Is that going to be your recommendation? Sidney should be second in command?" Heath asked, turning a corner and slowing down.

"No. If I'm right about Enos, he needs to be removed and Sidney put in his place. Then Sherman as second." She shifted to peer at the house where Trent lived. "There are two vehicles. I would think his wife would be at work."

They parked on the street and walked up to the front door.

Heath knocked and they stood on the stoop waiting for someone to answer.

The door slowly opened and Trent peered out. "What are you doing here?" His tone rose an octave as he said, "You're going to get us killed."

Heath shoved the door open, pushing Trent into the house. Dela followed and stopped inside the door as her gaze landed on Enos.

"What the hell?" She crossed her arms as Heath walked around her and shut the front door. "Have you been here the whole time? I thought you were at a party for your dad." Anger pulsed her blood, making a whooshing sound in her head. This was an anger unlike any she'd had before. Never had she felt so betrayed as standing here peering into Enos's unapologetic eyes.

Heath stood beside her. "Care to introduce me."

"Enos Apash, this is my friend, Tribal Detective Heath Seaver. He came here to help me discover who killed one of my best friends and find a child you could have kept from being kidnapped. Which caused my friend's death."

At least the man jerked from her accusations and his gaze drifted to the floor.

"Mr. Apash, I think it's time you had a visit with either the Lincoln City Police or the FBI," Heath said.

"We can't tell anyone," Trent blurted.

"I see you're healthy enough to be at work," Dela said in reply.

"You don't understand," Trent continued. "I didn't know about all of this until I came home from work and there was a note on my door saying something would happen to my wife if I continued to help you look into the kidnapping and murder. The easiest way to keep my wife safe was to stay away from the casino."

"You could have reported the threat," Dela said, glaring at the man.

"Where's the note?" Heath asked.

"I threw it away so my wife wouldn't see it. I didn't want her to worry." Trent cowered as Dela stalked straight toward him.

"Where is the note? Which garbage can?" she said through clenched teeth. If Heath weren't there, she would have knocked the man around just to get out some of her rage.

Trent's gaze flicked toward the kitchen.

"Watch them. I'm going trash can diving," she said and marched into the kitchen. It would be better to dig through the garbage than to hit the man. And she needed some distance from Enos so she could get her emotions under control.

She heard Heath ask Enos when he'd arrived back in Lincoln City. She stilled her movements to hear the man's reply.

It was low and muffled so she didn't catch it. Better if she just dug through this and got back into the room to learn more about why the man, who she thought was a stellar head of security, would do something like this.

She pulled the garbage can out of the cupboard under the sink and dumped it upside down on a rug. The slop and gunk that covered most of the trash would most likely have ruined the note, but she wasn't giving up until she saw it. If she didn't see the note, she'd believe the man was using it as a means to stay out of harm's way rather than a threat to his wife.

She found a pair of tongs on the counter and used those to pick through the contents. About halfway through the mess, she found a crumpled piece of paper. Picking it up she spied wording on the inside of the crumpled ball. The peanut butter and syrup on the outside may not have messed up the writing.

"Got it!" she called and using the counter, pulled herself to a standing position by the time the three men entered the room.

"Did you have to make a mess!" Trent exclaimed, staring at the pile of trash on the kitchen rug.

Dela shrugged and put the paper on the counter. She dug around in a drawer and pulled out a fork which she used to open up the paper. It was a typed threat. No way to use handwriting to find out who wrote it.

Heath inspected it and said, "Tell Dela why you left her to deal with something that could have been avoided." He started opening drawers.

"What are you looking for?" Trent asked.

"A plastic bag," Heath replied.

Dela held Enos's gaze, waiting for him to speak.

The man ducked his head, wiped a hand across his forehead, and finally opened his mouth. "My father isn't doing well. I was offered a lot of money to not be here this weekend. I didn't know for sure what was going to happen but I was promised no one would get hurt."

Dela snorted. "I don't give a crap that you were promised anything. You and I both know when someone is doing something illegal it never goes as planned."

He nodded. "I respect the person who asked me to vanish. I can't believe that they would condone murder."

"Who paid you?" Dela asked.

"She just wanted to get Asher away from Hugo. Can you blame her? He hurts her and treats the boy like a pawn in a chess game to keep her in control."

Dela put her hands on her hips. "Felicity had her boy kidnapped to get him away from Hugo?"

"Yes. There wasn't supposed to be anyone getting hurt. You would be here to head up the kidnapping, which would go cold when no one showed up to pick up the ransom. And I'd come back on Wednesday and pretend to be doing all I could. Then Jude and Felicity were going to go where she could get a divorce from Hugo and live in a country where he couldn't go because of his dealings."

Dela's mind was spinning. "Why didn't they just take the boy and leave? Why all this drama?"

Enos shrugged. "Drama follows Felicity."

Heath had the note in a plastic bag and had written in the corner where it was found and when. "I think the two of you need to go to the FBI and give a statement about your obstruction of this crime."

The two men's eyes widened.

"I don't think so," Trent said. "There is no need for anyone to know anything."

Heath shook the bag with the note. "This says someone thinks you know something. And they don't want you to help Dela find the truth. That makes you a witness to their crime."

"I haven't seen anything and all I did was drive Dela around. She's the one who knows everything."

Her mind had been spinning ever since she walked into the house and saw Enos. "Why are you hiding? If Felicity paid you and you were asked to stay away, why are you here? At Trent's house?"

"Because he called me when he found the note. Trent didn't know anything about the kidnapping. He was worried about helping you and wanted to know what to do. That's why I'm here and not helping move my dad into a retirement home. I told Trent I'd come see what I could find out."

"So have you spoken to Felicity?" Dela asked. She'd believed the woman ignorant of her husband's business but now she was thinking the woman had more cunning and acting abilities than she'd given her credit.

"No. After talking to Trent this morning, I tried calling her. The calls went straight to voicemail. I wondered if she and Jude had taken off already and drove to his place." He ran a hand over his face. "He's there and is also worried because he hasn't heard from Felicity since last night." Enos studied her. "I think Hugo figured out what she did and is forcing her to tell him where to find Asher."

Dela flicked a glance at Heath. Should she tell Enos what she knew and who was helping with the kidnappings and hiding the killer, or just get the two to the police?

She asked Heath, "What do you think? Fill him in or take him to the police?"

"Hey, all I did was step away for a few days, none of this is my fault," Enos said.

Shifting all her weight to her left leg, she spun, facing Enos. "How do you figure that when you could have told Felicity no and then told the police and FBI what she had planned? Not to mention that there has already been one fatality in this kidnapping and an assault and threat. This is not just a quick snatch-and-run kidnapping that would be a typical domestic dispute. This has escalated and who knows if Asher is even still alive. There could be two fatalities for all we know."

Enos ran a hand over his face. "I agree it has gone way beyond what I was told would happen. But I can't get thrown in jail even with the money I took to keep quiet, my dad will still need me to take care of him."

"You should have thought of that before you accepted the money to keep quiet," Heath said.

"Since the FBI put this notion of kidnapping into Felicity's head, let's call Special Agent Pierce," Dela said. She wanted him to see the mess his Feds had caused. Which also gave her the satisfaction of blaming him for Rowena's death.

"You sure that's who you want to call?" Heath asked, looking skeptical.

"Stedman should have picked up the two people

who can tell us more about the killer and kidnapping than these two. He's going to call me when they're ready to question them." Dela worried that Stedman wouldn't find Ferris. He seemed to be key to the whole thing in her estimation.

"We'd just be giving Special Agent Pierce two of the people he should know about if he orchestrated Felicity. And perhaps he is the one keeping her from everyone?" She threw that in to sway Heath's protector instincts to get what she wanted. She wanted Quinn here so she could rub his nose in the mess he'd made.

"Call him," Heath said. "Because if he doesn't have Mrs. Benedict, then we need to be looking for her."

She smiled inwardly. She knew Heath as well as he thought he knew her. Dela pulled out her phone, scrolled her contacts, and pressed Quinn's name.

The phone barely rang and Quinn answered, "Where are you?"

She could hear the sound of slot machines in the background. "Not at the casino."

"I discovered that. The little girl playing head of security wouldn't tell me where to find you."

"You could have called." She caught Heath watching her. She shrugged as if to say, I can't help pushing his buttons.

"That's what I was about to do when you called me. Where are you?"

"I'm at Trent Lawton's house. We would like you to come over here and clear up some things for us."

"Us? Who's with you?" His tone was wary.

"Heath, Trent, and Enos Apash, the head of security for the casino."

"I'll be right over." The call ended.

Dela smiled at Heath and said, "I have a pretty good idea he's going to vouch for these two." Which only put him higher on her list of shitheads. If he had condoned what happened and someone helping him cover up the kidnapping that killed Rowena, she was going to make sure he was arrested for Rowena's death as well. She didn't care if he was FBI.

Chapter Nineteen

While they waited for Quinn to arrive, Dela helped Trent clean up the mess she'd made with the trash. Heath and Enos sat at the kitchen table nursing cups of coffee. Once they'd cleaned up the mess, Trent handed her a cup and she sat down beside Heath.

Trent filled a cup for himself but he couldn't seem to sit. He paced back and forth and finally blurted, "I didn't know anything about any of this. You'll tell the FBI, won't you?"

"All you have to do is tell them the truth and everything that you know and you'll be fine," Heath said in his calm reassuring tone.

His calm voice and sincere tone had drawn out more than one person they'd questioned when he'd helped with crimes at the casino. Dela smiled at him. Those same two qualities were the ones that drew her to him the most. She always knew where she stood with him and he always told her the truth, even if she didn't like it.

Pounding on the door sent Trent jogging out of the room. He returned with Quinn and the other agent who had been tagging along with him all weekend. She'd yet to be introduced.

"What is going on here?" Quinn asked as the other agent pulled out a notepad and pen.

Dela glanced at Enos. "I should make introductions." She held her hand palm up toward Enos. "This is Enos Apash, head of security for the Siletz Bay Casino." She motioned to Trent. "I believe you met Trent during our investigation of the crime scene of Rowena Maxwell's homicide." She stared at the agent writing down the names. "But I've yet to be introduced to your sidekick." The man grimaced and studied her.

"Special Agent Buck Swanson, this sassy woman is Dela Alvaro, head of security for the Spotted Pony Casino. The man next to her is Tribal Detective Heath Seaver with the Umatilla Reservation—"

"Isn't that in the northeast corner of the state?" Swanson asked, interrupting Quinn.

"Yeah. He has no jurisdiction here but the two seem to always work together." Quinn grinned.

Dela glared back at him. "Enos has something to tell you about the kidnapping. That is if you didn't already know it."

Quinn gave her a quizzical look and shifted his attention to Enos. "What about the kidnapping?"

Enos went on to tell him what he'd told Dela about Felicity paying him to disappear for the weekend so she could kidnap her son.

"You know, the kidnapping you had Jude West put into her head," Dela said innocently.

He glared at her. "But she didn't kidnap Asher. She

was chewing us out for not stopping her husband from taking him."

"Who else would have been able to orchestrate the whole thing other than the mother?" Dela asked. "And why pay Enos to be gone if she didn't kidnap him?"

"If you want to play that game, why would she have someone killed?" Quinn asked.

"To keep the information she'd kidnapped her son from her husband," Heath said.

"She's got you believing I'm responsible for all of this?" Quinn asked, his gaze boring into Heath.

Heath shrugged. "She has come up with some good evidence that would point that way. I think the Lincoln City Police should be given all the facts and see what they come up with."

A surge of affection and gratitude flooded her at Heath's words.

"Why are you in Mr. Lawton's house?" Agent Swanson asked.

"Trent, tell him," Dela said.

Trent told how after helping Dela work the homicide and the kidnapping, he came home to find a note on his door saying that something would happen to his wife if he didn't back off and not help her.

Quinn's head snapped around and he peered at her. "What have you found out?"

"Not nearly enough. I know that an employee in surveillance, Oscar Xaviar, turned off the cameras during the kidnapping and the murder. The Lincoln City Police have him in custody. And they are looking for Peter Ferris, the P.I. from Portland. He assaulted a security officer last night and is caught up in the kidnapping and I strongly suspect the murder."

Heath cleared his throat. "And Hugo Benedict paid a housekeeping employee to ransack Dela's room and place a listening device in it."

Quinn smiled. "None of that points toward Felicity. It all adds up to Benedict. Ferris is his hired P.I. and we looked into all the employee's financials. Xaviar has had large sums of money coming into his account for the last six months from a business owned by Benedict."

Dela studied Enos. "You didn't see any large sums go into Enos's bank?" The head of security squirmed.

"No, we would have been on top of him if it had popped." Quinn also turned his attention to Enos.

"How did you get paid?" Dela asked.

"It was put into an account under my father's name at the retirement home. I didn't want it traced to me. In case something went wrong." Enos ducked his head. "It's amazing what we do for the parents we love."

The comment stung Dela's heart. She would never wish to cause her mom grief or unhappiness. Should she stop digging into the person she believed was her father? Grandfather Thunder said it would hurt her mom to bring him up. And now, after Heath investigated the newspaper records, she knew why.

"The important thing now is to determine who did kidnap Asher and find out who killed Rowena," Heath said, drawing her out of her sad thoughts.

"When was the last time you saw Felicity?" Dela asked. "Enos tried to see her today and Jude said he hadn't seen her since last night."

Quinn's gaze scanned each person's face. Then he glanced at Swanson. "Who was watching her last night?"

The other agent flipped back some pages in the notebook and said, "Winston."

"Give him a call and see what he says," Quinn said. "And see if anyone has eyes on Ferris and Benedict while you're at it."

Swanson nodded and stepped into the other room.

Dela studied Quinn. He wasn't faking the worry etched on his brow or the way the muscle along his jawline twitched. He didn't like the things he'd just learned.

"How long have you been watching Felicity and Ferris?" she asked.

"Since they both arrived in Lincoln City," Quinn said absent-mindedly.

Anger burned her cheeks. She swallowed the wad of rage in her throat and said, "Then you have an agent who witnessed Sherman being beaten and did nothing?"

Quinn's head jerked around and he stared at her. "What?"

She glared at him. "You heard me say Ferris beat up a security guard last night and you didn't even flinch. If you have people watching him, they should have reported the beating. And you knew about it. Why didn't they stop Ferris or offer Sherman some aid after the man had walked away?" She snapped her fingers. "He's working for you as well, isn't he?"

"I can assure you that Peter Ferris Private Investigator is not working for us. He might have been in law enforcement before, but he's a long way from doing anything legal." Quinn shoved his suit coat back and placed his hands on his hips, staring at Dela. "When you get rid of the notion in your head that I am behind every bad thing that happens, we might be able to figure this thing out."

She started to say something but felt Heath's presence beside her. She glanced at him and he gave her a barely perceptible shake of his head. He was telling her there was no sense wasting time arguing with the Feds.

She threw up her hands. "Fine. I'll be neutral until we find the person who kidnapped the child and killed my friend."

"That's all I'm asking," Quinn said as Swanson strode into the room.

"Winston said the last he saw Mrs. Benedict she had gone into her room for the night. He was relieved by Johnson who said he hasn't seen her all day." The agent peered at Quinn for two blinks of their eyes and then said, "The agent following Ferris hasn't reported in since this morning."

"Shit!" Quinn blurted. His eyes sparked with rage. "Tell Johnson to go up to the Benedict room and request to see Mrs. Benedict. Then get GPS tracking up on the agent following Ferris and find out where they are."

Swanson nodded and strode out of the room. The door closing resounded through the quiet house.

"It looks like this is more than you first thought," Dela said, studying Quinn and wondering what was going on in his head.

He nodded to Enos and Trent. "Make sure they get to the Police Station. We'll need their statements when we catch up with Benedict and Ferris."

Dela nodded.

"And when you drop them off, go get the security officer who was assaulted by Ferris. I want an in-person witness account." Quinn swept out of the room.

"You heard what Agent Pierce said." Heath waved his hand toward the door.

"What about my wife? If whoever wrote that note sees me going to the police station, they might hurt her." Trent balked.

"Call her and tell her the house isn't safe, the gas line is leaking. Tell her to stay with a friend. Don't even come home for clothes, you'll have someone drop them off at her work," Dela said.

He called his wife, then gathered the things she wanted into a bag. As they walked out to the car, Heath said, "Put that in the trunk. We'll drop it off after we take you to the police station. I don't want anyone following us from here to know where she works and figure out what is up."

Trent did as he was told and they headed to the Lincoln City Police Station.

At the Police Station, Dela and Heath ushered the two men in and asked to speak with Detective Stedman.

The detective walked down the hall toward them, a smile on his face. "Enos, good to see you're back. Now maybe we can get things figured out."

When Enos didn't respond, Stedman glanced at Dela. "What's going on?"

"I'd rather tell you somewhere private," she said, nodding toward the people in the waiting area and the woman behind the glass window.

With a nod, he headed back down the hall. He flung open a door and they all filed into what looked like a conference room.

"What's going on?" Stedman asked after they were

all seated.

Dela gave him a run-down of how they found Enos at Trent's and what they learned while there.

Stedman settled his gaze on Enos. "You could have come to me instead of calling in an outsider and making things worse."

Enos shrugged. "I knew Dela was good, but I didn't expect her to connect me to this mess."

"We told Special Agent Pierce what happened and that no one can find Felicity. Even Jude West. If he can be believed," Dela added.

"We're still trying to find Ferris. He hasn't been staying in any motels. No one has seen him except at the casino." Stedman pulled out his cell phone and made a call. "Bruce, bring in that folder sitting in the middle of my desk to the conference room. Thanks." He shoved the phone back in his pocket and continued. "I did have a buddy in Portland see if Ferris has been to his place lately. All his neighbors say they haven't seen him in over a week."

"I think that's the time he's been down here working for both Benedicts," Dela said.

Her phone buzzed. "It's Agent Pierce." She stood, answered, and walked toward the door.

"Dela, we found Felicity. She was gagged and bound to a chair in her room. She is near hysterics saying that Hugo has Asher and he threatened to kill her if she tried to get the boy back." Quinn was out of breath as he talked.

"Where are you going now?" she asked.

"We found Morton, the agent watching Ferris. He's being taken to the hospital. Someone beat him up and left him in the bushes outside the casino."

She sucked in air. That could have been Sherman or any one of the security officers. "What do you want us to do?"

"Get the guy who Ferris beat up to the police for protective custody. I think Ferris is getting scared and lashing out at anyone who might be able to place him at the kidnapping and possibly the murder." He said something muffled and a car door closed. "Gotta go."

Dela put the phone back in her pocket and faced the room of men watching her expectantly. "That was Agent Pierce. They found Felicity bound and gagged in her room. She says Hugo has Asher and will kill her if she tries to see him."

Enos shook his head.

Heath studied her. "What else?"

"They found the missing agent. He was beaten pretty bad. They're taking him to the hospital." She held Heath's gaze. "He wants us to bring Sherman in here for police protection. He thinks Ferris is lashing out at anyone who might be able to pin all of this on him."

"That's a good idea," Enos said, standing. "Let's go get him."

Stedman stood. "Not you. You're staying here until we get things figured out."

Heath rose. "Let's get going."

"What about Oscar?" Dela asked Stedman. "Can you keep holding him or do we need to try and talk to him?"

"We have him on tampering with tribal security footage. I'll have Enos talk to the tribal board and get an arrest warrant written up on him. He'll be here a while. I can hold off on the questioning as long as we have him arrested."

"I'll be back to talk to him in the morning. I'd like to learn a little more and have Ferris here to scare Oscar into talking."

"I'll make sure we have him arrested," Enos said. "I've sat on the sidelines too long on this one."

Dela studied the man and nodded.

Heath took her by the hand and led her out of the room, out of the station, and into her car. As Heath pulled out of the parking lot, she said, "If Hugo has Asher, did he discover where Felicity had the boy stashed or did Hugo take him in the first place?"

"Good question. Do you still think it was Felicity who had her son taken in such a dramatic way? Have a man take him out and hand him off to a scuba diver?" Heath maneuvered the vehicle through the traffic on Highway 101 as he talked.

"The setup for the kidnapping sounds exactly like what Felicity would orchestrate. And even though I said she must have wanted the photos to keep Hugo from finding out about the kidnapping, I'm thinking differently now." Dela's mind raced, putting together the things she knew.

"How differently?" Heath asked, turning off the highway and down a side street heading to Sherman's house.

"I saw Ferris watching the kidnapping from the side of the Otter building in one of Rowena's photos. He could have seen her taking photos at the time and surmised she had photos that would give him and Hugo information about where Felicity was taking Asher."

Heath pulled up to Sherman's house and parked. "I don't see any people sitting in vehicles or standing around watching the place."

"If Ferris is a good judge of character, as a good private investigator should be, he would know Sherman isn't going to give him up. I doubt he's here, but it's a good idea to get Sherman safely away from here." Dela walked ahead of Heath up to the door but waited while Heath rang the doorbell.

The door opened and the woman who had answered the door on her first visit scowled at Dela. "Now what do you want?"

"We need to talk to Sherman," Dela said, not pushing, realizing this woman was the pillar of the family.

"He's fixing the dryer. Can you come back?" she said, not budging from where she stood with one hip behind the door to keep them from entering.

"It's important we speak to him," Heath said, in his reassuring voice.

The woman studied him and slowly opened the door. "What could be so important?"

"Nina, who's here?" Sherman asked, walking into the living room and wiping his hands on a rag. His eyes widened at the sight of them. "Dela, what happened?" He tucked his wife under his arm, protectively.

Dela shot a glance at Nina and back to Sherman. "Did you tell her how you got the bruises? Which by the way, are turning a pretty purple and green," she said light-heartedly.

Sherman put a finger on the bruising around his eye. "Yes, I told Nina what really happened. Why?"

"The FBI and the police wanted us to bring you to the police station. They can't find Ferris and he beat up an FBI agent." Dela figured this was just like taking off

171

a bandage. She needed to just spit it out and let the fear pour forth rather than try and make it sound trivial. She wanted Nina to realize she and the children should stay with a friend or relative for a few days.

The short woman spun out of her husband's hold and stared at him. "You said the man was a drugged-out vagrant."

"Mrs.—" Dela stopped when the woman glared at her. "Nina, it would be best if you took the kids and visited a relative or friend in another town."

Tears glittered in the woman's brown eyes. "Will Sherman be okay?"

Dela nodded. "He'll be safe at the police station but that's no place for children."

"Nina, do this for me and the kids. I'll be safe and I want you to all be safe. Pack some bags and go straight to my brother." Sherman wrapped his arms around his wife and kissed the top of her head.

She nodded, rubbed her face on his shirt, and moved out of his embrace. "I'll pack."

"I won't leave until you and the kids are in the car," Sherman said. He faced Dela and Heath. "Do you believe we are in danger from that man?"

"It's best to be safe than sorry," Heath said.

Sherman nodded. "I'll go pack an overnight bag. I have faith you or the FBI will have him by morning."

Dela watched the man walk out of the room. She stepped closer to Heath. He put an arm around her shoulders. "We'll get Ferris," he said in a whisper and kissed her temple.

She needed his reassurance. Right now, she wasn't sure she was thinking with a clear head. Too many shocks in a short amount of time. First the pleasure of seeing Rowena, then finding her dead, and Heath's information her father was a serial rapist. She wanted to curl up in Heath's arms and sob for the loss of not only her friend but the hope she would learn her father had been Dory Thunder and that she was part of the proud Thunder Family. Which she could be, but knowing how she was conceived and what her father had done to so many women, she felt dirty and devalued.

Chapter Twenty

Dela entered the police station with Sherman. She'd realized they never had a chance to see what was in the folder Stedman asked someone to bring into the conference room when they were there earlier.

She waited until Sherman had been led off to hang out in the conference room with Trent and Enos before she asked, "That folder you asked to have brought to us earlier, can I look at it now?"

Stedman motioned for her to follow him. They walked into a cluttered office. "It's what was dug up on Ferris and Jude West." He picked up a folder and handed it to her. "One seems to be an angel and the other a devil. You decide which is which." He winked.

"Can I take this with me?" she asked, knowing Heath sat out in the car waiting for her.

Stedman shrugged. "I don't see why not. It's all been pulled from public records."

"Thanks." Dela walked out of the station and had a shiver snake up her spine. Stopping, she glanced around. There wasn't anyone paying attention to her except Heath waiting patiently in the car.

"What do you have there?" he asked as she slid onto the passenger seat.

"What Stedman dug up on West and Ferris." She opened the folder and started reading as Heath backed out of the parking slot.

She skimmed the papers, noticing most of the information was what she already knew. Except, the fact that Jude West hadn't existed, at least not this one, until eight months ago. "Curious."

"What?" Heath asked, turning off Highway 101 toward the casino.

"It appears the FBI's informant is completely made up. He didn't exist before eight months ago."

Heath glanced at her. "Surely the FBI knows this. They wouldn't just walk up to someone and talk them into being an informant without investigating them."

"Unless he has a reason to want to be on the good side of the FBI. But why would he be meeting secretly with Ferris if he knows the FBI are keeping track of him?" She put all the papers in order and closed the folder. "We need to check out Jude West."

Heath pulled into the casino parking lot. "We need to take a look around in the Benedict suite."

Dela held up her master keycard. "Remember, the security officer in the office the other day handed me one saying Enos told him to give it to me."

Heath put the car in park and studied her. "Is that when you knew he was mixed up in the whole business?"

"Yeah, that's when I began to suspect Enos knew something. Why else would he have left orders to give me the master key? Why did he think I would need it? Did he think Hugo would do what he did to Felicity when the boy went missing?" She'd contemplated Enos's motives ever since the security officer handed the card to her.

"Let's go to the Benedicts' room first," Heath said, opening his door.

They walked through the parking lot to the entrance of the Starfish building. Dela punched the up button and they stood in silence waiting for the elevator. On the third floor, they strolled down the hallway to the suite. No sense in having someone who might be watching think they were on a mission.

As soon as they turned the corner her hand fisted around her purse. There wasn't a need to use the card. Quinn and Swanson stood in the hallway outside of the room she and Heath wanted to enter.

"Are you still processing this room?" Dela asked.

Quinn motioned for them to stay where they were. He said something to Swanson who smiled and Quinn walked to them. He stepped between them and put an arm across each of their shoulders, turning them, and walked back toward the elevators.

"We have everything here under control. There's no need for the two of you to be here." He stopped at the elevator and smiled.

"What don't you want us to see?" Dela asked, knowing the man was hiding something. Possibly the fact the FBI was mixed up in this whole mess.

"I don't want you saying things to Felicity that will make her uncooperative with us. That's all," Quinn said, raising one eyebrow. "You have a way of turning people against the

FBI."

"For good reason," she said, remembering all the times as a youth that the Feds had swooped onto the reservation, taken down information about someone missing, and then never be seen again, as if they had only come to make them all think something was being done to look for a loved one.

"You are worse than the elders holding a grudge against agents who have long passed. We do care about missing people and we do work our asses off to find them. Even if it's just to find them shacked up with someone else."

"There's no call for that," Heath said, his color deepening and his eyes sparking with anger.

"I agree." Dela moved closer to Heath to show solidarity. "We'll keep our distance. Sherman is at the police station. Has anyone found Ferris?"

"Not yet. But we have agents all over the town looking for him." Quinn turned to walk away.

"Has anyone looked at Jude West's?" Dela asked.

Quinn spun around, his narrowed eyes glaring at her. "Why would you think Ferris would be there?"

"Because those two were meeting secretly at the casino the other night and talking about ransom. What if the two of them took the kid and then put the parents against one another?" She hadn't thought about it until just now. But as she flipped through what she knew trying to find something to goad Quinn, she remembered the meeting between West and Ferris. The two would make out well if they could get Felicity to pay ransom for her son, and West, helping the FBI could catch up Hugo with unlaundered money if he paid a ransom with what he could get his hands on quickly.

"I told you before, West is helping us. He wouldn't do anything to jeopardize our relationship." Quinn studied her. "And that's why you think this whole thing was played out by us. You can stop thinking that, because it wasn't. Go get some dinner and leave us to do our jobs." This time he strode down the hallway and disappeared around the corner.

Heath slipped his hand into hers. "Come on. That's the first right thing Quinn has said all day. Let's go get some dinner. We can discuss what we know and what we think over a nice salmon dinner."

Dela let him lead her into the elevator, outside, and over to the restaurant. She was hungry, and yet, she really wanted to go see Jude West.

♠ ♣ ♥ ♦

Dela walked beside Heath out of the restaurant and toward her car. They'd run through everything they, the police, and the FBI knew to this point. Or what the FBI was telling them.

"I think Jude West is the key to this. He is connected to everyone- FBI, Felicity, Ferris, Hugo, and Asher. And you heard him. He even knew Rowena." That was what had been niggling in her mind. Who had called her to take photos of Mt. Hood at the last minute? And why would she leave this job to take that one?

"We need access to Rowena's phone," Dela said, pulling her cell from her pocket. She dialed Detective Stedman.

"We're still looking for Ferris," Stedman answered.

"Good. What I'm calling about is do you have Rowena's phone or does the FBI?" Dela hoped she didn't have to ask for it from Quinn.

"We have all the evidence that forensics didn't find. Why?"

"I'd like to come by and check out the calls made to her." Dela glanced at her watch. "We can be there in fifteen minutes."

"Don't break any speed limits. I'll be here until late. We're trying to figure out what to do with the three men who need protection and keep Oscar from learning anything. Can't put them all in the cells together."

Dela hadn't thought about that dilemma. "Sorry to have given you so much trouble."

He sighed. "It's all part of the job. I'll grab the phone and have it in my office."

"Thanks." Dela ended the call.

"Head to the police station?" Heath asked.

"Yeah. I want to see who the last phone call was from." Dela settled back in the seat but the worry didn't ease in her gut. Something about all of this wasn't adding up. Had the husband kidnapped the son from the wife, or had the wife kidnapped the son and the husband found him? But what about the ransom note? Would Felicity have sent one if all she wanted was the child? Or would she send one to make Hugo think it was one of his business acquaintances who had taken their son? And where was the boy? Was he safe or hidden in some nasty place?

Her head started to pound as Heath turned the car into the police parking lot.

"Hey, are you okay?" he asked, facing her and massaging her shoulder closest to him.

"Just have a headache coming on. Stress." Saying the word started her stub aching and feeling like it had when the foot and calf were torn from the rest of her leg. She grimaced.

"That's more than your head," Heath whispered, leaning closer and kissing her. "Do I need to massage your leg? You have been putting a lot of hours on it and you heard more bad news today than any person should hear." He kissed her again.

He had a way of taking her mind off stress and therefore relieving the phantom pains that came with it.

"I'll think about you massaging my leg when we get back to the room and that should keep things at bay," she said, kissing him back and moving her hand to the door handle.

"I'll look forward to it," he said, winking.

It was times like this that Heath made her feel like the teenager who fell hard for him in high school. But she was older, more cynical, and too world-wise to let her emotions override her need to find justice for Asher and Rowena.

They exited the car and walked up to the police station door together. Heath held the door and she walked in. A different officer sat behind the glass window.

"We're here to see Detective Stedman," she said.

"Are you Dela Alvaro?"

She peered at his name tag. "Yes, Officer Talen, I am."

"Do you have some I.D.?"

She glanced at Heath who shrugged. Dela dug in her purse and pulled out her driver's license and her Head of Security card for the Spotted Pony Casino.

The officer studied them and nodded. "Go down the hall, second door on the left. I'll bring the evidence in to you." Officer Talen stood and walked out of the dispatch office.

Dela led the way down the hall to the room the officer had mentioned. Inside they found two chairs and a table. The click of hard soles on the flooring in the hallway grew closer and the officer walked through the door with an evidence bag on the top of a clipboard.

"Sign here," Officer Talen said, holding the clipboard toward Dela.

"Where is Detective Stedman? He said he'd be here," she asked.

"He was called out. But he told me you would be in to look at this piece of evidence." Officer Talen unsealed the evidence bag and slid the phone out on top of the clipboard.

Dela reached for the phone, but Talen stopped her. "Put these on," he said, holding out a pair of latex gloves.

She did as requested and then picked the phone up. She turned it on and spent nearly twenty minutes figuring out what the pin could be to open the phone. Finally using the date Rowena had left the Army. Dela knew it well because it was the same day she was shipped to Iraq.

The screen came alive with a gorgeous photo that she was sure her friend had taken. Dela scrolled for recent calls. The last call after her call at 10:18 was a voicemail at 10:45. Rowena must have left her phone in her room when she'd brought the cheesecake over. Her hands had been full with the dessert and hot chocolate. Tears burned the back of Dela's eyes. She blinked to clear them. Her friend had been so thoughtful and vibrant. Why would anyone want to kill her?

"Want me to do that?" Heath asked quietly.

"No. She received a voicemail while she was in the room with me. She must have left her phone in her room." Dela hoped it would be a clue. She hit play and speaker.

"Ro, my love. I'll be at Timberline until Wednesday. Come join me." The male voice had warm husky undertones. He sounded like a lover. But she'd said there wasn't anyone special in her life.

Dela raised her gaze to Heath's. "We need to find out who this number belongs to. If for no other reason than to let him know what happened."

Heath put his hands on hers and released the phone onto the clipboard. "Think about it." He nodded toward the phone. "She didn't call him back to tell him she was coming. She must have been going to surprise him. But he didn't try calling her again. You would think if it was a tryst, he would have called to see why she didn't come. I think that call was used to get her to leave her room."

A sob caught in her throat. She couldn't talk as she thought about how Rowena had lied to her in the note, saying she was going to take photos. Dela slowly drew the gloves off her hands as she composed herself. "She had to know his voice and his phone number." She studied Officer Talen. "Can you run this number and see who it belongs to?"

"I can try." He wrote the number down on a tablet, put the phone back in the bag, resealed the bag, and wrote on the clipboard before walking out of the room.

Heath pulled out his phone and typed in numbers. The phone dialed and rang.

The Pinch

"Hello? Who's this?" a voice Dela had heard before asked.

She grabbed the phone. "Mr. West, this is Dela Alvaro, I'd like to come by this evening and visit with you."

"You must have the wrong number." The line went silent.

Dela smiled. "He is messed up in this clear to the wrinkles around his eyes."

Chapter Twenty-one

Heath turned the car off Highway 101 seven miles south of Lincoln City. "We don't even know if he's home," he said again, as they wove their way toward the mansion where they'd last talked to West.

Dela leaned forward. "That's true. Especially since I told him I wanted to talk to him. But if he isn't home that might give us a chance to look around."

"Didn't you say he was Mrs. Benedict's lover? Wouldn't he be by her side if that were true?" Heath turned a corner and the mansion was lit up before them.

"Yes, but Quinn didn't say anything about West being there." Dela huffed and leaned back in the seat as she pulled out her phone. "I guess I should call and ask him."

"No. He'll wonder why you want to know. If you plan on sneaking in to look around, no one should know we're interested in West."

Dela smiled. "That's why I hang around with you. You keep me from being impulsive."

Heath parked the car two blocks beyond the house. Walking into the shadow between two neighboring houses, they found a back street, where they could backtrack to West's house.

At the fence behind West's house, Dela stopped. "A house like this should have surveillance cameras."

Heath gave her a leg up and then shimmed up the side of the six-foot high cement fence. They both used their arms to hold their heads above the fence and study the area beyond.

Heath pointed to the corners of the porch. "They're at the tops of the porch pillars."

Dela ignored the pull on her arms as she studied the back side of the house. The swimming pool had lights in it as well as a line of lights illuminating the way from the back patio to the changing shed.

"I wonder if we came in from the side if there would be less chance of getting noticed?" Dela dropped back to the ground and walked to her right. They rounded the corner and stopped to check things out again. The wall was higher here due to a gulley that ran alongside the wall.

Heath gave her a leg up to perch with her arms on the cement fence and her head high enough to see what was going on inside. She spotted someone walking toward the changing shed by the pool. A light went on as the person approached the building. She sucked in air.

"What do you see?" Heath whispered.

"Ferris just carried something into the changing shed. It looked like a tray of food." She stared at the spot where the man had disappeared. He returned without the tray and walked back toward the house.

Once he was inside, she dropped down.

"I think they have Asher in that shed. Why else would he take food to someone out there?" Dela's chest throbbed with sadness for the child and adrenaline tingled in her limbs as she surveyed the yard trying to find a way to get him out. "Ferris is working with West. Who is either working for the FBI or for his own gain."

"Let's make a plan," Heath said as they sat on the ground beside the wall. "We don't know how many people are in that house. The man who let us in the other day seemed more like a navy seal than a butler."

Dela nodded. "I had that impression too. I thought he might be an FBI agent here to keep tabs on West."

"That could be. And if it is so, then you were right about the FBI. But why would they use Ferris? He has a horrible reputation and you saw what he did to Sherman and heard what he did to the FBI agent. I can't see him working with the Feds. They don't take lightly to someone beating up one of the family." Heath stood. "I think West is in this for himself and no one else. We should let Pierce and Stedman know what we know."

Dela hated to give up that easily when the child was not that far from her, but having witnessed the brutality of Ferris, she also understood all the risks of the two of them trying to get the boy out.

"Ok. Let's go back to the casino, and I'll get Quinn and Stedman to come talk with us and we can tell them." She held up her hand and Heath pulled her to her feet.

"That was easy. Why did you give in so quickly?" He held onto her hand as they walked back to the car.

"I don't want anyone else I care about to get hurt." She stopped and drew him to face her. "Thank you for coming here and not trying to talk me into letting the Feds and city police take care of things."

He put an arm around her. "You are the best investigator I've ever met. I knew they weren't going to find the truth without your stubbornness to follow all the clues, not just the ones they wanted to see."

She snuggled against him. "That's why I—"

"Get your hands up!" someone shouted.

Dela froze as Heath's arms stiffened around her.

A light shone in their faces. "I said get your hands up!"

Heath released her and raised his arms.

Dela wobbled a minute but raised hers. "Who are you?" she asked.

"I'll ask the questions."

With the flashlight in her eyes, she couldn't see who the man was behind the bright beam.

"We were just out for a walk," Heath said, calmly.

"I'll be the judge of that," the voice said. "Turn around and walk toward that vehicle."

Dela put her hands down, grasping for Heath's hand as they walked toward a dark SUV. *FEDS*! She should have known.

When she started to say something about call Special Agent Pierce, Heath squeezed her hand. She glanced at him but he kept his face pointed toward the vehicle. What did he know?

At the vehicle, a man stepped out and frisked them. He glanced up at her when his hands felt the prosthesis. He took their phones and motioned for them to get into the SUV.

The hair on the back of her neck tingled. Feds gave her a gut ache, this was different.

"I don't know who you think we are, but we were just out for a stroll," Heath said.

"You're two people who keep sticking your noses in the boss's business. When we spotted you peeking over the fence, I called and was told to detain you."

Finally, they'd get to see who was really in charge of the kidnapping and Rowena's murder, Dela thought.

She tried to see who was behind the steering wheel, but the man's face was hidden in shadows by the brimmed hat he wore. The man who caught them stepped back and closed the door. The man who'd frisked them got in the front passenger seat. He dropped his arm across between the two front seats, blocking them from trying to grab for his weapon or the steering wheel.

Dela tried the door. It was locked. The child-proof locks must be set to keep anyone on the inside from opening the door while the vehicle moved.

The car started up and they drove north toward Lincoln City. Five minutes passed and the car turned off Highway 101, headed east into the coastal range.

She glanced at Heath. In the dark, she could barely make out the set of his jaw. However, the gleam of anger in his eyes blazed. He had the same thoughts she did. They were not coming out of this alive.

She grasped his hand and squeezed. If they both kept their heads, there was no reason they couldn't survive.

The vehicle continued for about twenty minutes then pulled in front of a log house in the middle of a stand of fir trees. The vehicle's motor died and the lights shut off. The building was a large dark blob in front of them surrounded by dark silhouettes of the trees.

"We're getting out here," the man in the passenger seat said.

The driver didn't move. If they were going to be left here with only one person watching them, they would have a chance to escape. Dela smiled in the dark before her eyes met those of the driver in the rearview mirror. He'd been watching her. Who was he? She wished she could see his face. There was something familiar about his eyes. The disdain shining in them reminded her of someone.

The man beaming a flashlight through her window had a gun pointed at her. He opened the door and motioned for her to get out. Luckily, she'd gone in with her full leg first and could push with it to get her body to the edge of the seat and out.

"Go to the back bumper and stay there," he said, motioning with the gun barrel.

She did as she was told. They didn't need to get shot before they had a chance to figure out a plan.

Heath slid out. As soon as his feet touched the ground, he held a hand out to her. She went to him, clasping his hand tight.

"Oh, so cute. Pretending to be lovebirds still." The man walked behind them, shining the flashlight so their shadows made dark figures inside the white circle of light. "Walk to the cabin door."

She made a note of the one-foot-high porch, the two stools to the right of the door, and the fact the door was carved in an intricate pattern.

"Step to the side," the man said, waving the light and weapon to the right. He put the flashlight in his mouth, dug with his left hand into a pocket, and inserted a key, all while holding the handgun on them with his right hand.

Dela glanced back at the SUV. The driver was talking on a cell phone. He lowered the phone and stepped out, walking toward them. He also had a gun in his hand. *Great...*

Once the door swung open, the first guy motioned for them to enter.

Heath stepped inside, drawing her along with him. Cedar and a spicy masculine scent filled the interior.

"Stay right there," the man said, and she heard someone walk by them his steps thudding deeper into the house.

Two minutes later lights came on, making her blink. She covered her eyes, with the hand Heath wasn't holding, until they adjusted to the light. Once she could tolerate the brightness, she moved her hand and stared at an opulently decorated interior. The room looked like a picture in one of the magazines her mom liked to read. She'd redecorated her new husband's house after the wedding and it looked a lot like this. Wood, wool, and artwork everywhere.

"Nice place you have," she said, not able to keep quiet.

Heath squeezed her hand. She supposed it was to tell her not to poke the bear.

The man with the wide-brimmed hat returned with zip ties. Dela groaned inwardly. Of all the things to be tied up with.

The first man set his flashlight down and shoved his gun in a holster under his jacket. He put a straight-backed chair behind Heath and told him to sit. Dela released Heath's hand and watched as the man tethered

Heath's hands together behind the chair's back and his legs to the front legs of the chair.

She peered into Heath's eyes, but she couldn't tell what he was trying to tell her. Only she knew he wanted her to do something. She raised an eyebrow.

He slumped as if she'd failed to understand.

When the man told her to sit, she dropped to the floor as if she'd fainted.

"What the hell did you do to her?" the man with the wide-brimmed hat asked. The hard edge of his voice was familiar.

"Nothing. She just dropped. I think she fainted." The man pulled her to a sitting position on the floor, but she remained limp, resisting the urge to fight him.

"Get her on the chair," the other man insisted.

"I'm trying. You could help. She's limp as a dead body."

His comment sent a wave of fear through her. How would this man know what a dead body felt like unless he'd killed someone?

The two of them set her on the chair. She lolled her head back and tried to get a look at the man in the hat, but he was busy securing her hands behind the chair. The man at her feet was securing her ankles to the chair legs.

When they had her secured, she moaned and slowly opened her eyes. "Who are you?" she asked as if waking from a dream. She wanted them to think she'd forgotten what was happening.

"I'm going to get the boss. You stay with them," the guy in the hat said and headed for the door.

She studied his height and stature. It was familiar, just like the voice. Who was he? She'd hoped they would both go get the boss.

The man left behind hauled wood in and started a fire in the fireplace. Then he went into the kitchen area that could be seen from where the chairs were set.

"Did they tighten your straps?" Heath whispered.

Dela moved her hands, they were snug but not tight. "There's a bit of wiggle room in my wrists." She tried her feet. The guy had only tightened the strap as much as her feet were pulled away from the legs. She could get her legs loose easily. "I can get my legs loose if he goes where he can't see me squirming."

"Good. We'll wait for the right time. He's coming."

Dela remained as limp as she could and not pull a muscle. No sense in the man seeing that she was tied loosely.

"What's with you two trying to get into Mr. West's place?" the man asked, apparently a talker.

"We weren't trying to get in. We just peeked over the top to see what the backyard looked like and continued on our walk." Heath said in his calm tone. "I told you we were just out for a stroll."

"Even though you two happen to be the two people the boss told us to keep an eye out for?" The man bit into the sandwich he'd made while in the kitchen.

"What two would that be?" Heath asked as Dela worked at getting her left thumb out of the zip tie.

"The lady who was friends with the dead lady," the man glanced at her and then over at Heath, "and her boyfriend." The man finished off his sandwich as Dela thought about what he'd said. He didn't use their names, only that Heath was her boyfriend and she was connected to Rowena. Was this about Rowena's death and not the kidnapping of Asher?

She drew her gaze from where she'd been staring in her lap and studied the man. He didn't look familiar. Not like the driver. The man stood and walked away from her. That's when she realized, she'd followed the man with the wide-brimmed hat up stairs and he'd given her the same look when he'd peered down at her from above as he had in the rearview mirror. Neither Stedman nor Quinn knew he was involved.

Chapter Twenty-two

The more Dela stewed about the number of casino employees who seemed to be connected with the kidnapping and murder, her anger grew.

The man hadn't even offered them anything to eat. It wasn't as if she'd eat anything the man prepared but she wanted him either out of the room or with his back to them so she could get out of her ties.

"I need to use the bathroom," she said, in the middle of the man's story about a fishing trip he'd taken on the Rogue River.

"I can't let you do that," the man said, glaring at her.

"Then I guess you'll have to tell the boss how his floor and chair smell like pee because you wouldn't let me go to the bathroom." She wiggled on the seat and pressed her thighs together as if she were trying to hold it in.

"That does look like a real expensive rug," Heath muttered.

"What did you say?" the man asked, pointing the gun at Heath.

"I said the rug looks expensive. It would be a shame for you to have to either replace it or pay for it to get cleaned." Heath brushed the toe of his shoe back and forth what distance the restraints on his ankles would let him.

Dela whined. "I really gotta go."

The man pulled out a knife and switched it open. He cut her feet loose and helped her stand. "You're gonna have to figure out how to get your pants down with your hands behind your back." He held her arm, shoving her toward a small hallway.

He pushed her into a lavish powder room decorated in forest tones. "No funny business," he said, closing the door.

The man stood outside the door. His breathing and the sound of boards creaking gave him away. She stood with her back to the door and clicked the lock.

"Hey! What are you doing in there?"

"I want to make sure you don't come barging in here when I'm struggling to get my pants down," she called. Then she walked into the toilet, making the seat clank.

The man chuckled.

Dela bent down and stepped back over her tied wrists. Now her hands were in front of her. Turning on the faucet at a slow trickle, she quietly looked through the drawers for something to either grease her hands or cut the ties. She found a tube of lip balm. Holding the tube in her hands, she pulled the cap off with her teeth then grasped the tube in her mouth and rubbed it on her hands below the plastic tie.

Turning off the water, she flushed the toilet and worked her hands out of the zip tie. Then she made a couple of stomping sounds, which brought another chuckle from the man outside the door.

She washed her hands, turning the water on full force. After drying her hands, she held the towel in her hand behind her back and unlocked the door.

"I'm done," she called and waited for him to open the door.

When he did, she tossed the towel on his head and grabbed the hand with the weapon, twisting his arm up behind his back. She shoved him against the wall, keeping upward pressure on his arm. The weapon clattered to the floor. She couldn't release her pressure on him to get the gun. A good kick with her prosthetic foot sent it far enough down the hall that she'd have time to get him under control before he'd get his hands on it.

Dela forced him down the hall ahead of her at the same time the front door and a door behind her flew open.

"FBI!" two voices shouted at once.

"Don't shoot!" Heath shouted.

Dela didn't release the man. "This man and another one abducted us," she said to the man in the FBI-emblazoned protective vest.

"Are you Dela Alvaro?" the agent asked, as another agent came up behind her and snapped handcuffs on the man she'd captured.

"Yes." She moved to Heath and used the knife she'd taken off the captured man to cut his zip ties. "And this is Heath Seaver."

"How did you know where to find us?" Heath

asked, rubbing his wrists.

Dela could see the lines in his skin where he'd been trying to break the ties while the man was keeping guard outside the bathroom. "Yes, how did you know we were here?"

The agent shook his head. "You'll have to ask Special Agent Pierce. He told us to come here and see what was going on. When we spotted Seaver tied to the chair and heard a toilet flush, we figured it was a good time to make our presence known."

Dela leaned into Heath when he put his arm around her. She was happy they'd both made it out of this mess alive. But it bugged her that Quinn had known where they were.

"We'll give you a lift. Where do you want to go?" The agent asked as they walked out of the house and a group dressed in forensic outfits walked in.

"Who owns this house?" Dela asked.

"On the tax roll it belongs to Felicity Carter," the agent said, holding the door to a silver SUV open.

The agent who had taken charge of their captor deposited him in another SUV and walked toward them.

"As in Felicity Carter Benedict?" Dela said. Was Felicity the mastermind behind all of this? That house might have been well furnished but it had the scent and feel of a man's house. Who was living in her house? Her lover, Jude West?

"I believe so," the second agent said, sliding into the driver's seat. "Where to?" he asked.

"Wherever Special Agent Pierce is. I have questions and answers for him." She leaned back in the seat, tucking her shoulder under Heath's arm. The drive time back to Lincoln City would give her time to collect her thoughts.

"Are you okay?" Heath whispered, touching her hair with his lips.

"Fine. Just confused," she whispered back. "I know who the driver was. Everything is so messed up. I don't know who the bad guys are and who the good guys are, other than us." She sighed.

Heath hugged her to his side. "I knew you had a plan when you asked to use the bathroom, but I was trying my hardest to get my hands loose while he was waiting for you."

She picked up his hand and gently touched the welts at his wrist. "I knew you would be trying to get loose. Lucky for me someone in that house likes lip balm." She leaned closer to whisper even quieter. "Did you get the feeling a man stays there and not a woman?"

"It wasn't a bachelor pad," he whispered back.

"No, but it smelled of masculine scents. And the bathroom had cedar air freshener, the towels were brown and dark green. Colors a man would pick. And the toilet seat was up."

Heath chuckled. "Then it must have been a man who used it last."

She punched him softly in the chest. "I'm serious. If that belongs to Felicity then I would bet Jude West has been living there."

The vehicle entered the south end of Lincoln City. Not to her surprise, the agents parked the SUV in front of the Starfish building.

"Is Agent Pierce still in the Benedicts' suite?" she asked.

"He and Swanson have set up a command post in the suite," the driver answered.

"I bet Hugo loves that," Dela said sarcastically.

"He disappeared after tying his wife up. No one can find him," said the other agent, opening the door for them.

Dela slid out taking this information in. Hugo was missing. His son was missing. Who was covering up the loose ends?

She and Heath followed the agents into the building, stood in the elevator with them, and then walked down the hall and waited as the driver knocked on the door.

Swanson opened the door and ushered only she and Heath into the room.

"Dela, Heath, good to see you're all right," Quinn said, walking toward them.

"How the hell did you know where we were? If you had an agent following us, why didn't they intervene sooner?" Dela stood in front of Quinn, her hands bunched to keep from punching him.

"If I tell you how I know where you were, you'll never work with me again. Let's just be happy that the agents made it to the cabin before anyone was hurt." Quinn handed Heath a cup of coffee. "Would you like one?"

"You know damn well I don't want a cup of coffee. For once in your egotistical, self-righteous life tell the truth. How did you know where we were?" Her palms hurt from her fingernails digging into them.

Heath put a hand on her shoulder. "Relax. Getting mad at Quinn isn't going to find Rowena's killer or the boy."

She drew in a breath and released it slowly. Her fists began to unclench.

Heath continued massaging her shoulder. "Tell Pierce what you saw."

Dela shook, releasing all the tension and focusing on what they were doing before they were abducted. "We were at Jude West's place."

"I told you he has nothing—"

"Shut up and listen." Dela glared at him. "We looked over the back fence and saw Ferris take a tray of food out to the changing shed by the pool. That is where Ferris has been hiding out. With his friend West." She raised an eyebrow as Quinn ran a hand over his face.

"You're sure?" Quinn asked.

"I have seen Ferris enough to know it was him. We were on our way back to the car—the car is still parked two blocks from his house." She spun toward Heath.

"An agent can take Heath to pick it up," Quinn said. "Tell me about what happened."

"As I said, we were headed back to the car when a guy flashed a light in our eyes and said we were to get into an SUV. The guy who was with us got out of the car and frisked us then shoved us in the back. The man driving was Reuben, a security officer here at the casino."

Quinn whistled. "Another one of the employees is involved. This is starting to look like there will be a huge shakedown when this is all over with."

Dela agreed. "Reuben drove off to get the boss. With all of your people crawling around the house, they won't go back." She scanned the room. "Where's Felicity?"

"An agent drove her to her house in Portland. Why?" Quinn asked, pouring himself a cup of coffee.

"The house we were taken to is owned by her. I'm sure you knew that when you sent your agents to *save* us." Dela took the cup of coffee that Swanson offered her. It was going to be a long night. She wanted answers. "You should be on the phone getting people over to pick up Ferris at Jude West's...Oh by the way, what is his real name? Stedman and I know that until eight months ago, he didn't exist." She sipped the coffee and watched Quinn and Swanson exchange glances.

Heath sat in one of the stuffed chairs in the seating area. "We're not going anywhere until you start giving us some straight answers."

Dela grinned, walked over to the chair not far from Heath, and sat. She smiled and said, "You should invite Detective Stedman here for coffee as well. He has three people in custody to keep them safe from the man who is staying at the house you are renting for an informant."

Quinn stared at them for several minutes, his jaw twitching.

Dela liked seeing him squirm. She and Heath knew more about the kidnapping and murder than the FBI. Or at least she thought she did. That prompted her to throw out another thing she knew. "The night Rowena died she received a call from Jude West to meet him at Mt. Hood. That he'd be there for three days." She sipped her coffee and furrowed her brow. "Didn't you tell me he had fallen for Felicity? Why would he make a call that sounded like he was setting up a tryst with Rowena? And why didn't she just tell me that rather than she had to go to Mt. Hood to take photos?"

Quinn rubbed the back of his neck with a hand and studied her.

"Tell her. She's dug up more information than you said she would. Hell, she is a better agent than everyone we have working on this case," Swanson said.

Quinn glared at the other agent.

"If you're not going to tell her, I will." Swanson sat down on the small sofa across from Dela and Heath. "Your friend was an FBI agent. She was commissioned by the casino to take photos by our urging. We needed someone Benedict and his people didn't know who could move around taking photos no one would pay attention to. It wasn't West who made that call to tell her to get out, she'd been compromised. It was our man who was staying in the house with West to keep an eye on him. When your friend left the photos she'd taken for you, we thought maybe it was because you weren't connected to the agency and no one would suspect anything. Now we think it was because she knew someone in the agency was working for Benedict."

Dela set the cup of coffee on the table and leaned back. Her stomach was churning from the acid and the information. Rowena had worked for the FBI. She hadn't said a thing. "Was her running into me in the restaurant a coincidence or did you tell her I was here and to keep an eye on me?"

"That was a coincidence. We didn't know you two knew each other until after your dinner and we asked her how she came to sit with you," Quinn said.

"You were watching her or me?" Dela accused.

"You. I wondered at the fact you were here when the kidnapping had been set up," Quinn added.

Dela shot out of the chair. "You have been part of the kidnapping, haven't you? I can't believe this. And you screwed it up, didn't you? Hugo found out and outsmarted you and now he and the boy are missing. I bet Felicity isn't about to help you get the goods on her husband now." Dela dropped into the chair. "Rowena lost her life for nothing. Nothing!" She glared at the two FBI agents. "I think I'm going to be sick." She shot out of the chair and into the bathroom.

Never in her life had she felt so gutted as right now. Leaning over the toilet, she let her empty stomach heave out the acidic coffee she'd drank. It was nearly midnight and she was tired. As tired as she'd felt after long shifts in Iraq. But her body was buzzing with adrenaline from getting the better of the abductor to learning the Feds had set in motion the murder of her friend.

"Are you okay?" Heath's soft voice asked behind her.

She sat on the floor with her back against the wall peering up at him. "I don't think I'll ever be okay again."

He knelt in front of her and took her into his arms. "Betrayal is the hardest emotion to deal with."

She wasn't sure what he meant, but she was drained and only wanted to be held.

Chapter Twenty-three

The next morning, Dela dressed while Heath showered. He'd brought her to their room straight from their embrace in the suite bathroom the night before. As he led her out the door, he'd told Quinn they'd decide today what they planned to do with what they knew.

Back in the room, Heath helped her undress, take a long soak in the tub, and go to bed. She'd curled up next to him and fallen asleep, secure knowing he wouldn't let anyone hurt her.

This morning, she had one thing on her mind. To find the person who killed Rowena. It was apparent the boy and his father were in some country that the FBI couldn't push around. She and Heath would have to find the murderer and bring all the questionable casino employees to light. All the Feds cared about was getting Benedict. After all, Rowena was a casualty of their cause. She snorted. Cause. It was a vendetta. Quinn wanted Benedict so badly that he would forget everything else that was happening.

A knock on the door brought her out of her angry thoughts.

"I ordered breakfast," Heath called from the bathroom.

Dela answered the door and found a person dressed in the casino uniform with a plastic bag.

"I brought your order," the young man said.

"Thank you," Dela signed the receipt and dug in her pocket for a five-dollar bill. She couldn't find a five and gave him three ones. "Sorry, it's all I've got in my pocket and I'm not sure where my purse is."

The young man nodded, but he didn't look very happy as he left.

Dela carried the bag to the table by the window and pulled out two cups of coffee, and two Styrofoam food containers. One had waffles, eggs, and sausage and the other had pancakes, bacon, and eggs. The meals were their favorites. She decided to split them, putting half a waffle and one pancake with one piece of bacon and half a sausage patty in each container. Then she began eating.

Heath entered the room towel drying his long hair. "Smells good. I didn't feel like going to a restaurant this morning." He sat on the end of the bed, brushing his hair.

"Would you like me to braid your hair?" she asked. While he'd been adept at braiding his hair since the age of twelve, she liked the intimacy of running her fingers through his long fine strands and paying homage to his culture.

He smiled. "You know I love it when you braid my hair, but I think you should eat. This only takes a couple of minutes and I'll join you."

She nodded and turned her gaze to the ocean waves curling toward the beach. A thought crossed her mind. "Do you think the scuba diver and the boat were Felicity's dramatic kidnapping but instead of passing him off to Felicity's man the older gentleman handed him to Hugo's man?"

"I've felt all along that the boy being smuggled out to sea seemed over the top. Especially when all the mom had to do was hand her son over to whoever was going to hide him." Heath sat at the table and opened the lid on his breakfast. He smiled. "I see you shared."

"I wasn't sure which one you wanted and I was hungry." Dela poured more syrup on her half of the waffle. "That could be what she did instead of saying she was showering for an hour. If Hugo paid Oscar to cut the cameras at the same time as Felicity was taking her son to be scuttled away, how had he known?"

"I think a lot of the answers are with West. As you said yesterday, he is connected to everyone involved." Heath spread butter on his food as Dela finished off her meal.

"When you get done, we need to get a ride to West's to get my car. We can do some snooping while we're there."

♠ ♣ ♥ ♦

Dela stared at West's house as the Uber driver drove past. Federal vehicles and agents were going in and out of the house. The Uber driver dropped them off at her car two blocks beyond.

Once she and Heath sat in her car, Dela said, "Did you see all the Feds at West's?"

"Yeah. Sure you want to go see what's going on?" Heath asked, starting the car.

"I do. I want to make sure they have Ferris." Dela studied the commotion as they pulled up at the curb and parked.

Heath met her on her side of the car and they walked up to the house together.

"No one is allowed here," said a female agent, flashing her badge.

"Call Special Agent Quinn Pierce and tell him Dela and Heath would like to talk to the person in charge here."

The woman studied them and shook her head. "We were told to keep any reporters or civilians away."

"We've been working this investigation with Special Agent Pierce and Detective Stedman of the Lincoln City Police," Heath said, showing his tribal badge.

The woman shook her head.

"Did you arrest Ferris? And is West in the house?" Dela asked, trying to get the woman to see that they were in the loop about everything.

"I have my orders," she said, though she glanced around nervously.

Dela pulled out her phone and even though she didn't want to call Quinn, she saw it as the only way to get answers.

"I see you," he answered.

She scanned the windows of the house. "You're inside? Tell this agent that we can enter."

"I don't see any reason for you to be involved in this case anymore," Quinn said.

"At least tell me you arrested Ferris and West." She needed to know the man she was pretty sure killed Rowena was under arrest.

"West is dead. His body was found in the pool shed. And it wasn't dinner Ferris took to him. It looked like he tortured him." The control in Quinn's voice told her he was frustrated and angry.

"He wasn't in the shed long enough to torture anyone."

Heath studied her.

"We'll have a better timeline of when he was killed after the medical examiner takes a look at the body." Quinn said something that was muffled.

"But you have Ferris?" she asked. He was the one person she didn't want to run into.

A deep sigh echoed through the phone. "No, we don't. He was gone when we arrived. There was only the body in the shed. We're going through the house trying to figure out where he might have gone."

Dela's chest squeezed. Where could Ferris be and who was he working for? "We'll leave you to find the answers." Dela ended the call and started back toward the car.

"What was that all about?" Heath asked, opening the door for her.

She sat with her feet out the door on the curb.

He crouched in front of her, his hands on her knees.

Dela peered into his eyes. "West was in the pool shed." She went on to tell Heath everything that Quinn told her.

"Ferris has to be the one who killed Rowena. But why would he torture and kill West?" She glanced over Heath's shoulder to the house beyond trying to put all the things she knew together in her head and have them make sense.

"You said that he was Mr. Benedict's private

investigator, yet Mrs. Benedict hired him to follow around her husband. I think she's lying. And I think she does have her son." Heath rose and motioned for her to put her feet in the car.

When he was seated behind the steering wheel, he asked, "Where to?"

"Let's talk with Oscar and find out if he turned off the security cameras for Hugo or Felicity," Dela said, knowing they needed to discover who really had the child. With Ferris torturing West, she believed Felicity had her son and Hugo was trying to find him.

♠ ♣ ♥ ♦

At the Lincoln City police station, Dela asked for Detective Stedman. He came to the lobby and escorted them to his office.

"How is the investigation going?" he asked.

"Another body and Ferris is still on the loose," Dela said.

Stedman nodded. "I called Special Agent Pierce this morning to see if I could let the three in protective custody go and he told me what happened." The man shook his head. "We rarely have a murder in this town, let alone two in the same week."

"I'd like to sit in your interview with Oscar and see who paid him to turn off the cameras. I have a hunch about why West was killed, but I don't want to say anything until I'm certain." Dela had another thought. "And I'd like to visit with the three in protective custody."

"Who do you want to talk to first?" Stedman asked.

"Oscar. I know you have to be present when we talk to him, but I think he'd talk to me easier if I'm the only one in the room with him." Dela didn't fear Oscar.

The man had shown he was a coward. And that cowardice is what had him keeping his mouth shut.

"I can get the room set up where we can start out with me in the room and I'll excuse myself and listen from another room." Stedman rose. "Wait here until I get everything set up and Oscar in the room."

Dela nodded.

When they were sitting in the office alone, Heath asked, "What are you thinking?"

"We need to find out if Oscar cut the cameras for Hugo or Felicity. If Felicity, then we know she has the boy. If for Hugo, then we know he knew what Felicity was up to and most likely has the boy, but I doubt it. Not with his hired heavy going around killing people for the answer."

"You'd think Felicity could just play the card of telling the Feds what she knows about the business to keep her son," Heath said.

"That's the thing, I'm not sure she knows. I think Hugo has kept her in the dark and that's why she resorted to kidnapping her son, to get them both away from Hugo and whatever he's mixed up in." Dela didn't think Felicity had the brains to outsmart her husband, but if she did have her son, she was doing a good job of doing just that.

Chapter Twenty-four

Dela and Detective Stedman entered the room where Oscars sat dejectedly behind a table. The bags under his bloodshot eyes and sallow complexion made her wonder if he'd slept since his arrest.

She and the detective sat across from Oscar. Stedman read Oscar his right to an attorney and that whatever he said could be used in a court of law. He also had the man acknowledge the meeting was being recorded.

When he finished, Dela said, "Hi, Oscar. I can see you're not dealing well with jail. All you have to do is answer our questions and I can try to get Enos to drop the charges against you."

His eyes widened as he peered at her. "You can get me out of here?"

"I might be able to if you answer my questions. Right now, you are in here for turning off the surveillance cameras as a crime was being committed. We don't want you. We want the person who told you to turn the cameras off."

Oscar's Adam's apple bobbed a few times as he glanced from her to Stedman and back to Dela.

"Are you thirsty?" she asked,

Stedman stood. "I can get a soda or water brought in. Would you like some?"

"Soda," he said.

He walked to the door and disappeared

Dela knew this was her chance to get what she wanted to know out of Oscar. "It's just you and me while Detective Stedman gets your drink."

"Why do you do double shifts?" Dela asked, trying to show him she wasn't just out to get him. "Don't you have a family to go home to?" She knew he lived with his mom, but she wanted him to think she knew nothing about him and that she cared. In the Army as an M.P., part of her job was questioning people to get to the reason they did whatever got them brought into the detention facility.

Oscar lowered his head, staring at his hands that were clasped together. "I live with my mom. I work to have an excuse to not go home."

"You also play the slot machines when you don't work overtime. Is that where your overtime money goes?" Dela kept her tone conversational even though she wanted to get back to her main question.

"As much as this casino boasts about big payouts, it hasn't been to me and I'm a regular." He continued to study his hands.

"Who approached you about turning off surveillance cameras?" she asked.

"Reuben."

This didn't shock her since he'd been in on her and

Heath's abduction. But how long had he been working for…she still didn't know who was pulling the strings on all of this.

"He saw me sitting at a machine after I'd put two hundred dollars in. I was thinking about how I'd never get out of my mom's house if I couldn't win anything."

Dela wanted to say, 'if you didn't play the machines, you would have enough to move out,' but kept her tongue. "I see. What exactly did he say?"

"That was months ago. I don't remember exactly." His head came up and his bloodshot eyes peered at her. "He just said, looks like you're losing. I know how you can make extra without doing more than pushing a couple of buttons. Or something like that. Made it sound easy and it wouldn't hurt anyone."

"Did you turn off cameras before this past weekend?" she asked, wondering how they tested him for the kidnapping.

"Yeah, three times, he passed me a note saying where and what time to turn off cameras."

Dela pulled a notepad over from the end of the table. "Do you remember those dates?" She slid the pad and a pen she picked up over in front of him.

"Not the first one. I thought that was the only time I had to do anything. When he slipped me the second note, I started paying more attention." He wrote the dates down.

"And this past weekend. Did you know they were going to kidnap Mrs. Benedict's boy?" Dela asked.

He shook his head. "I didn't realize that was what happened until Enos came into surveillance wanting to see the video. I was scared that they'd realize what I'd done and I'd get fired. When I tried to talk to Reuben about it, he just said, to keep my mouth shut and nothing would happen to me. Then that homeless guy who hangs out in front of the casino came over to me at lunch the day after and asked if I had any footage of the kidnapping. When I said I didn't, he said some horrible things to me, and the look in his eyes… I was relieved when he walked away."

Dela hoped Heath and Detective Stedman heard all of that. It appeared that Ferris and Reuben weren't working together. Reuben, it seemed, was working for Felicity, and Ferris for Hugo.

"Was the money Mr. Benedict paid you for turning off the cameras?" she asked.

"I don't know who paid me. During the day, before I was to turn them off, an envelope would appear in my locker with money in it. Then the next day would be the same amount."

Stedman walked in with the soda. He glanced from Dela to Oscar and set the can down in front of him. "What did I miss?"

She knew he'd been listening and had a reason for entering when he did. "Oscar said he was paid in cash," she said.

Stedman peered at the man across from him. "Cash? Then why were you also getting sums of money in your account from Hugo Benedict?"

Oscar's eyes widened and he stared at the detective. "What? Mr. Benedict wasn't paying me." His head shook back and forth.

"We have records of sums of money being deposited in your bank account from one of his accounts for the last six months." Stedman continued to study Oscar.

Dela noticed the man's hand holding the soda, shake.

"I haven't received anything other than my paychecks in my account." He said it with more assertion than he had anything else.

She believed he didn't know anything about the extra money in his account. Which meant he didn't keep very close tabs on his spending.

"Forget about the money going into your bank account. The money you found in your locker—Did you receive a payment after the night my friend was killed?" Dela asked, thinking she could get Sidney to watch video of the employee's breakroom to see who went near Oscar's locker all the days he wrote down and on Friday.

"There wasn't anything left in my locker on Saturday. And I didn't want it after I figured out what had happened." Oscar's red eyes appealed to her. "Will this help me stay out of jail?"

"I'll talk to Enos," she nodded to Stedman, "and the detective, and whoever else is involved and see what I can do. But we can't promise we can do more than give them your side of the story and see what happens. More people than me have to believe you were gullible enough to think no one would be harmed by what you did." Dela and Stedman stood. They walked to the door.

"Do you know who was paying me?" Oscar asked. "I mean besides Reuben."

"I think I know but I'm not prepared to say anything until I have more proof." She opened the door and was met by Heath.

"Nice work," Stedman said. "Sure you don't want

to come work for our city police?"

Dela smiled at Heath. "I like where I'm at, thank you. Now I'd like to talk to the other three, together."

"I can have them brought to the conference room," Stedman said, before stopping and instructing an officer to take Oscar back to his cell.

"That's a good place, less like they are in trouble. Other than Enos getting lost like he was told, the other two have been collateral damage. I'd like to hear all their stories and see all their reactions." Dela headed to the conference room. She stopped. "Can you have someone go out and get us coffee and donuts or pastries? I want this to be as informal as possible to get them to open up."

"I'll send Officer Talen to get that." Stedman strode down the hall as Dela and Heath entered the conference room.

As soon as Dela sat down, she texted Sidney to look into the footage of Oscar's locker in the employee breakroom.

Heath sat beside her, in a quiet voice he asked, "Are you getting a clearer picture of what went on?"

Dela nodded. "I think someone was putting money from Benedict's account into Oscar's without either of them knowing and then Felicity was paying him from cash to make it look like Hugo was paying Oscar to turn off the cameras. That way Hugo looks like the kidnapper."

Nodding, Heath said, "That's what I came up with as well. Stedman too. He commented on Felicity being more devious than he'd thought."

"I agree," Dela said, remembering how the woman had acted when they'd met.

The Pinch

The door opened and Enos walked in.

"Take a seat, we're going to have an informal meeting to see if we can put pieces of this mess together," Dela said, as Trent and Sherman walked into the room.

The three sat on the side opposite Heath and Dela. She smiled at them. "I hope they have been hospitable to you."

They all shrugged.

"It's not the Ritz," Trent said, "but we know we're safe."

"I talked to my wife this morning. She wanted to know when she and the kids can come back," Sherman said.

Dela sighed. "I wish I could tell you. I spotted Ferris last night but the FBI were too late getting there. He'd killed someone and vanished. As he seems to do." She frowned. How did the man get away so easily and hide out?

"Who did he kill this time?" Enos asked.

"Jude West," Heath said.

The three men glanced around at each other.

"Why him?" Enos stared at Heath.

"We think he was trying to get West to tell him where Felicity has the boy," Heath said.

Dela added, "West was tortured before he was killed. He was also an FBI informant."

Sherman slammed back against his chair. "Whoa, the guy who beat me up killed someone working with the FBI? They'll be after him for sure now."

"Only as long as he leads them to Hugo Benedict," Dela said sarcastically.

Enos studied her. "You haven't thought the FBI are

doing their best at catching the kidnappers. Why?"

"Because I know Special Agent Pierce well. He is only after the big fish. Always has been and always will be. Rowena, who by the way we learned was FBI, and West are only collateral damage to him in his quest to get Benedict." Dela knew she was sabotaging the FBI in the minds of these three men but she'd been pushed around and told her insights didn't matter one time too many from the FBI and Quinn.

Stedman entered the conference room with a carrier of paper coffee cups and a paper bag with grease stains.

He placed the drink carrier in the middle of the table and dug in his pocket, tossing packets of sugar and creamer alongside. He handed the bag to Dela.

"Thank you." She ripped the bag down the side and set it beside the drinks like a paper platter. "Dig in. This is a brainstorming session."

The men each grabbed a cup of coffee and a pastry. She, Heath, and Stedman did the same. Once everyone had a sip or two of coffee and a bite of their pastry, Dela started.

"We," she waved a hand across her side of the table, "believe that Felicity instigated the fake kidnapping and set her husband up to take the fall."

The three stopped chewing as they took in what she'd said.

Enos spoke first. "How did you come by that?"

Chapter Twenty-five

Dela told them all that she'd learned from Oscar, what they'd learned from the FBI, and about being abducted by Reuben.

"Come to think about it, I've seen Reuben talking to Mrs. Benedict several times," Trent said. He frowned. "And they looked friendly, if you know what I mean."

Sherman nodded. "Yeah. I have too. The two of them had their heads together in the hallway before she went in and told Enos her boy was missing." He glanced around. "At the time I thought she was complaining to him about something."

Enos cleared his throat. "When Felicity came to me with the suggestion I be out of town this past weekend and offered money to put my father in a retirement home, I hadn't known anything would come of this other than her, the boy, and Jude heading to another country. I felt I was helping a battered woman get away from her abuser." He peered into Dela's eyes. "I never thought it would become this complicated with murders, beatings, and abductions."

This was the Enos she remembered from their past encounters. The man who cared about others. Which was why he'd come back to help Trent when he'd called. She nodded.

"What we need to do is weed through the employees who we think are on either Hugo or Felicity's payroll," Dela said. "The FBI said only Oscar came up as someone who was getting paid by Hugo, but he didn't know who was paying him, other than Reuben. He received cash in an envelope in his locker before and after he turned off cameras."

"We can check that," Enos said.

Dela smiled. "I already have Sidney looking into it."

He nodded.

"We need to get more eyes on the video to see who Reuben has been pulling into this scheme. And we need to discover where Hugo and Ferris are." Dela glanced at Stedman. "Do you think you can get the State Police to help look for them?"

"I can ask. I'm sure if I tell them they are implicated in two homicides of FBI agents and informants it will get them interested." He stood. "I'll go make that call."

"Thank you," Dela said, before turning her attention to the three across from her. "I want you three to come to the casino and work in the back surveillance room looking at video. Sidney needs to be doing her job as assistant head of security."

They all three nodded.

"It's better than sitting in here doing nothing,"

Sherman said.

"And if we go in the back door to the security office, no one will know we're there," Trent said.

Dela's gaze met Heath's. She was definitely making sure Trent was demoted from assistant to the head of security. He didn't have the backbone for it.

"I think we can all fit in my car. We don't want any of your vehicles in the casino parking lot," Dela said. "It's best to keep you all out of sight."

Stedman met them before they made it to the lobby. "OSP is already looking for the two. They received the bulletin from the FBI."

"Good. At least they had brains enough to get help on this. Especially since Ferris was hiding from them with their agent." Dela motioned to the three men. "We're taking them to the casino to go through surveillance video to help us catch everyone involved in this."

"Good idea. But you can't get them all in your car. I'll drive over too. It won't hurt for me to check in with the FBI." Stedman motioned to Enos, "You can ride with me."

"Make sure you drop him off where he can't be seen and can get to the back security door," Dela said.

"I can do that," Stedman said, waving Enos to follow him to the back of the building where the police cars parked.

"Do you think we need to be picked up behind the building?" Trent said, slowing his footsteps.

"I doubt Ferris is sitting outside the police station looking for you. He's more likely blending in with the people at the casino." That thought had come to her last night as well. There was a good chance he was staying at the casino where he could keep tabs on everything and hear what was going on.

"Oh! Then do you think going there is such a good idea?" Trent asked.

Sherman slapped the other security guard on the back, making him take a step forward. "We are going in the back and will be in a room that can only be entered by one door. No one, not even Ferris, will be after us anyway. He has to know other people know more than us. Besides everything is pointing to Mrs. Benedict."

Dela liked the fact Sherman wasn't playing Doomsday like Trent. But she also worried more people in security were helping either Reuben or Ferris who might inadvertently find out about the trio in the back surveillance room.

♠ ♣ ♥ ♦

At the casino, Dela had Trent and Sherman get out by the beach and walk half a mile to the casino. She and Heath entered through the front and went to the security office.

Sidney sat at the desk on the phone. "Samuel, could you come in and cover for Trent tonight?" A pause and she smiled. "Thanks, we are down seven people between security and surveillance so all the help I can get is great." She ended the call and gave Dela a weak smile. "This being the boss is hard work. I've spent most of my time juggling work schedules so I can fill all the positions on all the shifts."

"Did Reuben call in sick?" Dela asked.

"He didn't show up for work. I know why Sherman, Trent, Enos, and Oscar aren't here but what about Reuben? And Dave hasn't arrived or called in either."

Dela looked around the room. "Dave? The old guy who usually sits in here?"

"Yeah. I called his home number and his wife said he left for work. I didn't want to upset her so I didn't say he hadn't shown up, I made up some excuse about wanting to change his shift and asked her if it would work."

Sitting down in the chair beside Sidney's desk, Dela skimmed over what she remembered saying while Dave was in this room. "How friendly were he and Reuben?"

"Not at all that I know of." Sidney shook her head. "I'm beginning to suspect everyone who works here." She glanced at the older woman sitting at the radio desk. "Except you Fern. I know you aren't taking bribes."

The woman smiled. "I only do this job to keep from having to stay at home with my old man. He's been driving me crazy ever since he retired. I don't need the money. He's rich. I told him I'm doing charity work when I come in for a shift. Then when I get paid, I give the money to a different local charity." She shrugged.

"That sounds wonderful," Dela said, returning the woman's good-natured smile. "I'm going to be letting Enos, Trent, and Sherman in through this door," she pointed to the back security door. "But no one is to know they are here."

Fern zipped her lips and acted like she was throwing away the key.

Sidney laughed and then sobered. "What are they doing here?"

"I've learned some new stuff and figured you

wouldn't have time to look for it with having to do their jobs, so they are going to go through surveillance video."

"Good idea," she said, smiling and nodding. "But how are you going to get them past all the people in the surveillance room?"

"I'm hoping there are more honest surveillance people than we've come across in the security side of things." Dela did hope they could get the men in and no one called to tell either Ferris or Reuben that they were here. She didn't want a showdown with either of the men at the casino.

A knock on the metal back door sent Heath striding toward it. He opened the door and stepped back. Sherman, Trent, and Enos all walked through.

"Enos caught up to us on the beach," Trent said.

"I'll go see if there's anyone between here and the stairs to the surveillance room. If it's clear, I'll text Heath and you can all head up there." Dela headed to the door when her phone rang. She saw it was Quinn and ignored it as she left the office and walked down the hall to the stairs and the short hall beyond that. Not seeing or hearing anyone she texted Heath a thumbs up.

When the men, followed by Heath, went up the stairs, she fell in behind. Dela wanted to know if any of the surveillance crew showed undo interest in the three.

She stepped into the room as the three were walking to the back room. Some people called out welcome back to Enos and others just watched the men walk by. When the group entered in the back room, Dela stopped at the door and faced the room.

"Could I have your attention?"

They all shifted their gaze from their monitors to

her.

"You all know your job requires secrecy and privacy to the patrons. You need to extend that to the three men who just entered the back room. They are here to help find the people who have threatened them for telling the truth. Please use discretion and avoid telling anyone they are here. Thank you." She watched as each person nodded and went back to their job. A sigh of relief whooshed through her lips and relaxed the tense muscles in her neck. This group seemed to be honest people ready to help their fellow counterparts in security.

In the room she found Enos hooking up cables to the three monitors along the far wall. "We can use the two backup laptops to have each of us looking at different monitors and videos. That will make the process go faster than three of us watching the same thing."

"I agree." Dela watched the older man as he settled first Trent at a laptop and then Sherman. He explained to them how to get into the videos and gave them a chart with the letters and numbers for each camera.

"How do you know so much about the surveillance cameras?" Heath asked.

"I worked surveillance here before I moved to security. Sitting all day in a chair watching monitors wasn't good for my health. I needed to be up moving around. Then I made it to head of security and now I wish for the days of sitting more than moving around." He smiled slightly. "I'm retiring in two more years. I hope to have someone ready to move into my position by then." He nodded toward the two men.

Dela said quietly, "The best person for the job is

down there taking care of a crisis."

Enos met her gaze and nodded.

"You have my number. Text if you find anything. Heath and I are going to work on another angle." Dela headed to the door. "And lock this door behind us. Only let Sidney or the two of us in here until we have eyes on Reuben and Ferris. Call her to bring up food when you get hungry and use the restroom up here for the surveillance staff."

The three nodded as images appeared on their screens.

"You do know what you're looking for?" Dela asked.

Trent said, "I'm seeing who put the money in Oscar's locker."

"I'm following Reuben to see who else he may have been working with," Sherman said.

"See if he and Dave, who sits in the security office, meet up outside of the office," Dela said. "He didn't show up for work today."

Sherman nodded.

"I'm going to see if I can't find cameras around the ones that were turned off that picked up the people involved in the kidnapping or the murder." Enos twisted in his chair and peered into her eyes. "I didn't for a minute think a life would be taken by Felicity taking her son. I want to find the person who took your friend's life."

Tears burned the back of her eyes. She'd never liked sympathy as a child when she discovered it made her feel vulnerable. "Thank you." She spun to the door and found Heath holding it open.

They stepped out. She waited until she heard the

lock click and then they walked through the room and down to the security office. At the door, she said, "Come have a cup of coffee with us," to Sidney.

Surprise registered in Sidney's eyes before she nodded and stood.

They walked out into the casino and over to the coffee shop. Dela directed the waitress to a booth in the back with no one else around. They ordered and as soon as the waitress walked away Sidney asked, "What else did you learn?"

Dela told her about the murdered FBI informant and how they now believed Felicity faked her son's kidnapping to get away from Hugo and he was using deadly force to find the child.

"I don't understand," Sidney said, "if he believes Felicity has the child, why isn't he going after her to get the boy back?"

"Because I don't think he is completely sure that's who has the boy. Remember there was a ransom note," Heath said, then leaned back as the waitress placed their coffee and sandwiches in front of them.

"Can I get you anything else?" the waitress asked.

"No, we're good," Dela said and waited for the woman to walk a good distance away before adding, "I think that's why Ferris is killing. To find the boy. They believe that one of Hugo's enemies has Asher."

"But what about Reuben? You said he had you two abducted. Why?"

"I think he and Felicity were trying to figure out how much we've worked out." Dela sipped her iced tea and then said, "If they're smart, they are long gone from here and Hugo. But we have to get Ferris for killing Rowena and West."

"What makes you so sure Felicity and Reuben didn't kill them?" Sidney asked.

Dela thought about the coldness she'd first witnessed in Reuben's eyes. "Nothing. I could see Reuben killing both of them, but Reuben was with us when Ferris killed West."

"We don't know that," Heath said. "He left to get the boss. He could have driven back down to that pool shed and killed West after trying to find out what the FBI knew."

A shiver ran down Dela's spine. That was true. He'd been gone long enough that he could have very well used the whole abduction as an alibi. "I need to find out what the guy the Feds took in said." She pulled out her phone and texted Quinn. *Did the guy from our abduction ever say who he was working for?*

She picked up her sandwich to take a bite and her phone pinged. She glanced down and slammed her food onto the plate.

I've been busy with the murder and haven't talked to him.

There are 35,000 FBI agents, I'm sure one of them could take a moment and ask the guy. She shot back.

Heath spun her phone to read the messages. He chuckled and pointed. "Good one."

They aren't all in Oregon. Quinn replied.

You're telling me with a murdered FBI agent and an informant you don't have the whole West Coast converging on Lincoln City?

No reply. She nodded. "I think Quinn hasn't told anyone other than locals about the murders. He wants to bag Hugo and be able to boast he caught someone no other agent could catch. I have always hated his hubris."

Heath nodded. "He needs to get a heart if he wants to make a difference as an FBI agent."

"You two must know him pretty well," Sidney said, picking up the second half of her sandwich.

"I met him when we were both stationed in Iraq. I was an M.P., he was a 'meat eater,' Special Forces. We butt heads a lot when he'd come to take away my prisoners so he could beat them up and get answers. I had a rapist in the DF, detention facility, and he said that his needs for the man were greater than the justice for the woman the man had raped." Dela swallowed the anger and frustration remembering that day. "He still believes getting the head of something is more important than who gets hurt along the way."

Heath put a hand on her knee and squeezed. "We are here to make sure everyone who gets hurt gets justice."

She smiled and patted his hand. "Yes, we are." She glanced across the table at Sidney. "Sorry, I got caught up in the past there for a moment."

The woman shook her head. "Don't be. I knew you were a good person the moment I met you, but now, I understand why Enos had you come when you did. I'm proud to help you find justice for your friend and Mr. West."

"And I hope we are right about Felicity having her son. I don't like thinking what could be happening to him if he is in the hands of one of Hugo's enemies." Dela had worried about that during the night when she'd awoken and couldn't go back to sleep. Her thoughts had spun through everything that had transpired since her arrival in Lincoln City.

"We'll discover that soon, too," Heath said, finishing off his sandwich.

Dela glanced across the table at Sidney. All communities she'd lived in had the same type of people. A casino would too. "Who is the person in this casino that everyone, workers and patrons, tell their ups and downs to?"

Sidney chewed on the bite in her mouth for half a minute, took a drink, and said, "It would have to be Carmela. She's one of the Keno runners. She'll listen to what anyone has to tell her and give advice. She gets around the casino running slips to and from the game room."

Dela smiled at Heath. "Give us a description."

"You can't miss her. She's only five feet tall but she wears her hair all ratted up on top of her head to make her look taller. She's in her fifties but doesn't look it. There is usually a flower tucked into her pile of hair. She's from the Philippines and will talk to anyone. Many go to her for advice. She works mostly from the restaurants upstairs down to the keno room." Sidney finished off her drink. "I'll get back to work and let you know if I hear anything."

"Thank you for all you've done so far." Dela meant it. The young woman had been the most useful person on the security staff.

"Ready to go look for Carmela?" Dela asked, picking up her drink to finish it off.

"Ready when you are," Heath said, putting money with the meal ticket and standing. "You think this Carmela will be your version of Rosie at the Spotted Pony?"

"That's what I'm thinking."

Chapter Twenty-six

They found Carmela visiting with a couple in their sixties as she waited for them to fill out a keno card while they stood in line for the buffet.

When she walked away, Dela caught up to her. "Carmela, when do you have a break?"

The small woman smiled at her and waved the keno tickets like a fan. "Honey, I don't take breaks because I visit with so many people."

"We would like to buy you a soda or water and visit with you," Dela said. "It would be a great help to Enos if you could visit with me about the Benedicts to help us find their boy."

The woman's smile drooped. "I heard about that. You know if people these days paid more attention to their children and less about themselves, we would be a much better world."

"I agree. Could you spare a few minutes, please," Dela asked, motioning to a padded bench seat along the wall leading to the restaurants.

"For the little boy, I will. But I don't know what I can tell you." The petite woman waved the keno tickets in her hand. "I have to take these to the keno room first. I'll meet you in the deli in five minutes." She strode away from them, her tower of hair quivering with each step.

"You heard the lady. We'll meet her in the deli," Heath said, putting a hand on Dela's back and directing her to the down escalator.

At the deli, they found an empty table in the corner. They sat with their backs to the wall and Dela waved when Carmela entered the area.

The tiny woman walked over to the counter, talked to the young woman at the cash register, laughed, and walked over to them with a drink. Sitting, Carmela said, "That's Trina, she's so fun. Always a happy face."

Dela had a feeling Carmela would find everyone fun. "We were wondering what you could tell us about Mr. and Mrs. Benedict. How happy was their marriage, who else did they talk to?"

Carmela released the straw and studied Dela. "You want the gossip or what I know?"

"Both. Sometimes gossip does have a touch of truth to it."

The woman nodded. "True, true. Gossip. They do not get along. He is a bully and she finds other men to make her happy. It's been said, she only had the little boy to get her way with the husband." Carmela sipped on her drink and continued. "Truth. He is mean to her. In public, he squeezes her arms and steps on her feet. I have seen this. A man like that, it is hard to say what he will do to her when no one is watching. She is not a woman who sleeps around. But she does use men."

Dela nodded. This was pretty much what she'd figured out. "Can you tell me which men she's been using? Especially ones who work here?"

Carmela leaned forward. "I saw with my eyes, her running her fingers over the back of Reuben in security and she was talking quietly in a corner of the restaurant with Enos one night. She also had a man, I saw him in here today, he has longish dark hair that sticks out and cruel eyes, but he was taking in all the sugar that woman was putting out."

Dela straightened. The description sounded like Ferris. "You saw that man in here today? Where? When?"

"He and Mr. Benedict were having lunch in the buffet about two hours ago. They were deep in discussion and that's not the only time I've seen the two of them together. I thought it odd that the man was also keeping time with Mr. Benedict's wife." She sipped her drink.

Dela glanced at Heath. They needed to get their eyes on Hugo and Ferris. But she had one more question. "Did you ever see Reuben being friendly with anyone else who works in the casino?"

"He met the old guy in security a few times down here in the deli. I see everyone who comes to the deli when I come down with tickets to take to the keno room." She smiled. "Some of my best conversations are by catching someone's gaze and talking with them."

"Did you see this older guy hanging out more than once with anyone else?" Dela had to know how this all fit together.

"Only Reuben and Mrs. Benedict," Carmela said,

standing. "I need to get back to work."

"Go ahead. Thank you and don't tell anyone you talked with us. It's for your safety."

Carmela stared at her for a moment. "Telling the truth is not dangerous. It is the lies that cause harm." She strode around the water feature to the up escalator and stairs.

"We need someone to see if Ferris is still in the casino," Heath said.

"I agree. We also need Stedman to send an officer to Dave's place and make sure he is hiding and not dead." Dela hoped the old man hadn't run into whoever was killing people to either hide the kidnapping or to get information about it.

They split up. Heath went to the surveillance room to ask Ray, the older man Dela felt was on the up and up, to find video of Hugo and Ferris together in the buffet.

Dela walked into the security office, and with the help of Fern found Dave's address. She put it into her phone as she walked out the entrance of the casino and looked toward the Starfish building for Stedman's vehicle. She couldn't see it so she called him.

"Detective Stedman," he answered.

"Hi, it's Dela. Are you still at the casino?" she asked.

"No. What's up?"

"An officer needs to go to the home of Dave Wheeler. I'll text you the address. He's an employee who didn't show up today and has been seen with Reuben on multiple occasions." She opened the app on her phone, copied the address, and sent it to the detective.

"You think something might have happened to him?" Stedman asked.

"He could just have been told to stay home by Reuben or he could have been tortured for information since he is on the Felicity team." She continued scanning the parking area. "When you were at the suite, did anyone see Mr. Benedict? He was here having lunch with Ferris according to a keno runner. Do you happen to know if the Benedicts have a place around here? That could be where Ferris has been staying. Other than under the FBI's nose by being in the casino while they are hunkered down in the Benedict suite." She found it both funny and asinine that the man the FBI was supposedly hunting for was right within arresting range.

"Hugo hasn't been to the suite since the FBI took over. I heard he is renting a place at Road's End. At least that's what he told the FBI." Stedman sighed. "This investigation has had so many twists and turns, that I'm not sure what I'm investigating anymore."

Dela had to agree with him, but she wanted Rowena's killer. "I'll wander over to the FBI suite and fill them in on what I know and see if they have anything."

"I'll go check on Wheeler." The call ended.

Dela texted Heath to let him know she was headed to the suite in the Starfish that the FBI had taken over. As she crossed through the parking lot, a vehicle started up. Using more caution than normal, she strode to the sidewalk and continued on it until she came to the laundry building and swimming pool. The hum of an engine still lingered in the air.

She surveyed the parking lot back the way she'd walked and then the area between her and the Starfish building. Several vehicles were moving around in the lot but none were pointed in her direction.

Dela stepped off the sidewalk and started across the parking lot. She spotted Quinn standing by an SUV talking to someone. She headed toward him when spinning tires squealed.

She couldn't move fast enough to get out of the way of the car barreling in her direction. Hoping she survived, she concentrated on the license plate.

Something hit her from the side, throwing her to the asphalt, smashing the air from her lungs, and holding her down.

"Get them!" a voice shouted from above her. "Are you okay?" Quinn's voice registered as the weight on her disappeared and a hand moved to sit her up.

She stared into Quinn's concerned eyes. "W-what happened?"

"Did you hit your head?" he asked, grasping her head and parting her shoulder-length hair.

"Get your hands out of my hair," she said, shaking off the shock and fear. She batted at his arms, getting him to stop touching her.

"That's more like it," Quinn said, standing and holding a hand down to help her up. "Who did you tick off this time?"

She scowled at him as he pulled her to her feet. "The same as usual, the bad guys." Pressing her fingers to the bridge of her nose she recited the letters she'd read on the car license plate.

"What gibberish is that?" Quinn asked, walking beside her to the sidewalk in front of the Starfish.

"That is the vehicle's license." She stopped and took a minute to assess. The shoulder that hit the ground ached, but she figured it would be sore and bruised from the force in which it hit the pavement. And it was the hip and upper leg attached to the prosthesis that took the brunt of being smashed to the asphalt from Quinn's weight. Her neck hurt from instinctively holding her head away from the hard surface as her body was flung to the ground. But she only had a small area of her temple and cheek that burned from being scraped.

Quinn was on the phone reciting the license to whomever he was talking with. He ended the call and studied her for a minute. "Any idea who that might have been?"

"That's for you to find out with the letters I gave you." The car coming at her flashed in her mind and she envisioned the person had unruly hair. That wasn't Dave. She glanced at the doors to the building. "I was coming over to see if you'd learned anything more about the deaths, Ferris, Reuben, the Benedicts. And to let you know the FBI killer was under your noses. A good source saw Ferris in the buffet with Benedict having lunch."

Quinn stared at her. "He was here? On the premises?"

"Yep. Heath went up to surveillance to see if they could catch him on a camera." She bent, wiping the sand off her pant leg, and said, "Thanks. I figured if I survived the hit, I could at least give you the license plate." She sobered. "I knew I couldn't move fast enough to get away from the car."

He grasped her arm, standing her to look at him. "As usual, you thought you would survive to give us evidence. Dela, when are you going to believe in yourself enough to know you can get out of anything?" He stood close, staring down into her eyes.

Something reflected in the dark depths but she couldn't see it clear enough to discover the emotion. "I know my limits physically." Her voice sounded rough and full of more emotion than she'd planned.

Quinn released her arm and stepped back. "The only person putting those limits on you, is you."

She stared into his eyes a few more seconds before a woman in a blazer walked out of the building. "Quinn, they caught the person driving the car."

Dela mentally shook off this exchange and asked, "Who was it?"

The woman glanced at Quinn. He nodded.

"A Dave Wheeler."

Dela stared at the woman. "You're sure?" It didn't make sense. Why would he try to run her down? Unless he was told it was her life or his by Reuben. "We need to find Reuben," she said.

"Reuben who?" Quinn and the woman said at the same time.

"Reuben Jones. He's a security officer at the casino but he's been working with Felicity on the kidnapping and he and Dave Wheeler were seen multiple times talking. If Dave was the one who tried to run me down, he was put up to it by Reuben and probably won't talk unless you have Reuben in custody." She faced Quinn. "I can tell you what Heath and I believe, but I need your promise you will act on it and not just go after Hugo Benedict."

Quinn flicked his gaze to the woman and said, "Go up and see what you can find on this Reuben Jones."

The agent was hesitant but finally pivoted on her

heel and went inside the building.

"Why did you say that in front of one of my colleagues?" Quinn asked in a tone that forgot that just minutes before she was about to be hit by a car.

"Because I want you to be looking for the killer, not trying to get something on a man that will be around doing his dealings and you can get later, but the evidence to the two murders will dissipate with time." She put her hands on her hips, even though her right shoulder protested the movement.

"Is that what you think? I'm only focusing on a way to get Benedict?" Quinn crossed his arms and stared at her.

"I know how you operate. You want the top dog, always. This time the top dog isn't the one who needs to be caught. It's the person who keeps killing." She crossed her arms and tipped her head. "I'd think that you'd want to find the killer of an FBI agent and informant even if you didn't know them well."

His gaze drifted over the parking lot and the tendon over his jaw twitched. He had known one of them well. She'd guess West.

"Did forensics come up with anything to help pin this on someone?" she asked.

"They found fingerprints from everyone we'd expect to find there. West's, Felicity's, Asher's, Morrison…" When she frowned, not knowing the name, he added, "The 'butler' I guess you would call him."

"What about Ferris or unknown sets of prints?" she asked. "Hey, where was Morrison when West was kept in the changing shed and killed?"

Quinn ran a hand across the back of his neck. "We

haven't been able to find him."

She stared at him. "You mean there could be a second agent who was killed? Man, your butt's in a wringer." Dela glanced at the building. "Is that woman you sent away someone who's here to make sure you avenge the killings?"

Quinn grimaced.

Dela grinned. "Oh, I bet you like having to follow her rules about as much as you like following any rules."

Her phone buzzed. It was Heath. "Yeah, what have you learned?"

"We found the video of Benedict and Ferris having lunch. They were in an intense conversation. Then we followed them. Benedict went out to his car and drove off. Ferris disappeared out of range of the cameras. He has where he can go undetected down to a science."

"He isn't on the premises and you don't know what he's driving?" She knew Dave Wheeler had been picked up in the car that nearly hit her, but she could have sworn it was Ferris driving the vehicle when she was studying the license.

"Yes."

Her shoulders drooped making her right side ache. "I'm coming back over to the casino. The Feds don't know any more than we do." Ending the call, Dela studied Quinn and then told him what Heath had said. She debated if she should tell him that she believed it was Ferris driving the car that tried to run her down. Since he'll insist Wheeler was caught behind the wheel, there wasn't any sense in wasting her breath.

"Want me to walk you back to the casino?" Quinn asked.

"I'm fine. I'll keep to the sidewalk in front of the buildings." She scanned the parking lot. "If Wheeler was picked up, I don't think I'm in danger at the moment."

Quinn stepped in front of her. "That's what worries me. You tend to get on people's nerves and they do careless things to put a stop to you. Be careful. Don't go anywhere alone."

She shrugged, flinched at the sting of pain, and walked away. What she wanted was to be in on the questioning of Wheeler but knew if the female agent Quinn had sent away to talk to her was in charge, there was no way she'd get to sit in on it.

Chapter Twenty-seven

"What happened?" Heath asked as soon as Dela stepped into the surveillance room. Several heads turned in her direction.

"Someone tried to run me down in the parking lot." She nodded to the monitor above Ray who Heath stood behind. "Did you find anything else interesting?"

"No, but the three in the back room have a lot of information," Heath said. He thanked Ray for his help and motioned for Dela to go before him into the back room.

"Hey, Dela, I found the car that tried to run you over," Dede said, waving her hand.

Dela pivoted and walked over to the woman. "Can you see who was driving? I think I saw Ferris, but the FBI said Wheeler was driving when they caught up to the car."

The woman clicked on the keyboard, backing the video up.

"Why didn't you see this when it happened?"

Heath asked, his tone accusing.

"We don't watch the parking lot on monitors, but we can pull it up if someone says their car was broken into." Dede stopped clicking when the car was parked and two men walked toward the vehicle. It was Ferris and Wheeler.

Dela pointed. "That's what I thought. I could have sworn I saw Ferris behind the wheel, but there was no sense trying to tell Quinn that. I was able to give him the license plate and an FBI agent took off after the car since he and Quinn were standing outside of the Starfish talking when it happened."

Dede ran the video forward.

"My God!" Heath exclaimed when Quinn shoved her out of the way just before the vehicle hit her.

Seeing it from this direction sent a shiver up her spine and quickened her heart.

"Quinn saved you," Heath said, putting an arm around her. "I'm going to owe him a steak dinner."

"That's all I'm worth," she said teasing.

"No, you are worth a whole lot more," he said, peering into her eyes.

She saw the fear and love shining in his dark brown eyes. If they hadn't been in the middle of a room of people, she would have sunk into his arms. "Let's go see what the guys in back have come up with. We have to get the killer before he strikes again."

Once inside the room, Heath pulled her into his arms and whispered in her ear, "Don't go anywhere without me until this is solved."

She nodded and he released her with a kiss on her left cheek.

Trent turned from the monitor in front of him and

studied her. "Did you get in a fight?"

"Yeah, with a car. But it was a draw. What have you found?" Dela sat on the left side of Trent in the chair Heath placed behind her. He stood behind the chair with his hands on her shoulders.

"From the footage I went over the days before and after the dates Oscar gave you, the only person other than the employees with lockers on either side of Oscar's who went near his, was Reuben."

"Then it's safe to say, Reuben was the one who placed the money in Oscar's locker," Dela said.

Trent nodded.

"Okay. Sherman, have you seen any pattern in the people Reuben talked to?" Dela asked, standing and Heath moved the chair to the far side of Sherman.

"Yes, he did have several visits with Oscar and Dave. They all looked as if he were threatening them rather than saying, here's money to do this."

"I don't think Reuben knows any other way to talk to people. Which makes me wonder how he came to be an item with Felicity. I would think after being with her brute of a husband she wouldn't fall for a man who bossed her around." Dela thought on that a bit. Felicity had acted like an airhead, but from everything the woman had pulled off, she was anything but.

Dela glanced up at Heath and then said to Sherman, "Did you watch any of the interactions between Reuben and Felicity?"

"I remember seeing something. I'll dig it up." The man reached for a small notebook where he had dates and times written down along with initials. "It will only take me a minute."

"While he's digging that up, here's what I

discovered," Enos said, motioning to his monitor.

Dela stood and moved between Sherman and Enos to watch the middle monitor.

"Nothing conclusive, but Felicity and the boy left the Starfish at the time she said she was showering. She came back at one-forty-five. The cameras came back on and it showed her at the door calling for the boy. I think it's pretty clear she took the boy to someone who waited down by the beach before taking the boy elsewhere."

Dela snapped her head around to look at Heath. "We need someone who knows what the boy looks like to take a look at Rowena's photos. They could have used a different boy with Asher's dog to wait around and make it look like he was taken to the boat. This was a very elaborate sleight of hand."

"I can call Quinn and get a photo," Heath said, pulling out his phone.

"We'll talk to him," she said to keep Heath from calling.

"I can get the disk you gave me of the photos," Trent said.

Dela couldn't hide the sly grin. His disk was useless. "Heath and I will get the photo. But first, what else did you learn?" she asked Enos. "Anything from cameras during Rowena's death?"

He nodded. "That's a toss-up. Cameras in the Otter lobby caught Ferris, Reuben, and Hugo going up the elevator. Ferris and Hugo got off on the third floor and Reuben got off on the second floor." Enos peered over his shoulder at her.

"There was a sandy print on her balcony. Whoever strangled her came from below the balcony. What were the times you saw the three go up in the elevator?" Dela asked.

"All after she'd checked out," Enos said.

"How long after she'd checked out?" Dela knew from what she'd witnessed at the crime scene, Rowena had come back from delivering her note and checking out to start packing. There had only been a few items in the suitcase before she was strangled.

"Twenty minutes for Ferris and Hugo and fifteen for Reuben." Enos spun his chair. "I'd say it was Reuben who strangled her and the other two found her already dead and unable to answer their questions."

Dela pulled out her phone and punched photos. She scrolled to the photo of Rowena. "She's facing the door. She wouldn't know Reuben, why would she let him in and then him come at her from behind clear across the room?" She shook her head. "I think the killer is the one who left the sand print on the balcony. Someone who came up from the outside. I know when I am getting ready to leave my room the last thing I do is lock the balcony door. My guess is either the killer was already on the balcony waiting when Rowena came back or they somehow made it up with a rope or some climbing apparatus and killed her from behind after coming through the sliding door."

"That makes sense," Heath said.

"But who else could it have been?" Enos asked. "We've been suspecting Ferris and Hugo all along. And then Reuben."

"West," Dela said. "He was part of the equation until someone killed him. And he was alive when Rowena was killed."

Heath huffed out a breath. "I don't like it. That

The Pinch

means there are two murderers. Because West didn't kill himself. And he didn't kill the other agent."

Dela nodded. "True." Her mind spun with thoughts.

"Then there has to be another person we don't know about," Enos said.

"One that has been using all the others to hide their tracks." Dela walked to the door. "Come on Heath. Let's get that photo."

"I have the video of two of Mrs. Benedict's visits with Reuben," Sherman said.

Dela spun back around and strode over to Sherman. "Show me."

The monitor in front of him showed Felicity and Reuben standing in a corner of the casino. She was backed into a corner of a wall and a slot machine. The only reason Dela could tell it was Felicity was her head leaned out toward Reuben. She only saw the security officer's profile.

Felicity's hand appeared and she stabbed a long fingernail in Reuben's chest. It was clear she was giving all the orders. Rueben said something and she fisted her hand in the front of his shirt and pulled him close. The slot machine hid whatever they were doing, but Dela imagined they were playing tonsil hockey.

"Okay, the next one," she said.

Sherman brought up the other video.

Again, it was a dark corner of the casino. "How did you find these, they wouldn't stand out just looking through videos," Dela said.

"You had me following Rueben and this is where he ended up several times."

Dela realized it was the same bank of machines and

247

the same corner.

Nicely done. This time there wasn't any kissing going on. Felicity was upset. She didn't hide as deep in the corner and did a lot more fingernail poking to Reuben's chest.

"A lover's spat?" Heath said, in an amused tone.

"When was this?" Dela asked.

"The day you put Sidney in charge and told Reuben to go home."

Dela had an idea they'd been looking in the wrong direction all along.

Chapter Twenty-eight

As Dela walked through the surveillance room, Dede waved her over. "Did you find something else?" Dela asked.

The woman nodded. "Yes. I don't know why someone didn't think to look at the parking lot footage when the boy went missing. I found this." The woman pointed to the monitor directly in front of her and the parking lot in front of the Starfish appeared.

A van drove up to the building and Felicity walked out with her son. She and the child got in the van and a man with another boy stepped out, the little boy holding a stuffed dog. The van drove off and the man and child went between the buildings to the beach.

"Does that van bring Felicity back?" Dela asked.

"No. She's dropped off by the fancy limousine." Dede fast-forwarded and the long dark car drove in about ten till two by the time on the bottom corner of the video.

"West was in on the kidnapping," Heath said.

"Did he help Felicity and not the Feds or was he helping her for the Feds?" Dela asked not expecting an answer as she peered into Heath's eyes.

"If helping the Feds, they've known all along where the boy was. Why go along with the charade?" Heath said, anger vibrating his words.

"They knew Rowena was taking the photos. It has to have been someone in Hugo's payroll who killed her. He is the only person who would want to know what happened to his son." Dela's anger at Quinn and the FBI grew. "We need to have another talk with our friend."

Heath held onto her arm as they descended the stairs. With him keeping her steady she could move faster.

"Don't go after Quinn like a pit bull. He'll only bristle up and clamp his mouth shut," Heath said at the bottom of the stairs.

"I'll be as subtle as I can considering I was right all along and the FBI planned the whole thing and then left their agent out to dry when they should have been keeping tabs on her." Dela marched out the front entrance and straight across the parking lot, even though she'd nearly been run over not that long ago.

Heath kept up with her stride for stride. "You know he may not even be in the suite."

"Good. Then I'll talk to the agent who came here to clear things up." Dela stepped up onto the sidewalk as that woman strode out of the Starfish building.

The woman stopped the other two agents behind her and said, "Ms. Alvaro, I didn't expect to see you again today. Did you get looked over after that fall you took?"

"I need to talk to Special Agent Pierce," Dela said.

The woman's gaze landed on Heath. "We've met before, haven't we?"

Dela glanced at Heath. He studied the woman.

"You do look kind of familiar," he said.

"I'm Special Agent Cora Leland." She smiled. "We butt heads at Pine Ridge eight years ago."

Something flickered in Heath's eyes before he said, "Agent Leland. Yes, I remember."

"What are you doing now? Still undercover or…" her gaze flit to Dela and back to Heath, "on vacation?"

Dela decided if the two had history, she'd use it to her advantage. "We wanted to talk to Agent Pierce about the kidnapping. But if you have time to listen…"

Heath's hand pressed on her back as if he was urging her to move along.

Special Agent Leland turned to the two agents behind her. "You two go on. I'll catch a ride with someone else." When the other agents walked away, she motioned to the building. "Come on up. We'll have the suite to ourselves and you can tell me what's been happening around here. I don't feel like I'm getting the truth from any of the agents who have been here."

Heath held onto Dela's elbow, slowing her pace. He whispered in her ear, "Be careful. You can trust her less than you can trust Quinn."

Dela glanced into his eyes before stepping onto the elevator and realized, that the emotion she'd seen flickering in his eyes was distrust. What had happened in Pine Ridge that had him cautious of the woman? Now she wished she hadn't been so bold and had instead asked to see Quinn. At least they knew why he did what he did.

At the suite, Cora invited them to take a seat while she made them coffee. As soon as the woman walked into the kitchen area, Dela leaned over and asked, "Why not trust her?"

"In Pine Ridge, she was taking money to look the other way. If she's been monitoring this whole operation, she could be the person giving whoever is killing people the information."

When the woman walked into the room with three cups of coffee, Dela took the first one and Heath the second. Cora sat on a chair across from them, sipped from her cup, and studied them.

"What did you need to tell Agent Pierce?" she asked.

"It wasn't telling him so much as asking him something," Dela said, now trying to figure out what to say that wouldn't give the woman more information to pass on, if indeed, she was still on the take.

"I've been monitoring the operation from the beginning. I should be able to answer your question."

Heath cleared his throat as if warning her to tread lightly.

"Whose idea was it to help Felicity Benedict fake her son's disappearance?" Dela decided to go with the obvious.

"I don't know what you're talking about. Hugo Benedict kidnapped their child. We're trying to help her get him back." The woman's expression was neutral, but her eyes were boring into Dela as if she could read her mind.

Dela laughed. "Ok. For the sake of making you happy, we'll say Hugo took his son. Then if he took his son, why are he and his muscle man still around here killing people to find the boy?"

Heath held out his phone. "Excuse me, I need to take this call."

Dela caught his warning glance and wondered what he was up to.

Cora's gaze followed Heath. "How do you and Heath know one another?"

"We were high school sweethearts who reconnected when we both moved back to Nixyaawii." She smiled. They were more than sweethearts, they were soulmates, but she'd only told her best friend Molly that.

"How nice. Then he told you about his time at Pine Ridge?"

Dela could tell the woman wanted to say something to put a wedge between her and Heath. "He did. I felt for him when he said his father had died before he was able to see him."

The woman's eyes widened and then she regained her composure. "Yes, that's what brought him to Pine Ridge. But he stayed. Did he tell you the reason for that?"

Heath walked back into the room. "Dela and I keep no secrets from one another. She knows everything that happened at Pine Ridge."

Dela steeled her expression. She knew something had happened there that Heath had yet to tell her. And she had things that had happened to her in the Army that she'd yet to disclose as well. She nodded and smiled. "Whatever friction you're trying to put between us, you might as well give it up. We make a good team in our private life and our professional lives."

The door to the suite opened and Quinn strode in.

"Cora, I thought you and your people were going back to Portland."

"I was waylaid by Ms. Alvaro. She wanted to tell me something." The woman smiled with a full set of teeth that looked as sharp as a shark's.

Quinn faced Dela. "Did you want to talk to Cora or to me?"

She realized Heath had called Quinn and he'd hurried here to stop her from telling this woman anything. While she didn't trust Quinn, she trusted Heath and if he thought giving this woman any information would hurt their efforts, she'd abide by that. "Yes, we wanted to talk to you. I'm glad you made it back." She stood and studied the woman. "It was interesting meeting you."

Cora glared at Quinn and held out her hand. "I hope we meet again."

Dela shook hands, noticing the woman had a firm grip.

Quinn walked to the door. Dela and Heath followed him out into the hallway. "Let's go for a drive," Quinn said, leading them to the elevator as Cora followed them down the hallway.

All four of them rode down in the elevator. When they stood on the sidewalk, Cora asked, "I don't have a ride back to Portland. Do you have anything you want me to do, until a ride picks me up?"

Quinn smiled and waved his hand. A tan-colored SUV pulled up in front of the building. "Agent Smith will take you to Portland."

The woman glared at him again and climbed into the passenger side.

"We can go back up to the suite now," Dela said.

"No, we can't. She might have bugged the room." Quinn pointed to a federal vehicle parked close to the entrance. "We'll take my vehicle, myself or Swanson has been in it the whole time she's been here so she or her little gremlins couldn't touch it."

Dela studied Quinn. He had the same distrust of the woman as Heath. "I see there is no love loss between you two." Dela climbed into the front passenger seat where Heath held the door for her. He slid into the back seat behind her.

Quinn slid in behind the steering wheel and pulled out of the parking lot. "You don't know the whole of it. She is my ex-wife's niece, and she believes that Cora just needs to grow up and she'll make a great agent. What my ex-wife doesn't see is her darling niece will do anything for a buck. Even if it means going against the agency's policies and taking money from the people we are supposed to be catching. We, Swanson and I, believe Cora is on Hugo's payroll. We try to keep her out of everything we do to catch him, but she always pops up." He glanced over at her. "What have you learned?"

Dela wished Heath had sat behind Quinn so she could take cues from him if she said too much. "I want a straight answer. Did the FBI start out helping Felicity kidnap her child and then she took things into her own hands?"

Quinn glanced at her as he turned south, driving through Lincoln City. "Yes. We, along with West, had planned the kidnapping to put Benedict in a bind and have him use unlaundered money to pay for the boy. Only Felicity decided to use the kidnapping as a way to get herself and the boy away from Hugo."

"Did she know Rowena was filming the kidnapping?"

"Not unless West said something to her. Why?"

"Because we saw the video today of Felicity driving off with Asher in a van after a man and a boy Asher's size got out of the van. Someone taking photos would be able to look at the photos and know the boy seen with the man wasn't Asher. The only other person who would have reason to want the photos would be Hugo to discover what happened to his boy, but he and Ferris entered the building after Rowena was already dead." Dela had decided Felicity killed Rowena after hearing the information Sherman, Enos, and Trent had found out. She was the only person with something at stake that wasn't accounted for at the time of Rowena's death.

Quinn chuckled. "You think Felicity killed Rowena? She was helping us."

Dela shook her head. "Think about it. Was she helping you? Or was she helping herself? If Hugo had taken the bait and used unlaundered money as ransom for his son, she would be rid of him legally and have her son without Hugo continually taking her to court for custody of the boy."

"That makes sense," Heath said. "But who beat up the agent and killed West?"

"I think the agent was beat up by Ferris. He discovered he was being followed and wanted to get away. That's when he disappeared and was at West's house. I believe he tortured West to find out what Felicity had done with the boy, but I suspect it was either Reuben or Felicity who killed West. They had the most to lose if the agent told Hugo that Felicity had the child. He was the one who brought Felicity back after she'd driven away in the van with Asher. He had to know the kidnapping hadn't gone as planned by the FBI."

"But what about Ferris beating up Sherman and threatening Trent?" Heath asked.

Dela shrugged. "He's a thug. He beats up anyone he thinks isn't helping him. And you and I both figured out Trent is a coward. I'm sure Ferris saw that and used that to get what he wanted, Trent not helping me."

"But that doesn't make sense?" Heath leaned between the two seats.

Dela twisted in her seat, wincing, and stared into his eyes. "Why?"

"Because he could have followed you around and learned what they wanted to know. You were on the inside and could learn things he couldn't. If he was a good P.I. he would have recognized you as a person that would help him get the information he wanted.

Chapter Twenty-nine

Dela thought about why the P.I. had hurt Sherman and threatened Trent when he could have, as Heath said, just followed her around to find out information.

Quinn pulled into a restaurant on the south end of the town. It sat by itself with a good ocean view. The parking lot was a distance from the building, but Dela didn't mind breathing in the briny ocean breeze.

"Let's grab dinner and continue this discussion." Quinn stepped out of the vehicle and came around to the passenger side as Dela and Heath slid out. "I like this place. There's an ocean view and we can talk without worrying someone from the casino will overhear what we say."

They followed the agent into the restaurant and he asked for a quiet corner table. They were given one on the far side of the restaurant. It was nearing dinner time but she hoped the restaurant didn't get so packed they'd have to lower their voices to not be heard at the next table.

After ordering, they continued their conversation.

Quinn placed his forearms on the table and leaned forward. "If I go along with you, that Felicity killed Rowena, how did she do it?"

"She's strong. She does yoga and works out. There has to be a rope that was used for her to climb up to the second floor and wait for Rowena to come back from the registration office. Then when Rowena's back was turned, she could have already had the door slightly ajar and quietly opened it before wrapping the cord around my friend's neck and killing her. Then she looked for the disk and smashed the camera before leaving the same way she came. It would account for the sandy footprint on the balcony. And why all the men we suspect weren't in the building soon enough."

"Since finding out Rowena was FBI, I believe she left the card for me and put an empty one in her camera. That would be what was flushed." Dela had made this determination shortly after discovering Rowena had worked with the FBI.

Heath put up a hand. "But how had they all come to enter the building after she was killed?"

"Hugo could have had someone in the registration office who contacted him about Rowena leaving." Dela snapped her fingers. "If you believe Agent Leland is being paid by Hugo, he would have known Rowena was FBI. He and Ferris could have gone up to find out what she knew since she'd gone to check out."

Quinn nodded. "There is that."

"And what about Reuben being on that floor after she checked out?" Heath asked.

Dela, even though she wanted to sigh, knew that when Heath posed these questions it helped her to see things clearer. "He was either there to check and make sure Felicity didn't have any trouble or he wanted to make sure Rowena was dead."

"Why didn't Felicity go out the door and down the hall, if as you say, she was the killer? She had the cameras all turned off." Quinn leaned back as the waitress returned with their drinks.

Dela waited until the woman was gone and answered. "That time of night there could have been people returning to their rooms and they would have seen her."

The food arrived as they debated whether Felicity had normal motherly instincts if she would use her child for bait and then kill someone to keep him safe.

The aroma in the restaurant had started Dela's stomach growling, now she could savor the flavors she'd been breathing in. The food was delicious, she chewed and watched the waves roll toward the sandy beach and rocky river outlet.

When they'd sated their hunger, Quinn posed a question, "Do you also believe Felicity killed West and did something with Morrison? We know that Ferris beat up Morton and was most likely the person who tortured West and killed him. I'll give you Felicity might have killed Rowena, but she wouldn't kill West. I think she genuinely had fallen for him and him for her. Why else would he help her go against the plan we'd provided?"

Dela thought about that. "I think she is a very good actress. She can turn her feelings and her personality on and off like a faucet. She had me and several others convinced she was the victim of abuse. But I would venture to guess she made it look like that to get away from Hugo."

"When did Hugo's business really take off?" she asked Quinn.

"You read the information I gave you." He picked up a cup of coffee and glared.

"Yes. His business didn't pick up until after he married Felicity."

"That's because she brought in capital. She was from a rich family," Quinn argued.

"Don't you think she also helped him make decisions?" Dela asked.

Quinn stared out the window for several minutes.

Dela and Heath sat in silence, sipping their coffee as Quinn stared.

Heaving a sigh, Quinn said, "You may have that right. Thinking about the times we brought him in for questioning, it was Felicity who arrived with the books or information that cut him loose. Not an accountant or legal representation, his wife."

"I think she's the brains behind it and is trying to get loose of Hugo short of killing him." Dela thought about that. With all the people she had to know, why hadn't she just paid someone to knock off her husband? Did she care about him and want him alive? Could they use him to get her to play her hand?

"She wouldn't want to bring Hugo's father down on her. He is very influential among the people she and Hugo consort with. If something happened to his son, he'd take it out on her." Quinn shoved his coffee cup to the center of the table. "I'll take you back to your room. There is no sense in us sitting here hashing the same thing over and over. I need to check in with Swanson and see if they've had any luck with finding Morrison."

"What about Felicity? Do you still have someone

watching her?" Dela asked. She was the person of interest in Dela's estimation.

"She's at their home in Portland," Quinn said.

"Are you sure? I would think she would be with Asher and she can't have him at the home if Hugo thinks she kidnapped their son." Dela didn't for one minute believe she was sitting at home.

"I'll check in with the agents watching her," Quinn said.

They all walked out to his vehicle and climbed in. He'd pulled out of the parking lot when his phone rang. He glanced at the name and put an earbud in his ear.

Dela figured it was FBI business he didn't want her to hear.

"Yeah, I had hoped to be back by now," Quinn said. He chuckled. "Yes, I told you that I'd be doing less of this kind of stuff."

Dela leaned around the front seat, peering at Heath and raising an eyebrow. This was not a business call.

"I'm driving and have passengers. I'll give you a call back in about an hour." He smiled. "I miss you too. See you hopefully in a couple more days." He sighed. "Yeah, it's a tough one." He smiled. "I'm looking forward to it. Talk to you soon." He ended the call and the smile remained on his face.

Dela couldn't help poking at his happiness. "That sounded like a nice call."

He twisted his head and smiled at her. "It was. I have a special someone in my life and I'm trying to slowly get out of these long intense cases. She doesn't need two people she loves in dangerous situations all the time."

The word love coming from Quinn struck her as

funny. She chuckled.

"You think it's funny I found someone?" Quinn asked.

"No, I think it's interesting that you are speaking of love. I didn't think that word was in your vocabulary." Dela couldn't stop smiling at the way the word had been spoken as if he said it a lot.

"It just takes the right person to bring out the happiness and desire to spend the rest of your life with them." Quinn smiled as he continued driving toward the casino.

"I agree," Heath said from the back seat.

Dela felt awkward. She used the word love with Heath in everyday conversation, but she'd never actually told him she loved him.

Quinn pulled in front of the Otter building. "Talk to you tomorrow when I have updates."

"Thank you for listening to us," Dela said, getting out and standing beside Heath. Her body was tightening up from her crash to the asphalt earlier. What she needed was a good hot bath. Or a shower if Heath joined her and helped her stand.

They closed the door and entered the building.

"I'm glad Quinn found someone to want to grow old with," Heath said as they stepped into the elevator.

Dela peered up at him. "Me too. It's nice to have someone you can trust to lean on." She stepped closer to Heath, and he hugged her as the elevator bounced to a stop on the second floor and the doors opened.

Walking down the hall, Dela spotted someone lurking in the shadows of the door across the hall from their room. "To the right," she whispered.

Heath nodded. As they approached their door,

Hugo Benedict moved out of the shadows.

"Mr. Benedict, what are you doing hanging around our room?" Dela asked.

"I have some questions for you and thought we might have a private conversation." He walked over to the door of their room.

"Aren't you forgetting you had the maid put a listening device in my room?"

Hugo's eyes narrowed and he huffed out, "I'm sure if you know about it you have destroyed it."

"You should know whether or not we've found it if you've been listening." Dela remained, not opening the door. For all she knew he could have Ferris standing in there to deal with them. "How about we go next door to the restaurant and sit at a table in the bar?"

Hugo glanced up and down the hallway. "Yeah. Sure."

"Lead the way," Heath said, moving next to Dela and motioning for the man to walk down the hall to the elevator.

"I'd rather take the stairs and meet you there," Hugo said.

Dela noticed the wariness that appeared in Heath's eyes as she felt her chest squeeze with apprehension. "I think we'll all go down in the elevator if you want to talk with us."

"I'd prefer the stairs. I don't trust being in an elevator with people I don't know." He again glanced up and down the hall as if he was expecting someone.

His actions made the hair on the back of her neck tingle. Before she could again insist he go with them, Heath grabbed the man's arm and twisted it behind his back.

"Oww!" Hugo whined.

"We're all three going down in the elevator," Heath said, moving Hugo ahead of him down the hall.

Dela fell into step right behind him, glancing over her shoulder every two steps to make sure someone didn't come charging up from the fire stairs.

When they were outside on the sidewalk, Heath released Hugo, dusting off the man's shoulders and smiling. "See, that wasn't so bad and we're all three standing."

Hugo glared at him. "I came to talk to you about my boy and you treated me like a criminal."

Dela moved in front of the man and said, "You were acting like someone was going to come down the hall and assault us. We had to be certain we weren't hurt. There have been several people associated with your son's kidnapping that have died."

Hugo's head dropped and he stared at his shiny shoes for several seconds before he looked her in the eyes. "That's what I want to talk to you about. The FBI has it out for me and won't listen. I have had nothing to do with the body count."

Heath nodded toward the restaurant. "Come on. Let's talk about this inside."

They walked into the restaurant and over to the small bar section. Dela followed Heath to a table in a far corner where they could keep an eye on the door and the other occupants.

Once settled with coffee for her and Heath and scotch and soda for Hugo, Dela studied the man. His gray complexion, wary eyes, and more than a day's growth of whiskers, said he wasn't standing up well to his son's disappearance.

"What did you want to tell us?" she asked.

Hugo held his drink in both hands, peering down into the amber liquid. "If my son isn't back to me in two days, my father is going to start looking for him." His gaze rose. Wet, dull eyes stared at them. "My father never lets anything get in the way of what he wants."

"Are you saying there will be more deaths if your son isn't back to you in two days?" Heath asked.

Hugo nodded. "What I fear more than my father's actions is Felicity hurting Asher to make sure I never get to see him again."

Dela straightened. "Then you know that Felicity has your son?"

"I figured it out. There isn't anyone else who could have him. I've checked up on all the people who would want to hurt me and know she put one over on the FBI, so she has to still have him."

"Where do you think she would hide Asher?" Dela asked.

"I've looked everywhere that I can think of." Hugo swallowed the contents of his glass and waved the waitress over for a refill.

"I have a question," Dela started. "Who runs your business? You or Felicity?"

The man flinched. "My father thinks I'm the brains, but it is all Felicity. She pretends to be dense and that I'm rough with her. She tells me to treat her that way. I don't care for it, but it makes me look like I'm in charge which makes my father happy."

Dela now knew why Felicity had been drawn to Reuben. She liked the thrill of pain. A shiver swept through her. The two together would be horrid to the boy and who knew what kind of torture they would do to others.

"Did you stay at the cabin thirty minutes north of here?" She wondered if the boy was being kept right under all of their noses.

"No. That's in Felicity's name and she keeps her boy toys there. I'm not allowed. But Ferris said he saw her and Reuben Jones go there multiple times." Hugo's face screwed up in disgust.

"Do you think she has her claws in Ferris? That he could be helping her?" Heath asked.

Hugo's gaze shot to Heath. "Why would you say that?"

"She told me Ferris was working for her to get the goods on you for a divorce," Dela said.

An unkind smile replaced the disgust on Hugo's face. "Ferris told me everything she said and did. Right up until the kidnapping, she thought she had him believing everything she said. Then somehow, she realized he wasn't really helping her." He raised a hand in supplication. "That's when I started to see she was out of control."

"What do you mean?" Dela asked.

"I believe once she killed the FBI woman who took the photos, she liked the feeling."

"We know that Ferris beat up Sherman, a casino security officer, and an FBI agent. What was he doing at the house where West was staying? Did he torture and kill West?" Dela asked.

"He roughed some people up but he didn't kill anyone. He went to West's to find out where Felicity had taken Asher. But when he arrived, he found no one in the house and while searching the outbuildings found West near death from someone torturing him. West told

Ferris it was Felicity. She'd gone crazy wanting to know what West had told you and the FBI." Hugo took the drink the waitress brought over and drank half of it before he continued. "Ferris took water and bandages out to West and was getting ready to call the authorities when he heard something. Knowing the FBI was looking for him, he took off. But he said West was alive when he left him."

Dela wondered if there was anything in the house where West stayed that might give them an idea as to where Felicity might be. She also planned to ask Stedman for a list of all the places under Felicity's name. She wasn't hiding, she was waiting for her moment to put the dagger in Hugo and twist.

"Thank you for all of this information." Dela shoved her cup of coffee to the middle of the table. "My best advice to you is to keep Ferris close for protection. My guess is Felicity won't be happy until you are either dead or behind bars. That means you will need someone for an alibi or to keep you alive."

Hugo's eyes widened. "I can't go home, that's probably where she is."

"I'd go stay with your father, if I were you," Heath said. "He seems to be your best protection. And we'll see what we can do about Asher." Heath stood and put a hand on the man's shoulder. "It's not always easy to find the right woman."

Hugo snorted. "The funny thing. I didn't want to marry Felicity, my father insisted."

Chapter Thirty

Once they were outside the restaurant, Dela turned to Heath. "I want to go to West's house and see if we can find something that might tell us where Asher is being held."

Heath stopped and peered into her eyes. "I'm sure the FBI went over that house thoroughly. After all, an informant was tortured and killed there."

As much as she didn't want to admit Heath was probably right, she gave in. "Okay. But what about the cabin where Reuben took us?"

"If the FBI are doing half their job, they have someone watching it," Heath put an arm around her shoulders. "Come on, let's get a good night's sleep and we'll work on it tomorrow."

Dela couldn't shake the feeling they had to find Asher before his mother did something horrible to him. "Can I at least call Stedman and get a list of properties that Felicity and Reuben own?"

"I don't mind if you do that. It will give us places

to start looking tomorrow." Heath led her out of the elevator and down the hall to their room. This time no one was lurking in the recess of the doorway across the hall.

Once inside Dela called Stedman.

"You believe that Mrs. Benedict is hiding out somewhere with the child?" the detective asked.

"It's the only explanation, unless they left the country. However, from what Hugo says, I think Felicity is trying to take over the business his father started for them." Dela had thought about this as she'd listened to Hugo. The woman had been smart enough to figure out how to get her hands on a very lucrative, if illegal, business.

"I'll get someone working on the property angle. The FBI agent is ready to be released from the hospital. He confirmed that Ferris beat him up, but he kept asking him what he knew about Mrs. Benedict taking the boy." Stedman slurped a drink and continued, "Your thoughts that she took her son seem to be spot on."

Dela smiled. It was good to hear someone besides Heath praise her.

"The State Police and FBI are looking for Ferris. He seems to have disappeared. Oh, and looking up information on the security officers as you asked earlier, we discovered Trent Lawton is a shirttail relative of Felicity Benedict."

Dela stared out the window at the waves rolling under the moonlight, carrying glittering white caps toward the beach. "That's interesting. I wonder if Hugo knows that? Thank you for the information." Dela ended the call and faced Heath. "I believe our coward wasn't hiding from Ferris but from Felicity."

Heath studied her. "Trent?"

"Yeah. According to Detective Stedman, Trent is related to Felicity. We need to have a talk with him. He might know a family residence that Felicity is hiding at."

♠ ♣ ♥ ♦

The next morning, Dela dressed as quickly as she could with a prosthesis, while Heath called to find out where Trent had spent the night. It turned out he'd stayed with Enos.

Dela called Enos as she and Heath headed out the door.

"Dela, do you have good news?" Enos asked.

"Yes and no. Can you and Trent meet Heath and me at the pancake house? We have information and a few more questions." She wasn't going to put Trent on the run by saying they wanted to visit with him.

"We're up and having coffee. We can be there in fifteen minutes."

"Thanks. See you then." Dela ended the call and slid into the passenger side of her car.

"Pancake house on the highway?" Heath asked.

"That's the one," Dela said, fastening her seatbelt.

"Do you think Trent will be straight with us?" Heath asked as he navigated out of the parking lot.

"I hope so. He did find good information when he was looking at video footage. My take is he knows enough about Felicity to be scared of her. And I bet she didn't try to pull him into her plans because she knew he wouldn't be able to keep her secret. It was best to just scare him away from the investigation." Dela settled back and thought about what she would ask Trent.

The parking lot at the restaurant had plenty of parking. Dela liked that the place wasn't going to be crowded. She had no idea how Trent would act when she asked him about Felicity. If he tried to bolt, Heath would be able to stop him in a less populated environment.

It took them less than ten minutes to drive to the pancake house. They exited the car and walked to the entrance. Inside they asked for a table for four and said two more would be joining them.

Dela scanned the other occupants and then flicked her gaze to the front. When Enos appeared with Trent behind him, she waved a hand. The two walked over and took the empty seats.

"Morning," Enos said, nodding at Heath.

"Looks like a nice day," Heath replied as they all picked up the menus and read.

Dela tried not to let Trent see her watching him. He seemed relaxed.

Once they'd ordered, Dela told them a little bit about what they knew so far, leaving out anything about Felicity. When Trent was listening intently, she said, "Why didn't you tell us you were related to Felicity?"

In the seconds it took for her words to sink in, Trent's expression went from relaxed and focused to wide-eyed fear. He pushed the chair back to stand as both Enos and Heath grabbed an arm, holding Trent in his seat.

Dela lightened her voice. "Trent, we know you had nothing to do with what Felicity has done. But now it makes more sense why you were so scared to be involved in all of this. But why didn't you tell us you were related?"

Heath stood and scooted Trent and the chair back up to the table like an adult making a child stay at the table to finish his meal.

Trent glanced at Enos and then settled his gaze on the table in front of him.

"We aren't accusing you of anything other than withholding the truth," Dela said. "We are hoping you can help us."

His face rose and he studied her. "Help you? Do you think Felicity would let me live or not try to hurt my wife if I helped you?"

"She won't hurt you or your wife. She won't know you helped. And if I'm right, she'll be behind bars for a long time." Dela leaned back as their breakfast was delivered.

Trent pushed his plate to the center of the table. "I don't know that much about her. Only that as kids she was mean to everyone and everything. She could act sweet and innocent when her parents were around. When us kids were outside, she'd pinch us and push us down and then say we were bullying her."

"She's still that way," Dela said, working to get the man's confidence.

"The first time I saw her and Hugo walk into the casino I about peed my pants. I swear she is the devil in a model's body."

Enos pushed Trent's plate back in front of him. "It sounds like to me, that you need to help us put her away so you don't have to live in fear of her."

Trent's gaze landed on his boss. Dela hoped Trent would remember Enos had come to his rescue when he'd received the threat. That all of them wanted to help him.

Picking up his fork and stirring it around in his scrambled eggs, Trent asked, "How do you think I can help with?"

"Felicity has to be hiding Asher somewhere close so she can keep tabs on the investigations. Are there any family properties along the coast or inland from here?" Heath asked.

Trent shoved the eggs around for about a minute and said, "She inherited a cabin a bit north of here in the coast range."

"Is it the one where she keeps her men?" Dela asked.

"I wouldn't know that. It was given to her by her aunt on her mom's side." Trent pulled out his phone and started scrolling. He held the phone up. "Here. That's where the cabin is."

Dela, Heath, and Enos all leaned over the table to look at the decrepit shack Trent had pulled up on a map app. The roof was covered in moss and the front porch roof sagged.

"That's not the one we were taken to the other night," Dela said.

"It doesn't look as if anyone has lived in it for some time." Heath pulled out his phone and put in the address from Trent's phone. "Are there any other places?"

Trent thought a minute. "I think she also inherited our great-grandfather's house in Garibaldi. I can ask my mom for the address." He started typing on his phone.

Dela exchanged a glance with Heath. Garibaldi was closer than the shack in the forest. She had a feeling that would be their first stop.

"Here is the address," Trent said, holding his phone

out to Heath.

"Thank you," Dela said. "We won't tell anyone where we found this out. I have Detective Stedman looking into the property Felicity owns so they would most likely come up on his report."

"Just find her before she hurts someone else. She acted like she was a good mother but she can turn vicious without warning," Trent said.

When they paid and walked out of the restaurant, Enos said, "Take my keys, I'm going with Dela and Heath." He held his keys out to Trent.

"No. We need you to contact Detective Stedman and Special Agent Pierce. Give them the two addresses and let them know that Heath and I are headed to the one in Garibaldi first. We will let them know if we find anything." Dela could see conflict flickering in Enos's eyes. "Please. We don't need any more people hurt."

He peered into her eyes. "What about you two?"

"We'll wait for backup when we find them. We won't move in on them unless we have to," Heath said, putting a hand on Dela's shoulder.

She knew it was a reminder that they would follow the rules of his police training. She would, unless someone was about to be hurt.

Enos studied Heath and then nodded. "I'll head straight to the police station and talk to Stedman. He can contact the FBI."

"Make sure he talks to Pierce or Swanson. Someone on the FBI has been feeding Hugo and Felicity information," Dela said.

"I understand," Enos said, pivoting and walking to his car with Trent following beside him.

Dela headed for her car. She felt like they were

finally going to get some answers.

Chapter Thirty-one

Dela's nerves started jumping as Heath drove into the small coastal town of Garibaldi. "According to the GPS, you'll turn left across from the gas station," she said, reading off the directions on his phone.

He turned and they followed the directions up several streets when it told them to go right. At the end of the street was an old two-story house with a fence around a flat area on the very top. It looked a bit like a larger version of a crow's nest on sailing ships.

"That's it up there. The one with the crow's nest on top," Dela said.

"Let's park here and see how close we can get on foot." Heath pulled the car next to the curb on the downhill side of the road. He leaned over her, opening the glove compartment. His semi-automatic, a box of ammunition, and his backup weapon filled the compartment.

"When did you put those in there?" she asked.

"After we'd arrived at your room and found it

ransacked. I didn't want anyone finding these." He checked the backup weapon, clicked the magazine in place, and handed it to her. "We're only using these if we fear for our lives." He checked his weapon and shoved it into his jacket pocket.

Dela slipped the weapon Heath gave her into her hoodie pocket. Luckily it was a smaller version of Heath's semi-automatic. They locked the car and walked up the sidewalk. The large house was at the end of the street. She didn't see any vehicles parked in front of the garage door in the hill underneath the house. Dela wondered if that had been for a carriage at one time and was now used for cars.

There were trees behind the house but to go along the side of the yard they'd be seen.

"Do you have a plan?" she asked, as Heath led them to the last house before the end of the road.

"Let's go down between these two houses and see if we can work our way around the side without being seen. Keep an eye on the windows to see if anyone is inside and to make sure we aren't being watched. You take the bottom floor and I'll keep an eye on the second floor." Heath grasped her hand, leading her between the houses.

In the backyard of the house closest to the one they were interested in stood an elderly man watching them.

"Hello," Heath said, smiling.

Dela smiled at the man.

"Why are you sneaking around between the houses? You gonna rob me?" The old man held up the hoe he'd been leaning on.

"We were hoping to get to the back of the house at the end of the road. The architecture is interesting,"

Heath said.

The man studied them. "Are you cops? The only people interested in that house are cops."

Dela glanced at Heath and shrugged.

Heath pulled out his badge and flashed it too quickly for the man to see he was a tribal officer. If the man knew much about law enforcement, he'd know Heath didn't have any authority here.

"I knew it. As soon as I seen them two and the boy show up, I was sure there'd be cops coming around." The old man nodded enthusiastically.

"When did the couple and little boy arrive?" Dela asked.

"Night before last. But I knew they'd be showing up. The man had been here earlier carrying in sacks of groceries. The only reason someone would stock up on food was if they planned to stay for a while." The man set the hoe back down and leaned on it.

"Have they gone anywhere today?" Heath asked.

"Not that I saw. They parked the car in the garage when they came the other night. I only know that because when they backed it in, the lights shone in my living room window."

"Thank you. It would be best if you stayed in the house until we can determine if these are the people we're looking for." Heath motioned to the house.

The man studied him for a few seconds and headed inside.

Dela walked to the back gate in the fence. She needed to get her eyes on either Reuben or Felicity before they could let Stedman or Quinn know that this was the right place.

Keeping to the trees on the uphill side of the house,

they made their way to the back of the property. A small shed that appeared to be as old as the house, sat at the edge of the trees.

"Think we can get down behind that and keep an eye on the windows?" Dela whispered. Even though they were a good thirty yards from the house, the wind was blowing, and she didn't want her voice to carry to any of the occupants.

"It wouldn't hurt to try and get an eye on them or even hear what they might be saying." Heath took the lead, his hand in his pocket, toward the backside of the shed.

Dela had a hard time going downhill and keeping the windows in sight. She needed to watch where she placed her right foot or tumble to the bottom.

Heath pulled her in behind the building when they stepped out of the trees. They stood still, listening.

The sound of someone moving around inside the shed had her staring into Heath's eyes. She mouthed, *"There's someone in there"* and pointed.

He nodded and crouched down, pressing his ear against the wall.

Dela pressed against the building and leaned, peering around the corner toward the house. A curtain fluttered at a window on the second floor. The back door opened. Felicity walked out carrying a plate of cookies and a glass of milk.

Dela pulled back and tapped Heath's leg with her foot. *"Felicity is coming,"* she once again mouthed.

He nodded and kept his ear to the wall.

Dela pressed her ear to the back of the shed. She heard sniffling.

"Mommy brought you some milk and cookies,"

Felicity said, in a singsong happy voice.

"I want to go in the house with you, Mommy," a child's voice said.

"Shhh, I told you that your uncle doesn't like children. I have to be nice to him for just a little longer and then the two of us will go far away from him."

"I want Daddy. Where is Daddy?" the small voice questioned.

"Quiet! There will be no talk of Daddy. That makes me angry and you know what happens when I'm angry." Her voice sounded like one of the evil characters in a cartoon.

"Don't hurt me, please, Mommy," the child pleaded.

"I won't if you stay here and eat your cookies and drink your milk like a good boy." There was the sappy sweet tone again.

It was enough to make Dela want to vomit.

The door closed, shaking the building. Dela slid back to the corner and peered around. Felicity walked up the three steps to the porch and entered the house.

Dela moved back to Heath who now stood. "We need to get the boy out of here," Dela whispered in Heath's ear.

He nodded and put his mouth to her ear. "I'll come up with a distraction in the front of the house and you take the boy to the neighbor we talked with and call Quinn."

Dela shook her head. "I should do the distraction. What if the boy is slow or refuses to go with me? You could pick him up and pack him. I can't carry him up that hill." She pointed to the hill that would need to be traversed to stay out of sight.

Heath frowned. "I don't like the idea of you trying to distract them. They know you. They haven't met me."

"Reuben has. Remember, you were in the office with me the day Sidney took over." She pointed to the corner of the building. "I saw someone move a curtain upstairs when Felicity came to the shed. That means Rueben is most likely in there with her."

"I'm sure I can get them both occupied if I walk up to the door and knock on it. They are going to want to see what I know." She didn't care to be that easy of a target, but the boy and Heath had to get away. She'd also text Quinn before she walked up to the front door.

Heath scowled. "You wouldn't walk up to that door and knock on it, would you?"

"Can you think of any better way to keep them occupied while you get Asher out of here?" She smiled, even though her insides were icy with fear.

"I think we need to figure out a better way. Like call the Garibaldi Police and have them do a drive up and knock on the door." Heath pulled out his phone and typed Garibaldi Police in the browser.

"Damn!" Heath peered into her eyes. "There isn't a City Police at this time. You have to call the county. They'll take as long as trying to contact the State Police."

"Let me text Quinn and see how quickly he can get here," Dela brought up her messaging and texted Quinn. *At the house in Garibaldi. So are Felicity and Reuben. Found the boy. Need assistance.*

She waited several minutes with no response.

"Call him," Heath said.

"If he's not answering my text, he's not going to

answer a call." Dela peered into his eyes. "He'll get my text and be here in time to help. I'm going to the front door. I'll go up into the trees and come out near the front corner. When I do that, you go into the shed and get Asher."

"Dela, I don't like this. We can just wait." Heath reached out to her.

"We can't wait. What if Felicity comes back out here and hurts the boy when he asks about his father? I won't risk it. I'd rather have her take out her anger on me than on that child." As much as she didn't want to face the monster she knew Felicity to be, she would never forgive herself if she stood here and the woman came back and hurt her son.

Dela kissed Heath and took off for the trees, her hand holding the weapon in her pocket.

Chapter Thirty-two

Dela stopped and caught her breath as she peered through the trees to the shed. Heath was watching from the back corner of the building. When her breathing was normal, she walked out of the trees and straight for the full-length porch on the front of the historic house. Any other time she would have been enamored with the woodwork.

Right now, her gaze hovered over the windows and the front door as she approached. It would be foolhardy to think she could just walk up to the door and knock when a murderer and her henchman were inside plotting more deaths.

The door opened quickly and Reuben stuck out his head and a hand with a revolver. "What the hell are you doing here?"

"I came by for a chat. I think I have this whole thing figured out and wanted to make sure you were here before I called in reinforcements." She didn't smile or let her lips tremble wondering if this had been such a good idea. At least Heath and the boy would be safe.

Reuben moved his head, looking around. "You wouldn't come here alone. Where's that Indian that's been dogging you?"

"My friend headed off to contact the FBI as soon as you stuck your head out the door." She tipped her lips in a smug smile even as her insides quivered.

"You know one more body doesn't make any difference to me," Reuben said, opening the door wider and motioning with the barrel of the gun for her to walk in.

She didn't have time to pull her weapon out and shoot before he could get a shot at her head from this close range. If she dived down in front of the porch, she'd have only seconds more time to get her weapon out and aimed. All she could hope was that Heath made it to the neighbor's quickly and came back before the two people in this house killed her.

Dela stepped through the door and found Felicity standing spread-legged with her arms crossed like some female action figure.

"I should have known you wouldn't leave us alone. All your questions and prodding answers out of people. What kind of do-gooder are you?" Felicity asked.

"I believe in justice."

Felicity laughed long and hard before getting herself under control. "Justice is as elusive as a leprechaun. People just talk about it but there isn't any justice."

"I happen to believe it is real and it is something that needs to be fought for." Dela wasn't going to let this woman's poison taint her belief that she could make a difference, one person at a time.

"You know all about fighting, don't you?" Felicity relaxed her stance and walked over to a table. She picked up a folder. "I've learned you were honorably discharged from the Army after an explosion." Felicity's gaze traveled down Dela's legs. "It seems you are one-legged. Is that why you seek justice? Because the Army you'd put your hopes in caused you to be a freak?"

The evil smile that spread across Felicity's face made Dela's guts twist and her mouth dry. Heath had been right. She should have waited. She clearly had underestimated Felicity.

Shaking off the fear, knowing that was what Felicity fed on, Dela smiled and said, "I'm no more of a freak than you are, going around playing the insecure helpless mother of a missing boy and then keeping him locked up in a shed and pretending to love him."

Felicity's eyes sparked with rage. Apparently, she could dish out insults but not take them. Her head snapped toward Reuben. "Go check the shed."

"Sure you're okay alone with her?" Reuben asked. "Maybe you should go check the shed?"

"I can handle a one-legged justice seeker. Go!" Felicity pointed to the back of the house.

Reuben took one more glance at Dela and headed down the hall.

Felicity walked toward her. The woman didn't have a weapon. Dela decided to see if she could get the upper hand. As soon as the door closed in the back of the house, she pulled her weapon out of her pocket.

"How about you stop right there, unless you want me to be the last thing you see." Since Felicity knew she'd been in the Army, she would know Dela knew how to use a gun.

The woman stopped. Her eyes narrowed. "All I have to do is scream and Reuben will be right back in here."

"And he'll find you bleeding out on the carpet from the bullet to your heart. Oh wait, you don't have a heart." Dela had moved close enough to grab Felicity's wrist and twist her arm up behind her back. The woman was of average height making it easier to control her. She slipped the gun back into her pocket and shoved the handkerchief she'd put there to use on her head into the woman's mouth just before she grabbed her other arm and wrenched it behind Felicity.

Dela had to get the woman secured before Reuben returned.

A shot from the back of the house surprised her and Felicity used that to break free.

Had Heath been unable to get the boy out of the shed? Did Reuben shoot him?

"What did you do with that gun?" Felicity asked, grabbing at Dela's clothing.

She punched Felicity in the face, knocking her backward toward the door.

Dela ran to the stairs and started up. Her hand felt inside her pocket and found the gun missing. Frantically she glanced around and saw where it had landed.

Felicity was headed up the stairs after her. At least she didn't have the gun.

Dela sprinted to the top, nearly toppling twice when her prosthetic foot landed odd, but she grabbed the banister and kept moving upward. At the top of the stairs, a hand grasped her left foot, making her have to use her partial leg to pull and hold her while she kicked with her left foot. It struck something hard and pain shot up her leg, but the hand released.

Running down the hall, she opened and closed doors that would only get her cornered. Then she opened a door to a set of stairs. They were steep and she used both her hands and her legs to get up them. At the very top, her right leg was stuck. She glanced back and saw triumph blazing in Felicity's eyes as she held tight to Dela's prosthetic foot.

Felicity gave a hard yank.

Dela had been pulling with all her might, knowing she had upper body strength from all her workouts. Her body flung through the door at the top like a slingshot and onto the crow's nest.

Her prosthesis was gone, she couldn't stand. She pushed with her left leg, scooting her butt across the boards and over to the low fence.

Felicity came through the door, holding the prosthesis with Dela's walking shoe in the air over her head like a trophy. "Now you will get what's coming to you," she said, swinging the leg at Dela.

Rolling to her left side, Dela avoided the leg that hit the fence, shattering the wood. She now was parallel to the fence, and the only way she could get away was to roll to the right.

Felicity took another hard swing.

A voice called out, but Dela didn't have time to think about it. She rolled to her right and used her left foot to shove Felicity into the fence.

The wood cracked.

Felicity screamed as her body fell.

Dela scooted to the opening in the fence and looked down.

Felicity lay on the gray shingles, her blonde hair

strewn over bright green patches of moss, one of her arms sprawled at an odd angle.

Dela's prosthetic skittered down the roof, landing on the lawn.

"Dela! Dela!"

She looked to the front of the house and spotted Heath with Quinn. Swanson was handcuffing Reuben. She waved and called, "I'll be right down."

"Stay there, I'll come get you," Heath said, disappearing.

She smiled, her knight was coming to her rescue, but she really didn't need him. She scooted toward the door and her hand pressed down on something that felt like a rock. Raising her hands, she found a small device stuck to her palm. She dropped it into her hoodie pocket and continued to the door and down the stairs on her butt.

She met Heath at the bottom of the stairs to the crow's nest.

He wrapped his arms around her, pulled her up to her one foot, and kissed her. Then he snuggled his face in the crook of her neck and whispered, "I thought I'd lost you when I walked to the front of the house and saw Felicity with your leg in her hands."

She hugged him tight. "Truth is I was wondering if I'd see you again when I heard the gunshot."

There was a clatter outside on the roof and Felicity screamed for medical help.

"Do you want me to carry you or be your crutch?" Heath asked, turning them to walk down the hall to the other set of stairs.

"I'll walk. And you are never a crutch. You're my soulmate."

Heath stopped and stared into her eyes. "Did I just

hear you correctly? You said I'm your soulmate?"

She smiled and kissed him on the lips before drawing back and saying, "And I love you. Let's go give our statements and get back to Nixyaawii."

Heath picked her up, spinning them both around three times, then he set her on her foot and tucked her beside him. "This, other than you nearly getting killed, is the best day of my life."

Dela laughed and laughed even harder when Quinn bounded up the stairs and studied them like they were aliens.

"What are you laughing about? You just about got yourself killed by trying to be the hero." His tone told her Heath had already filled the Special Agent in on why she'd been in the house.

"Asher? Is he okay?" she asked.

"I think Felicity must have been drugging his milk. He was out when I snuck in to get him. I carried him out and put him behind a tree. Then when I started back to see if you needed help, Reuben came out of the shed. I caught him by surprise, but he managed to get off a shot."

"That's what I heard. It startled me and Felicity got the jump on me. As we raced up the stairs she kept grabbing for my feet. She had my Army records and knew one of my legs wasn't real. She is vicious. Make sure she doesn't get out of prison for a long time," Dela said, narrowing her eyes at Quinn.

"I think we have more than enough to keep her in for life. Reuben was very helpful once he was caught. He didn't want to go down for the murders and made sure we knew who did them and where to find the evidence." Quinn smiled and said, "You two need to come to the suite when you get back and give your statements." He turned around and jogged down the stairs.

Dela held onto the banister and Heath as they descended the stairs. At the bottom, she found a pair of crutches with a note. *We need your prosthesis for evidence. Once photos and prints are taken, you can have it back. Swanson*

"It looks like I'm on crutches until they return my leg." Dela placed the small device she'd found in the crow's nest in Heath's hand. "Between now and then we need to decide if we want the FBI knowing my every move. I believe this flew out of my prosthesis when Felicity struck the fence."

Heath dropped it to the floor and crunched it under his heel. "We'll be checking your prosthesis when you get it back. I don't like the idea of them following you around when we are trying to find out more about Dory."

"That's a thought." She stuck a crutch in her armpit and shook her head. "They're too short."

Heath pulled out his knife and unfastened the screws, pulled the pieces farther apart, and tightened it up. He held it out to her. "You know I could carry you to the car and you could use your crutches back at the hotel room."

She smiled. "And you know I won't go out of this house looking vulnerable."

Heath grinned and lengthened the other crutch. "And I wouldn't have it any other way."

Thank you for reading book five in the Spotted Pony Casino Mystery series. If you enjoyed the book, please leave a review where you purchased *The Pinch*. Reviews are the best way to let an author know you enjoyed the story.

As I continue the series there will be surprises about Dela's heritage and more murders that she, Heath, and their friends will solve.

Paty

Other books in the Spotted Pony Casino Mystery series:
Poker Face
House Edge
Double Down
The Squeeze

If you enjoyed this mystery series you might like my other mystery series:

Shandra Higheagle Mystery Series

Double Duplicity	*Haunting Corpse*
Tarnished Remains	*Artful Murder*
Deadly Aim	*Dangerous Dance*
Murderous Secrets	*Homicide Hideaway*
Killer Descent	*Toxic Trigger-point*
Reservation Revenge	*Abstract Casualty*
Yuletide Slaying	*Capricious Demise*
Fatal Fall	*Vanishing Dream*

Gabriel Hawke Novels

Murder of Ravens

Mouse Trail Ends

Rattlesnake Brother

Chattering Blue Jay

Fox Goes Hunting

Turkey's Fiery Demise

Stolen Butterfly

Churlish Badger

Owl's Silent Strike

Bear Stalker

Damning Firefly

About the Author

Paty Jager grew up in Wallowa County in NE Oregon and has always been amazed by its beauty, history, and ruralness. She has always had an interest in the Indigenous people and their culture and enjoys learning more every time she writes a book.

Paty is an award-winning author of 55 novels of murder mystery and western romance. All her work has Western or Native American elements in them along with hints of humor and engaging characters. She and her husband raise alfalfa hay in rural eastern Oregon. Riding horses and battling rattlesnakes, she not only writes the western lifestyle, she lives it.

By following her at one of these places you will always know when the next book is releasing and if she is having any giveaways:

Website: http://www.patyjager.net
Blog: https://writingintothesunset.net/
FB Page: Author Paty Jager
Pinterest: https://www.pinterest.com/patyjag/
Twitter: https://twitter.com/patyjag
Goodreads:
http://www.goodreads.com/author/show/1005334.Paty_Jager
Newsletter- Mystery: https://bit.ly/2IhmWcm
Bookbub - https://www.bookbub.com/authors/paty-jager

Windtree
Press

Thank you for purchasing this Windtree Press publication. For other books of the heart, please visit our website at www.windtreepress.com.

For questions or more information contact us at info@windtreepress.com.

Windtree Press
www.windtreepress.com

Printed in the USA
CPSIA information can be obtained
at www.ICGtesting.com
LVHW011530290324
775847LV00043B/717